THE GIFT OF LOVE

"Very well, then," Nicholas said. "I'll stay at least until after Christmas and that silly thing you Brits do the next day. What do they call it?"

"Boxing Day," Priscilla said. "And good, that will make it easier. Then you can claim you have been called back to New York sooner than you expected—a family illness or some other lame excuse. People will not believe it, but it will serve."

"And you will come with me?" He began to stamp his feet. It was beginning to seem cold to him, and he realized he had run out without a coat or boots.

Priscilla looked at him, noting he had come to seek her without an overcoat. It gave her a thrill to think he would pursue her so recklessly.

"Just like that?" she said, the thrill she had felt giving way to a slight pout. He had not yet told her he wanted to marry her. She thought he did. Lucinda had said so, and Lucinda was very intelligent. Jeffrey seemed to think so too, though of course he was not very happy about it.

Nicholas had asked her to go with him to New York. Surely that meant marriage. But she wanted— needed—to know he loved her, to be asked to marry him on bended knee, with an engagement ring, no matter how paltry. She was more than happy to give up her mother's dream for her, but she still had her own dream: to be the love of Nicholas's life, the person he would give up everything for. . . .

BOOK YOUR PLACE ON OUR WEBSITE AND MAKE THE READING CONNECTION!

We've created a customized website just for our very special readers, where you can get the inside scoop on everything that's going on with Zebra, Pinnacle and Kensington books.

When you come online, you'll have the exciting opportunity to:

- View covers of upcoming books

- Read sample chapters

- Learn about our future publishing schedule (listed by publication month *and author*)

- Find out when your favorite authors will be visiting a city near you

- Search for and order backlist books from our online catalog

- Check out author bios and background information

- Send e-mail to your favorite authors

- Meet the Kensington staff online

- Join us in weekly chats with authors, readers and other guests

- Get writing guidelines

- AND MUCH MORE!

**Visit our website at
http://www.kensingtonbooks.com**

A MERRY LITTLE CHRISTMAS

Martha Schroeder

ZEBRA BOOKS
Kensington Publishing Corp.
http://www.kensingtonbooks.com

ZEBRA BOOKS are published by

Kensington Publishing Corp.
850 Third Avenue
New York, NY 10022

All Kensington titles, imprints and distributed lines are
available at special quantity discounts for bulk purchases
for sales promotion, premiums, fund-raising, educational or
institutional use.

Special book excerpts or customized printings can also be
created to fit specific needs. For details, write or phone the
office of the Kensington Special Sales Manager:
Kensington Publishing Corp., 850 Third Avenue, New York,
NY 10022. Attn. Special Sales Department. Phone: 1-800-
221-2647.

Zebra and the Z logo Reg. U.S. Pat. & TM Off.

First Printing: October 2002
10 9 8 7 6 5 4 3 2 1

Printed in the United States of America

*To Louise Sonnenberg with affection and gratitude.
You were there when the need was greatest, and
you continue to be both healer and friend.*

One

It wasn't fair.

That was all there was to it. It simply wasn't fair that her dreary cousin Lucinda should marry a rich and handsome man who adored her, while she, Priscilla Harrowby, with her blonde curls and china blue eyes, should languish unmarried at the advanced age of twenty. Not only was she prettier, Priscilla thought, her face a thundercloud of resentment, but she was an heiress while Lucinda hadn't a penny to bless herself with.

Of course, now Lucinda had everything while Priscilla, who certainly deserved the finest life had to offer, was relegated to receiving congratulations on her cousin's behalf.

"Oh, Priscilla, isn't it wonderful about your cousin? So brave to go to the Crimea, and how romantic that she found true love on the battlefield!"

"Oh, Priscilla, aren't you thrilled? Think of all the millionaires you'll meet!"

Pish and tush! If she heard one more person tell her how brave her cousin Lucinda was, what a heroine she had been to nurse soldiers with Miss Nightingale, Priscilla vowed she was going to drum her heels and scream! Nursing was a horrid, dirty job, and no lady would ever engage in it if there was anything else she could do.

As for meeting millionaires, Lucinda had been married a full month and nary a millionaire had Priscilla laid eyes on—except for Lucinda's husband, Jeffrey, and he looked at her and frowned, as if she weren't worthy to be Lucinda Bancroft's scullery maid, let alone her cousin!

Pish and tush!

There was a brisk knock at her door. Priscilla ignored it, wanting only to stay and sulk a little longer, nursing her grievances as if they were her dearest friends.

"Open this door, young lady!"

Her mother.

Mrs. Edwina Harrowby might look as if a strong wind would blow her over, but when it came to getting her own way, she could give lessons to Queen Victoria.

Priscilla sighed. She would have to open the door and listen to another scold. As slowly as she could, she slid off the bed. Ignoring the rumpled satin bedcover, she dragged herself over to the door, amid a fusillade of knocking. She jerked it open, almost propelling her mother, who was beating impatiently on the door, into the room fist first.

"Yes, Mama." Priscilla scuffed her toe in the rose-strewn carpet and hung her head, seeking to hide her puffy eyes from her mother's gaze.

"Stand up straight and look at me, young lady." Edwina's voice was naturally high-pitched, and anger made it even shriller. "We have received an invitation at last, and I won't have you pouting!"

"I am not pouting!"

"You are, you are! And you must not!" Edwina began to wring her hands, a sign she would very soon begin to cry. "We have an opportunity now to marry you off to someone with money and position. Mr. Bancroft knows everyone, and now that Lucinda has married him, she can help us. This invitation shows she will do so, if you will only be nice to her. Oh, why were you so mean to her when she lived here?"

Priscilla gave her mother a disgusted look. "Pish and tush, Mama! You were every bit as revolted by Lucinda as I was. Reading newspapers and discussing them with Papa! What kind of behavior was that for an unmarried girl? I heard you say so to Papa many a time. Vicar's daughter or not, she was no lady, and you thought so too!"

"But we should have been nicer, Cilla, my pet. Taken her about with us and tried to help her. But no matter!" Edwina smiled brightly and waved the heavy vellum invitation card in front of her daughter. "We are invited to an evening reception on Thursday next. That should be enough time to have Madame Dumaire make a new gown for you—pink, I think, with rows and rows of ruffles. And you must call on Lucinda before the reception and make your peace with her."

"Make my peace!" Priscilla scowled and turned away from her mother with a whish of her pink dimity skirts. She looked around for something to throw. The idea of going to Lucinda and eating humble pie was beyond revolting. It was abominable!

"Yes, Cilla, my pet, make your peace. You must." Her mother followed her across the room and put her hand on Priscilla's just as it closed around a Meissen shepherdess. "Do not throw that, my pet. It cost above fifty pounds. Yes, you must call on Lucinda. Then you may be asked to dinner and have a chance to meet more of those wealthy friends of Mr. Bancroft's and talk to them, enchant them, *make them propose."*

The last phrase was said with a kind of desperate passion Priscilla had never heard from her mama before. "What do you mean, Mama? How can I make a gentleman propose? What can I do that I have not done before? I am well dressed and I smile and cast my eyes down and pretend interest in whatever the gentleman is interested in. What more can I do?"

Edwina's brow puckered in obvious consternation. "I do not know, my pet. It is most discouraging, I confess. Many men show interest, but the only ones who propose are bounders who wish to marry your father's fortune."

Priscilla tossed her curls. "Much I care. All I want is wealth. They can be interested in whomever they please once I have achieved it." Her words were brave, even a little brash, and Priscilla saw her mother wince. But she had to put a brave face on her failure—for that was what it was. She had failed in the only test a woman had to pass.

What had she done wrong? There must be rules to follow, rules she had somehow had not learned. Edwina was of no help. Priscilla thought for a moment. If her mother couldn't tell her what they were, perhaps Lucinda, her erstwhile despised rival, would.

Priscilla would ask her.

"There aren't any rules, Cilla, or at least none that work." Lucinda sounded amused.

Priscilla gripped her hands in her lap. She was trying very hard not to hate her cousin, but it was difficult, especially when Lucinda refused to help her and gave her that faintly amused look. *As if I have done something stupid and she is trying not to laugh,* Priscilla thought resentfully.

"I don't see why you won't tell me." Priscilla tried to smile. "After all, you're married. What can it hurt to tell me how you did it?" She gazed at her cousin and tried not to envy her elegant new afternoon dress of dark blue watered silk. Only a single row of lace about the neckline, but that was of the finest French manufacture. Somehow it made Priscilla wonder if her mother, who insisted on ruffles and bows on everything, was really as fashionable and elegant as she thought.

Lucinda sighed, as if she found Priscilla provoking. "I fell in love. That's really all there is to it."

"But love has nothing to do with marriage." Priscilla was very sure of this. She thought for a moment. "Love really has nothing to do with anything. I mean, what good is it?" She warmed to the topic. "If you marry for love, you're liable to end up not just with a lot of children you have to take care of but poor as well. If you try to find love after you are married, your husband can take away your children and leave you penniless. So, I ask you, what good is it?"

"My goodness, Cilla," Lucinda said. "That was quite a speech. I think I had better ring for tea. You must be very thirsty." She smiled again, as if she knew a secret joke that Cilla would never understand.

Priscilla flushed. "You always did make fun of me. You think I'm stupid, don't you?"

Lucinda paused with her hand on the embroidered bellpull and turned to her cousin. This time her look was grave and sincere. "If I gave you that impression, I am sorry. I think I was trying to get my own back.

You used to tease me rather a lot about being a poor relation."

Priscilla's heart sank. She had been afraid this would happen. She knew Lucinda really had very little reason to help her. She *had* resented Lucinda, who had arrived at the Harrowby's with her dark-haired beauty and her judgmental air, and had taken over the management of the household at the age of fifteen. She had talked to Priscilla's papa, of whom Priscilla stood in considerable awe, with ease and had even made him laugh.

But Priscilla was not about to admit a fault and give Lucinda an advantage over her. "If I teased you a little, it was because you deserved it. You took over our house and our lives and you always thought Mama and I hadn't a brain between us."

Lucinda took a deep breath, and for a moment Priscilla thought she might order her out of her house. Instead, she smiled at Priscilla, a smile of such happiness and joy that Priscilla caught her breath. Lucinda had always been lovely, but this smile transformed her into a luminous creature who radiated some quality Priscilla only wonder at. Could it in fact be love?

"Oh, Cilla," Lucinda said, reaching out to take her hand, "you don't know, of course, never having experienced love. But I assure you, when you do, you will recognize it and it will change your life."

"Love?" Priscilla said. "It is love that has made you happy? Not all the money and the fact that you beat out all the other girls and snagged the catch of the year?"

"Of course it was love."

"Pish and tush, Lucy!" Priscilla was triumphant. "I remember when you first met Mr. Bancroft, you tried to catch him! Then you voiced some opinion about the army or the war or some other topic you had no business having an opinion about and he snubbed you!"

Again, that transcendent smile. "You are right. It was after that, in Turkey, that we quarreled and kissed and fell in love. So you see, my attempts to snag him, as you put it, were a dismal failure. It was only when I began to love him that I caught him. And he caught me."

Priscilla pursed her lips and considered. All of this sounded suspiciously like a fairy tale. Lucinda's story was not remotely what her mother had told her about marriage, nor what she had seen when her friends had become engaged. They often talked of love, but she had noticed that the financial settlement their fathers had negotiated was much more often the topic of conversation than their fiancés.

Was it possible Lucinda believed this ridiculous farrago of nonsense? Or did she have a more sinister motive in espousing it?

"Are you trying to make a fool of me, Lucy, with this romantic tale?"

Lucinda smiled and shook her head. "I should have known you would never believe me. Not after Aunt Edwina has been filling your head with mercenary ideas since you were in short skirts. But think, Cilla. Would you not be happier if you married someone you could actually care about?"

Priscilla gave this idea a moment's thought. "Perhaps," she conceded. "I might. If he were rich."

Her cousin laughed aloud and Priscilla, who always suspected that Lucinda laughed at her, jumped to her feet. But Lucinda only smiled at her and Priscilla sat down again, feeling foolish.

"I am not making fun of you, Cilla," Lucinda said,

her violet eyes reflecting her own happiness and compassion for Priscilla's dilemma.

Priscilla was torn between hating the idea of pity from anyone and a hint of warmth that her cousin felt any positive emotion toward her. Her mother, always sharp even while she doted, had recently begun to carp at Priscilla for failing to capture a rich husband.

Just then there was a noise and the door to the drawing room was flung open. "My love, I'm back at last and have brought—" Jeffrey Bancroft strode into the room, wearing a smile so warm that Priscilla felt *her* cheeks redden, though he had eyes only for his wife. He checked his steps and stopped speaking when he saw Lucinda was not alone. When he looked closer at their guest, his dark eyebrows joined together in a ferocious frown.

"Priscilla." His voice was icily polite. He inclined his head a bare inch in her direction. "I did not expect to see you here." His tone made it clear that she was not a welcome visitor. "I have brought Nicholas Cannon with me, my love, as I told you I would."

Dismissed, ignored, Priscilla found herself pasting a smile on her lips and telling herself to sparkle. It was always her mother's advice when she felt herself to be on social quicksand.

"Cilla," her cousin was saying, "may I present Mr. Cannon? He is a friend of Jeffrey's, come to visit from America. Nicholas, this is my cousin, Miss Harrowby."

The late afternoon sun shone in Priscilla's eyes as she sparkled up at the tall, dark man whose face she couldn't discern. "All the way from America, sir! What a long voyage you have made."

There was a short silence. Even Priscilla knew she had said something inane, but she had said the only thing she could think of. Her brain simply refused to work. She wasn't sure why until the faceless blur took her hand. Then she felt a shock like the tingle of lightning as it strikes close by.

She looked down to see his long, warm fingers closed over hers. Could that be what she had felt— simply his hand clasping hers? It was an unusual action for a man to shake a woman's hand, but Priscilla, usually the most conventional of women, found she liked it. Liked it so much, in fact, that she did not immediately withdraw her hand as proper etiquette indicated she should.

"Yes," the man holding her hand said, his voice a deep rumble, thunder to match the lightning of his touch. "It is a long trip. But a worthwhile one. I am by way of returning home, you see."

"Home?" Priscilla said. This was his home? "Here?"

He smiled. She could see the flash of strong white teeth and responded almost without thinking. She smiled up into his face, which suddenly came into focus as the butler silently drew the heavy velvet curtains across the windows against the coming evening. She gave a little, involuntary gasp that she hoped no one noticed. He wasn't handsome, but there was an excitement about him, an energy that seemed to fairly crackle from him so that one scarcely noticed the piercing eyes and craggy features. Priscilla felt compelled to respond to that energy.

"Not this exact place," he said, his smiled widening. "I don't mean I used to live in this house. I meant Britain. I was born in Scotland, as it happens."

She blushed. How foolish he must think her. With Lucinda, she was used to sounding silly. She almost tried to live up—or rather down—to her cousin's expectations. She knew she was less intelligent than Lucinda, but she believed that was a good thing, that men preferred it. So she hadn't worried about it, had refused to compete, to meet Lucinda on her own ground. Instead, she had played the empty-headed but adorable child-woman to perfection. So well, in fact, that now she thought it was not a pose.

"So you have returned to Britain," she said, knowing this remark was no more intelligent than the one before. "Are you here to see your family, Mr. Cannon?"

His face tightened and his mouth turned down. This time she had said something worse than inane, though she had no idea what it could be. Her lack of brains was beginning to bother her. Lucinda had that effect on her, and now it seemed Lucinda's friend did as well.

"Perhaps," he replied at last.

"Oh." It was the only safe thing she could think of to say. She cast about for something else. "You have arrived at a good time. We have been having a particularly warm autumn this year. Will you stay for Christmas?" She gave him her brightest smile and waited.

There was a short, uncomfortable silence, one Lucinda finally broke. "We do welcome you, sir, to our home." She moved with enviable grace to the bellpull and signaled for tea to be brought. "Do you find London much changed from your visit five years ago?"

"Thank you, Mrs. Bancroft." Relief was evident in his voice. Priscilla shrank back a little. Why could she not have thought of something to ask that he could respond to?

"Not so much excitement as there was during the Great Exposition," he said, and smiled at Lucinda, a friendly, warm smile that lit his face and erased the sharp lines that showed when Priscilla had asked about his family. "And I saw this afternoon to my surprise that they have moved the Crystal Palace."

Conversation flowed on around her. Tea was brought. Priscilla sat mute, unable to overcome the sense that she had failed a test, that this Scottish-American man who intrigued her had dismissed her as unworthy of notice or conversation. Why did she care? What about this particular man made her want to shine in his eyes?

She didn't know, but the very fact began to annoy her. He was a stranger and, as far as she knew, not rich or important, though he couldn't be poor and be welcomed as a business equal by Lucinda's millionaire husband. Priscilla declined another cup of tea and made her farewells with only a small smile. With a great deal to think about, she left for home.

Later that evening, Jeffrey and Nicholas sat at ease in front of a brisk coal fire in Jeffrey's book-lined study. Each held a snifter of brandy.

"You seem very contented," Nicholas said with a smile. "When I was last here, you seemed to be in a great hurry to get somewhere."

"Yes, I was. But now I know that in Lucinda I have found my destination." Jeffrey was afraid his answering smile was downright fatuous. "You, my friend, seem no happier than when you were here before. Tell me, have you been crossed in love again? Is that why you have come back? Are you going to the Highlands to visit your ancestral home?"

Nicholas frowned. "No! I am not here as a tourist

or visiting businessman and, unlike my last visit, I am not nursing a broken heart." He smiled a little wryly. "I found it was not broken after all, by the way. The beautiful Helen merely bruised it, I discovered when we met again. No, I am here on family business. Actually, I am English—at least, my father was English—and it is his family I have promised to contact."

Restless at the thought of his unpleasant errand, he rose and moved around the room, coming to rest at last in front of the tall windows that looked out over the tidy grass of Grosvenor Square.

"And that makes you unhappy? I saw how you frowned at my wife's nincompoop of a cousin when she asked you about your family."

Glad to find a more congenial topic of conversation, Nicholas grinned at his host. "I take it you are not fond of the lady."

"No, not at all. She is foolish beyond endurance and she was not very nice to Lucinda when they were growing up. Made sure Lucinda knew she was the poor relation." Jeffrey tossed off a large sip of brandy and reached toward an inlaid humidor that lay on the table near his chair. "She is a giggling, silly, mean little piece of worthless baggage."

"Whew! I had no idea you could be so infuriated by one small female. I'd have thought she was too insignificant to be worth being angry at." Nicholas found himself only partly amused at his friend's cold fury. In the back of his mind, he remembered the yearning he had sensed in Miss Harrowby's china blue eyes. He felt a little sorry for her.

"She's only insignificant when she doesn't have a hold over you. When you have to put up with her tantrums and demands, I assure you, she's as important as a snake in your path." Jeffrey turned a cigar over in his fingers. "And just as nasty."

Two

There was no party she had to attend that evening, and Priscilla was glad. Usually, she worried if an evening went by without some social engagement. It could be the beginning of the end, notice that the fashionable world was looking at her as a bit long in the tooth, that whatever party was being given was for younger girls.

That set her to brooding about her future. Where was the rich gentleman she could marry? The one her mother would approve of? The one her father would congratulate, talk to, smile approvingly on? Was he attending a party tonight, meeting another young lady? It was her constant fear.

But tonight she was going to forget her worries and engage in a secret pastime.

She retired to her room soon after dinner, pleading a headache. Once inside, she slipped off her shoes and managed to unbutton and step out of her dress and petticoats. She left them on the floor for the maid to take care of and reached inside a drawer in her chiffonier. From under a pile of chemises, she withdrew a book and carried it carefully over to the bed. Sighing in anticipation, she curled up and began turning the pages.

She knew her friends, not to mention her mother,

would be astonished to find her reading, but no one would be surprised that she hid the fact. It was not something a well-brought-up young lady did. Only fashion papers and improving tales, such as were found in *Godey's Lady's Book* or *Household Notes,* were acceptable fare for women.

But Priscilla was reading—or, more accurately, looking at—the drawings in a book of travel reminiscences. She had discovered the book in her father's library and had sneaked it upstairs in her reticule and hidden it in her lingerie drawer.

No one knew of her fascination with faraway places. No one must ever know. She had discovered a section of travel books in the library quite by accident one rainy day. She'd wandered in with no idea except that both her father and Lucinda found books fascinating, so perhaps, just perhaps, there might be something there to while away an hour or so. Underlying that reason was the idea that by reading she might gain the love and approval her father had given Lucinda so easily.

In so doing, she'd discovered a world.

For some reason, the idea of a world very different from the one she lived in fascinated her. If she allowed herself, she might almost wish to go to those places, where people wore fantastic costumes every day and lived in tiny cottages or teepees. Where they danced in an exciting, open way that looked very different from the decorous ballroom waltzes and quadrilles she was used to.

Where people were free.

So intent was she on the world she was looking at that the door was beginning to open before she noticed. With the quickness of guilt, she shoved the book under

the heap of pillows on her bed and smoothed her face
to blankness as her mother entered the room.

"Priscilla, what is wrong with you?" Edwina's
querulous voice pierced her dream journey like a sharp
pin. "What gave you the headache? Did Lucinda serve
you something that disagreed with you? Tell me about
her."

"She seemed well." Priscilla's response was halfhearted. For the first time she found herself unwilling
to gossip with her mother about her cousin.

"What did she say to you to overset you? Did she
rescind her invitation?" Edwina twisted her hands.

"No, Mama. We are still going to the reception."
Priscilla smiled and her mother relaxed.

"You are sure?"

Priscilla nodded, but her mother's eyes sharpened.

"What is that under your pillow?"

Oh, no, she had been discovered! "Nothing,
Mama."

What a foolish thing to say! Of course it was *something*. Why did she always crumble into stupidity
whenever she was frightened or embarrassed? She
could hear a silly, stupid giggle come out of her mouth
and see her mother frown. How many times had that
happened?

"What have you hidden under your pillow?" Edwina's voice was as sharp as a knife.

Priscilla could do nothing but smile and shrug. Why
could she never think of anything to say when con-
fronted like this? Why could she never do what her
father advised—tell the truth and shame the devil?

Her mother did not wait for a reply. She hurried
over to the bed and, before Priscilla's frozen brain

could respond, snatched the book from under the pillow.

"A book!" Edwina could not have sounded more horrified if Priscilla had been hiding one of the mummies pictured in the book. "What are you doing with a book? Is this Lucinda's work?" Red-faced, she waved it in front of Priscilla. "Did she give it to you? How many times do I have to tell you that you will never get a husband if you are known to read books!"

At that moment, Priscilla's tongue unlocked. "Lucinda did," she said.

"Lucinda!" Edwina pronounced the name with loathing. "Will I never hear the end of Lucinda? She has behaved like a hoyden— nursing men of all classes and conditions and proud of it. Heroine, indeed! She is no heroine to me, nor to any true woman. She is not what a lady should be. She is not what you *must* be. Do you hear me? Lucinda is not a model for any gently reared young lady. It is probably the fault of her father. He no doubt taught her all those outlandish ideas before he died."

"Her father was a vicar." Priscilla could not seem to keep her thoughts to herself.

Edwina's face grew even redder. "I do not care what her father was. I know what she is!"

"Her husband is wealthy." Priscilla could not seem to leave this subject alone.

"I don't care! I don't care! You are not to be like Lucinda! You are not to learn housekeeping or nursing! You are not to have opinions!" Edwina took a deep breath, her chest expanding like a pouter pigeon. "And above all, you are not to read books!" With a swish of her silk skirts, her mother marched out the door, bearing the book with her.

Priscilla pouted, looking around her room for something to do. No matter what her mother said, she didn't think it would hurt if she just looked at the pictures. What harm could it do? She had looked forward to looking at the illustrations and even reading a bit about the travels that were the subject of the book. Now she had nothing to do. Her needlework, which she did not enjoy anyway, was downstairs. She sat up and wrapped her arms around her knees.

Her mother was angry. She had been angry for some days, and Priscilla thought she knew why. Her daughter had as yet failed to capture a likely bridegroom, while her niece had done a brilliant job. Her mother had seemed quite desperate, and Priscilla thought that at this point any candidate would do.

She was glad she had not told Edwina about Mr. Cannon.

The large reception room of Lucinda and Jeffrey's mansion off Grosvenor Square was lit by a dazzle of gaslights. The dining room had sconces lit by gas, but they were turned down to a quiet glow and large silver candelabra gleamed instead on the deep mahogany of the table and buffet. Priscilla and her mother and father had been invited to the dinner party preceding the reception, a mark of distinction and a sign Lucinda intended to honor the relationship. Priscilla had a feeling, judging by the frown on Jeffrey Bancroft's face and the chilliness of his greeting, that he did not agree with his wife's decision to welcome her family.

"Priscilla." He took her hand and raised it to his lips in a courtly gesture, but his eyes held an expression of disdain cold enough to freeze her bones.

"Jeffrey." She sparkled up at him, her lips curving in their familiar, meaningless smile. "It was so nice of you to invite us."

"Lucinda invited you." He let her hand go and his expression grew even more unwelcoming.

"I know that, silly. It's always the hostess who invites the guests." Priscilla heard her own high, fluting voice as if it came from someone else. Her mother perhaps? The thought made her giggle.

Jeffrey turned to the next guest to arrive and Priscilla found herself facing her cousin. Lucinda had heard Jeffrey's greeting and she looked carefully at Priscilla. "Come with me and let me introduce you to the guests you haven't met." She sounded so kind that Priscilla feared she looked sad and that Lucinda was—perish the thought!—sorry for her.

She smiled her very best false smile at her cousin and said the first thing that came into her head. "Your husband looked very cross, Lucy. Have you been feeding him some outlandish Turkish food?"

Lucinda shook her head, grimacing slightly. "No, of course not. Jeffrey does not enjoy entertaining very much, that is all."

"You mean Jeffrey does not enjoy entertaining me."

What was the matter with her? Words kept coming out of her mouth that she was scarcely aware she thought. Insulting her husband was not the way to win over Lucinda. She covered up her embarrassment with a giggle.

Lucinda frowned at her. "If you would stop that annoying giggle, he might not be so sorry to see you coming."

Priscilla clapped her hand to her mouth. "Oh. Oh, my."

"Well, it is true, and you might as well know it. Not all men are enchanted by a childish woman, Cilla, and you do somewhat overdo it." Lucinda raked her new pink dress with a jaundiced glance.

Priscilla looked down. She had thought that perhaps this new confection was a little too loaded with ribbons and bows and ruffles, but as usual her mother had ignored her and ordered what she wanted. Was Lucinda right? It seemed possible. After all, Lucinda had married a wealthy and handsome man. Her ideas might have merit.

"Plainer, do you think?" Priscilla said.

"A simpler style, yes," Lucinda said. "But also, perhaps, a subtler color to bring out your features. And a simpler hair so everyone would see your eyes and how shiny your hair is."

Priscilla gaped at her cousin. Why was Lucinda offering her all this advice? Her mother would suspect that she wanted Priscilla to be less attractive rather than more, but Priscilla doubted that. After all, Lucinda had achieved all that she could hope for in marrying Jeffrey Bancroft. Why should she be jealous of Priscilla? No, it was just possible that Lucinda meant her advice to be genuinely helpful.

She would have to think about it. Without looking around to see if there were any men nearby, Priscilla made her way to a group of chairs in the corner of the room. She sat down and looked to see what other women were wearing, and how men seemed to react to them. For the moment, she gave no thought to her own appearance. There was a tiny frown between her brows as she contemplated Lucinda's friends. Observing others was a new idea to her, and she found the results intriguing.

The women seemed to be interested in the men, but also interested in each other. They greeted each other with what appeared to be real pleasure, with none of the tittering and high-pitched squeals Priscilla was used to hearing when women encountered each other.

Their clothes were elegant and made of sumptuous fabrics but, like Lucinda's, relatively unadorned. Men seemed attracted to them as much as they were to the kind of girls who were at the parties Priscilla usually attended. Yet they did not play with their fans or flutter their eyelashes or smile coyly.

She knew several of these women had been in Turkey with Lucinda and Miss Nightingale and they had married handsome, wealthy men. So it was not just Lucinda. These other women knew the secret, too. Perhaps if she could talk to them—

"Miss Harrowby, good evening."

She looked up in surprise to meet the dark pirate's eyes of Jeffrey's friend, Nicholas Cannon. She had been so deep in thought she had not seen him approach. When was the last time that had happened? She opened her eyes as wide as she could and prepared to sparkle, when out of the corner of her eye she saw Lucinda smiling gravely at her husband, not a hint of coquetry in her glance.

Why not try Lucinda's method, just for this one evening? Priscilla thought. After all, most of these people were not her friends. If they thought her strange, she didn't care. And Mr. Cannon would be returning to America soon, so what did it matter if he found her boring and dull?

"Good evening, Mr. Cannon." She gave him a small, friendly smile. "I hope you are enjoying your stay in London."

"It is for the most part a business visit, Miss Harrowby. I have to see some of my father's relatives." He frowned a little, then shrugged and gave a little half smile. "I think I mentioned that the other day. I am not looking forward to it. I find it concerns me so much that I have difficulty concentrating on anything else."

Priscilla thought for a moment about Mr. Cannon's problem. "Perhaps," she said, a little shyly, unused to giving advice, "if you just got the visit over with, you could enjoy the rest of your stay."

He looked down at her, an arrested look on his face. "That is very good advice, Miss Harrowby. Bancroft and his wife have given me the same suggestion. I begin to think I will have to heed it."

"Sometimes the more you think about something difficult, the harder it gets. I often feel that way about going to the dentist." Priscilla held her breath, afraid he would laugh scornfully at her. What girl talked about the dentist to a young man?

But Mr. Cannon smiled a friendly smile, as if they shared a secret and said, "I know exactly what you mean. I feel the same way about the dentist. The doctor, too, as a matter of fact."

Priscilla smiled back, a huge, friendly smile, and let her breath out in relief. He had understood. And all at once, that current of electricity that had seemed to run between them the other day became even more pronounced. Now it ran not just between a man and a woman but between friends.

"I believe dinner is served," Mr. Cannon said after a long, electric silence. "May I escort you?"

"I don't think so," she said with regret. "I'm sure Lucinda has arranged for you to take some important lady in to dinner, since you are an honored guest from across the sea."

"Yes, she did want to do that, but I requested you." He smiled down at her and patted the hand he had placed on his arm. "Unless you object, Miss Harrowby, we are dinner partners."

Her heart sang and, unaware, she gave a little skip of joy. "No, sir. I have no objection at all."

Once seated, Priscilla decided to ask the questions she wanted answered, for once not worrying that she would offend a man—the cardinal sin in her mother's eyes.

"Why do you not wish to see your family here, Mr. Cannon?" she asked. "Have they offended you in some way? Do you have to see them?"

He looked down at his plate for a moment. "My mother asked me to see them. They are my father's family. After he died, she asked that I pay a visit to them and see if the quarrel that has separated us for twenty-five years could be resolved. My mother is a great one for family." He smiled, as if at a pleasant memory.

"Then, of course, you must see them. Do you think they will snub you? Treat you as if you were some poor relation? You aren't a poor relation, are you?" Realizing what she had said, Priscilla lowered her face into her napkin for a long moment. "I shouldn't have said that. It was very rude, and none of my business."

Nicholas looked at her. "Is money so very important to you, then, Miss Harrowby?"

She thought for a long moment. It was important that she answer truthfully. She had been having the first truthful conversation of her life with a man, and she did not want to spoil it. She knew she ought to say, *No, money doesn't matter at all,* but she also knew that Nicholas Cannon would see right through her if she did. So, she opted for the truth, insofar as she knew what the truth was.

"I am afraid so. It is only unimportant when you have a great deal."

"And do you not have a great deal?"

Again, she considered. "I have never thought about it before. My father does. I assume my husband will. That should mean that I am rich, shouldn't it? But it does not. Why does it seem as if I do not have any money? Do you understand why that should be?"

She had been looking into those dark eyes of his that seemed fathoms deep and mysterious. Now, as servants passed silver dishes around for the second course, she looked around and realized if she did not begin talking to the gentleman on her other side immediately, she would risk being regarded as very rude and perhaps even fast. She would certainly hear from her mother at some length about her want of conduct. She did not want her mother to ruin this evening.

Smiling a little ruefully at Nicholas, she turned to the man on her left. She widened her eyes and began to sparkle.

When she once again turned back to Nicholas, after the fish course had been consumed, she was delighted to find they could continue their conversation as if nothing had intervened.

"I have been thinking," he said to her, his voice grave, as if he had been considering her statement since they last had spoken. "And I can understand what you mean. My father made a tidy fortune, but I did not feel as if any of that money was mine. I think perhaps you have to earn your own before you think of money as belonging to you."

Priscilla gave an impatient little shrug. He didn't understand, after all. "Perhaps that is true for you. You are a man. But there is no way for a woman to earn her own money."

His smile was rueful. "Because we speak the same language, I forget how different our lives are. In America, even women can earn their living if they have to." He paused for a moment as if considering his next remarks. "My mother earned a considerable sum as a baker and cateress before my father met with his success."

"What an amazing thought!" Priscilla had never so much as contemplated such a thing. Of course, now that she thought about it, she realized women worked for their bread every day in London. Just not women one knew. Seamstresses, governesses, shop girls, maids, and housekeepers—all earned their keep, she supposed. But a woman who gave birth to a man like Mr. Cannon, a man who spoke intelligently, whose manners were impeccable and who was a friend of Jeffrey and his friends—that was a revelation.

"You think it impossible that such a woman could be a lady—if not a lady born, then one formed by character and circumstance," he said.

"No, I think it is wonderful!" The words were heartfelt. "How admirable and courageous such a woman must be."

Priscilla was astounded. These were ideas she had never entertained. She had laughed when Lucinda had voiced them. Now she felt as if she had journeyed to one of those countries she'd read about, where customs were different and people seemed happy and liberated.

It was not something could happen here, of course. Not something she could ever do. Not babyish Priscilla, who always made mistakes, but someone free and brave. Like Lucinda.

Her heart sank.

Nicholas's face had been turning darker by the moment, his brows drawn together and his mouth clamped in a thin line. At her words, his expression cleared as if by magic. "Then you do not think it disgusting? It does not sink her beyond reproach in your eyes?"

"No, of course not." Priscilla frowned a little. "But I am not sure everyone would feel as I do about it."

"I am sure they would not." Nicholas smiled at her. "I am amazed that you do. You are a very enlightened young lady."

Priscilla preened at his praise. No one had ever thought her enlightened before. Indeed, no one had ever believed she had a thought in her head aside from ruffles and ringlets.

"Like your cousin, Mrs. Bancroft, you have a large view of life."

All Priscilla's pleasure evaporated. Would she always be compared to Lucinda? Could she never do anything that made people look at her, just her?

"You don't like to be bracketed with your cousin, do you, Miss Harrowby?" His eyes were shrewd but sympathetic and his smile warm.

Priscilla felt as if she could speak honestly to this man. He understood. "Would you like it if you were always weighed in a balance and it always tipped the other way? I am tired of being the lightweight, Mr. Cannon."

"So it is not your cousin you are angry with, it is the people who think you are alike."

"No one thinks we are alike." Bitterness crept into her voice and for a moment she didn't care. It felt so good to be able to share her feelings with someone. "Everyone thinks Lucinda is good and clever and beautiful. Downright perfect, in fact. And the same people think I am a silly little rattlebrain, selfish and mean, but not bright enough to be really bad. No one hates me. They all despise me. Your friend Jeffrey despises me. My own father despises me."

At that, her voice broke, partly from the tears that welled up and choked her, and partly from the horror she felt at having exposed her ugliest and most vulnerable side to a virtual stranger.

She took a deep, cleansing breath. "You must forgive me. I never spill all over someone the way I just did with you. It must be because I know you are going home to America and I will never see you again." There was a tiny stab of pain at the thought.

He laughed a little. "That's a compliment if I ever heard one. You have confided in me and now wish me at home in America, or perhaps better yet at the bottom of the ocean."

"Oh, no, never that!" Without thinking she reached out and laid her hand on his arm for a moment, then snatched it away.

It was the mere whisper of a touch, gone in a heartbeat, yet Nicholas felt it all the way to his heart. For the first time since he had left New York, he felt a warm, welcome physical contact. Something about the instinctive sympathy with which Priscilla had sought to reassure him meant more to him than he could say. Leaving his mother and brother and sister behind, with the prospect of meeting relatives who would despise him and his family, had left him feeling as if he were encased in ice.

"Thank you," he said, his voice heartfelt. He watched as she lowered her eyes to her plate. For a moment he thought she was trying to flirt with him. Then he chanced to look up and catch the gaze of Priscilla's mother boring into her daughter, a look of profound disapproval on her face.

Nicholas knew he was regarded by many people who met him in company with Jeffrey Bancroft as an upstart American. Jeffrey had kept his word and said nothing of Nicholas's burgeoning wealth. Clearly, Mrs. Harrowby was not pleased that her daughter was wasting her time on a mere colonial nobody.

Later he found it was worse than he knew. After dinner, when the gentlemen joined the ladies in the large drawing room, he contrived to make his way toward Priscilla, only to note her mother had taken her aside and was giving her what could only be a severe scold. They stood in an alcove, secluded from most of the room, but Mrs. Harrowby's tone of voice could be heard some yards away, where Nicholas stood. He could not make out the exact words, but Priscilla stood, her shoulders slumped, saying nothing as her mother went on and on in a high, hard voice.

Nicholas could think of nothing to do that would not make the situation worse. He looked around to see if there was someone else who might be able to go where he could not. To his relief, he caught Lucinda Bancroft's eye. She glided gracefully over to her aunt and cousin and took them both by the arm. Smiling happily, she led them out into the room. Before Mrs. Harrowby could protest, she found herself making up one of a table for whist, while Priscilla was led over to a group of young women who were gathered around the pianoforte, singing along to the accompaniment of one of their number.

Nicholas managed to talk briefly with Lucinda. "I am sorry I caused your cousin to suffer such a scold. Does it happen often?"

Lucinda looked at him curiously. "My aunt is determined to make her daughter into a replica of herself. Whenever Cilla tries to be her own person, in any degree whatsoever, she hears about it at great length."

"I didn't realize. What prompted it this time, do you know? Just her interest in our conversation?" Nicholas could not explain the guilt he felt at having caused such a scene.

Lucinda smiled. "You do not understand the rules of society here. Priscilla so far forgot herself as to actually touch you. That marks her as fast and may not be condoned. Her mother felt it necessary to remind her she should not think for one moment she can behave like her disreputable cousin Lucinda."

Nicholas's eyebrows shot up. "I had no idea you were a blot on the family escutcheon, Mrs. Bancroft."

"Yes, indeed. Only my husband's wealth insulates me from my aunt's strictures. She is hoping I will introduce Cilla to one of Jeffrey's wealthy friends." Her smile faded and she looked at Nicholas very seriously. "Aunt Edwina is a serious problem for Cilla. She has no use for you now, but I would be very careful if I were you to make sure she does not find out how wealthy you are, or she will make a dead set at you. The only thing worse than Aunt Edwina scorning you is Aunt Edwina fawning on you. Be warned!" Lucinda patted him on his arm briefly and left him to digest her words.

Three

The next morning, Nicholas found himself taking Priscilla's advice, getting ready to call on his father's family, the Connaughts of Grosvenor Square. His father had changed his name when he left for America. Bartholomew Connaught had thought Cannon was a more forceful and democratic name, and he did not want to be identified with the powerful Connaught family.

Nicholas was not sure he did, either. He had his parents' marriage certificate from a small parish in the north of England, made out in the name of Connaught, and a silver frame that closed like a box, containing small paintings of a man and a woman Nicholas supposed were his grandparents. There was a sealed letter, the ink faded on the envelope that his mother told him his father had written but never sent to his own father.

Nicholas turned the yellowing paper over in his hands. It was addressed to Lord Bartholomew Connaught, the Marquis of Bellingham, at an address in Grosvenor Square, the address to which Nicholas was making his slow and hesitant way on this crisp, bright morning in late November.

As the large, imposing mansions of Grosvenor Square came into his view, he paused for a moment to get his bearings. The trees in the central square had lost their leaves, but there was still an air of opulence and plenty about the place. A picture of his own family's new home on Fifth Avenue in New York came to him and he smiled. It was every bit as large and, to his mind at least, far lovelier than these palatial buildings.

He didn't need these people. He was paying them a visit only to please his mother. If he was received pleasantly, she was prepared to call on them or perhaps even visit them when she came with him to Britain, which she had promised to do in the next year.

Nicholas smiled. He found he was eager to show his mother London and go with her to visit her family in Scotland. They had not approved of their daughter's marriage to an improvident younger son, but they had reconciled with her and were eagerly awaiting her visit.

He would brush through this, get it over with, no matter how the high and mighty Bartholomew Connaught, Marquis of Bellingham, treated him. In a few weeks he would be on his way back to New York, to his familiar life.

Satisfied that he had relegated his unknown relations to their proper place, at the periphery of his life, he climbed the steps to Number 121 with a jaunty air, feeling much lighter of heart. What did these pompous scions of the old world matter to him anyway? They had no way of knowing the extent of his wealth, so Nicholas could see how they behaved to a man they could only believe was a poor relation.

He raised the heavy brass knocker and rapped briskly. The door was opened after a short interval by an elderly man whose bearing almost made Nicholas believe here was the marquis himself. He nodded to the butler and extended one of his visiting cards.

"Mr. Nicholas Cannon to see the marquis on a matter of family business," he said.

The butler's face remained impassive for a moment. Then, breaking all the rules Nicholas thought he had learned about the behavior of proper British servants, he smiled.

"You are Mr. Bart's son," the old man said, standing aside and ushering him into an enormous hall tiled in black and white marble, with a sweeping, double staircase leading upward. "I would know you anywhere. The spit of him, you are. I am Dalton. I've been here since your father was a lad. Welcome, Mr. Nicholas."

"Thank you, Dalton." Nicholas returned the old man's smile. No matter what the family thought, here was one person who recognized and accepted him immediately.

"The marquis isn't well, Mr. Nicholas," the butler said. "But I make no doubt this will chirk him right up. Mr. Bart's son come to see him." He shook his head in wonder. "Better than a tonic, it will be."

Nicholas was not so sure about that.

"If the marquis is not receiving visitors, perhaps the earl would see me." Nicholas's mother had told him that Granville Connaught, his father's older brother and the heir to the marquisate, was an earl. The earl of Ashden. A courtesy title, she had called it.

"If you'll wait in here," Dalton said and showed him into another enormous room, this one furnished with stiff-looking chairs and tables with porcelain ornaments set on them in rigid, geometrical perfection. Downright chilly, Nicholas found it. Not like the opulent, upholstered receiving room on the ground floor of his house in New York, where newspapers awaited the visitor and the butler would offer you tea or Madeira. Not very hospitable, these noble relatives of his.

"I understand you claim to be some sort of relation," a cool, bored voice said behind him.

He turned, but not too quickly, though he had been startled. The man standing just inside the door, leaning negligently against the door frame, looked to be his father's age. He was almost as tall as Bart Cannon had been, and there was a distinct resemblance in the high cheekbones and long, mobile mouth, though his coloring was a pale, washed-out version of his father's rich brown hair and dark eyes. This man's expression of chilly disdain made him look like a caricature of Nicholas's charming, openhearted father.

"I don't believe I have said anything beyond my name," Nicholas responded with equal disdain.

"Which is, as I understand it, not Connaught." The man—Nicholas assumed he was Granville Connaught—pushed himself off from the door and began a slow and careful walk across the room to where Nicholas stood.

Nicholas eyed him with carefully disguised interest. "No, my father changed it before they landed in America. He wanted a fresh start, with no ties to anyone who would not welcome my mother." As he approached, Nicholas was happy to note the man was at least several inches shorter than he was and did not enjoy being looked down on, as Nicholas was doing. He also detected brandy fumes, which explained the careful walk. His Uncle Granville, it seemed, was drunk—at eleven o'clock in the morning.

"You, of course, have documents to prove this." The voice was still bored, but Nicholas noted Granville's hands opened and closed convulsively, as if he wanted to wrap them around Nicholas's neck. "They all do."

"There are people who wish to be associated with your family?" Nicholas allowed his disbelief to show in his lifted eyebrows.

"You sound surprised." Granville Connaught did not extend a hand or introduce himself. He stood a few feet away from Nicholas and swayed gently. His voice, however, was not slurred. Indeed, he spoke with exaggerated precision, which made him sound even more patronizing. "Yet why else are you here except to claim an allowance, or one of the smaller properties? I sometimes think every young man who comes from the colonies to visit London claims to be related to my brother. His—shall we say—separation from his family is well known."

"I am surprised." Nicholas clenched his fists, then forced himself to relax his hands. He was pleased his voice was as even and cool as Granville's. "I myself have no desire to be other than a citizen of the American republic. But if you made the others as welcome as you are making me, they must have all been happy to return home."

He didn't bother to smile but stood, his arms crossed, awaiting the next barb. A few more minutes of this and he could leave. He would tell his mother the marquis was sick and the earl drunk. He would explain he had tried.

But he hadn't. Not yet. He had to show this arrogant ass the papers and paintings that would prove his case. He was reaching into his pocket to reveal them when Dalton again entered the room, his step brisk and his eyes bright.

"The marquis wishes to see you, Mr. Nicholas," he said.

"What!" Granville's mask of civility slipped, and his voice lost its tone of aristocratic boredom. He clenched his fists and swayed toward the old butler. "What the devil do you mean by this, you old fool? What did you tell him?"

All expression was wiped from Dalton's face in an instant. He became the perfect servant, stolid and deferential—except for his eyes. Nicholas could see the wintry twinkle.

"The marquis wishes to see Mr. Nicholas," Dalton repeated, speaking slowly, as if to a slightly backward child. Then he beamed at Nicholas. "If you will come with me, sir."

"What have you told the marquis? Did you tell him this young imposter is Bart's child? How do we know Bart even had a child?" Granville's voice was no longer a bored drawl. Instead, it became more frantic with each word. By now he sounded drunk.

"The marquis is waiting, Mr. Nicholas." Dalton ignored Granville, gesturing for Nicholas to precede him out the door.

He left no time for Nicholas to say a polite good-bye to his uncle, who had not, in any case, demonstrated anything like what his mother would consider good manners.

After ascending the gently curved staircase two flights, they came at last to the marquis's room. Nicholas had been expecting splendor. Instead, he was greeted by what could have been an enormous monk's cell, so cheerless and bleak did it seem. The only chair was a straight-backed wooden one, and a single gas lamp stood on the chest near the bed. The only comfortable element in the room was a huge mahogany bed on which a tall, gaunt figure lay.

"Here is Mr. Nicholas, my lord," Dalton said, raising his voice a little.

Nicholas stood in the doorway, waiting, though he could not have said what he waited for. A kind word from the man who had disowned his father? Surely not. He was a grown man. He no longer needed his grandfather's acceptance, if indeed he ever had.

"Come here, boy, and let me have a look at you." The voice was a harsh rasp and was followed by a deep cough. "Dalton thinks you're Bart's boy, but Dalton's a fool." The man in the bed gestured feebly with one narrow, long-fingered hand, a hand very like Nicholas's father's—and his own. "Well, what are you waiting for? Afraid of me, are you? They all are. I thought you might be different. Too bad."

The voice grew steadily more feeble until, at the last words, it fell silent altogether. Nicholas made his way over to the bed. "I am here, sir. Can I do anything for you?"

The old man opened his eyes at the sound of Nicholas's voice. Those eyes, set in the gaunt, paper-white face, were as alive as any twenty year old's. They were brown eyes, not pale like Granville's, but a deep, brilliant brown, sparkling with life. Nicholas couldn't help but stare. They were the exact color of his father's eyes and held the same expression of curiosity and impatience.

"I think the boot is on the other foot, boy. The question is, can I do anything for you? Or, more precisely, will I?"

"You needn't do anything for me, sir. I can take care of myself." It was on the tip of Nicholas's tongue to tell his grandfather just how well he could take care of himself, his mother, and his siblings. But caution made him hold his tongue.

The gaunt face creased in a smile. "He's Bart's boy all right, Dalton. You were right about that."

"Yes, sir," Dalton replied. "That I was."

For a moment, Nicholas watched the two old men share a silent grin of triumph. They looked, for all their gray hair and wrinkles, like a couple of schoolboys who had pulled off a prank.

"Granville won't be happy," the marquis said.

"That he won't," Dalton replied.

Both men grinned.

There was a long pause while the two old men savored their private communication. Then the marquis turned his head and surveyed Nicholas. "I suppose you'd better show me your proofs, boy, whatever documents you have, so we can show them to Granville and the solicitors. They won't be convinced by a face. In fact, nothing will convince Granville."

Something about the mysterious smiles and shared silence between Dalton and the marquis made Nicholas uneasy. He had no desire to become a pawn in whatever game the marquis seemed to be playing with his son. Nicholas had no family feeling toward Granville—or indeed toward Granville's father—but he disliked being used, whatever the reason.

"Let us talk for a bit first, if you don't mind, sir." He could feel his brows contract into a frown. Usually, Nicholas Cannon's frown made those around him eager to make any effort to erase it. This time, however, he was met by an equally formidable frown on the face of his grandfather.

"Why? Don't tell me you have no proof, boy. Bartholomew would never be so feckless."

"I have proof, sir."

"Then hand it over."

"First tell me the reason why you are so eager to have me as part of your family." Nicholas wasn't sure why he was pushing a sick old man this hard, but there was something in those bright brown eyes that told him there was more to this than the return of a long-lost branch of the family. "You disowned my father. You have not heard from him for twenty-five years. You haven't asked about him now." Nicholas stared at him hard.

"I know about Bart and his family," the marquis said, his smile no longer mischievous, but twisted and sad. "I know Bart died last year. I know there are three children and the oldest is called Nicholas. I will tell you why I took the trouble to find you." He sighed a little, and the light in his eyes faded. "Granville's wife, Emily, died last year in childbirth," the marquis said. "It was a terrible blow and quite unexpected. She was very young, should have had years ahead of her and several sons at least. But it was not to be. Your coming like this is the answer to a prayer."

Nicholas was quite sure Granville Connaught would never consider finding Nicholas compensated him in any way for any loss whatsoever. But perhaps finding his other son's family did make up for the marquis's loss, although he did not seem like a man who would grieve over his son's wife. It seemed to be the loss of the child that affected him. Was that the reason why the marquis was so pleased to see Nicholas—the substitution of one grandson for another?

"I do not plan to settle here, sir. My home is in America, and so is my family and my business."

Again that smile. "We'll see about that. A Connaught's home is always here or at Bellingham Place."

Nicholas was not going to argue with a sick old man. When the time came he would simply leave, Connaught of Bellingham Place or not. But first he must make sure of the most important thing. "Where I go, my mother and my brother and sister go as well. If you welcome me, you welcome them. If not, I will bid you good-bye now."

The marquis smiled. "I am glad you see it that way, boy. Of course your family is welcome here. You are the heir, after all."

"What are you talking about?"

"You are my heir now that Bart is dead and Granville has no son."

"Surely Granville is your heir." Nicholas could feel the hair rise up on the back of his neck. The heir to a marquisate. He could all but feel the dead hands of a hundred Connaughts weigh heavily on his shoulder. He shook them off.

"Granville is—ill."

A new voice entered the tense conversation. "Not so *ill* as to welcome an imposter, my lord."

Granville Connaught entered the room. It seemed to Nicholas as if his uncle had drunk considerably more brandy in the few minutes since Nicholas had left the drawing room. At any rate, the fumes seemed stronger. The marquis coughed again as his son ambled forward to the bed, ignoring Nicholas.

Again, that mischievous smile, so at odds with the parchment white face and the thin body under the bedclothes. "Granville, I understand you have already met your nephew."

"Has he produced any 'evidence'?" Granville's voice put the word in quotation marks. "Some artful letters, perhaps, or a picture of a woman vaguely resembling Mama?" There was a hectic flush on his cheeks and his mouth was drawn into a thin, sardonic smile.

Slowly, reluctantly, Nicholas withdrew the papers and the silver frame from his pocket. "Here," he said as he grudgingly handed the carefully saved mementos over to Dalton to give to his grandfather.

"I'll take those, Dalton, if you please." And before Nicholas or the marquis could move, Granville's long fingers had plucked them from the butler's hands and the earl was moving with uneven steps over to the long, uncurtained window to examine them.

"You be careful with those, Granville," his father said sharply. "Anything happens to any of those papers, I'll recognize Nicholas Cannon as my grandson immediately. Do you understand?"

"Most clearly, my lord."

Nicholas wondered if anything was clear to his uncle at this point. Granville took his time looking at the marriage certificate. He turned the letter over in his hands several times and smoothed his fingers over the address, but he did not open it. Then he opened the silver case and gazed unblinking at the portraits for a few seconds before he snapped the case shut.

He turned to the others and extended the mementoes to Dalton. "Here. Take them to his lordship." He turned away and looked out the window. Nicholas wondered if he was aware his hands opened and closed convulsively on the window frame.

Nicholas found himself almost disappointed that the earl had not denounced him as a fraud. Then he could leave this place, with its strange relationships and family secrets. Granville and the marquis didn't seem to like each other. Granville's sorrow, if he had felt any, at the loss of his wife and stillborn child had turned to bitterness and an escape into drink.

The marquis took the portraits and papers. He immediately looked at the letter, turning it over in his hands for a few moments before opening it with hands that shook uncontrollably. Without a word, Dalton reached over, opened the letter, and handed it to the marquis with a pair of spectacles.

There was silence for a few minutes while the marquis read the letter. When he finished, there were tears on his cheeks. He looked up at Nicholas and said, "He wanted us to be reconciled. He was sorry we were estranged."

"But he was not sorry he went to America or married my mother." Nicholas was determined that whatever happened, the Connaughts would know where he stood. On the deck of a ship heading for New York, that was where he wished he stood.

He looked around at the huge room. The ceilings must be twenty feet high, he mused. There were no rugs on the floors or curtains at the windows, no knickknacks on tables or books on shelves near to hand. The people were not much more comfortable than their surroundings. The marquis looked frail and shaken as he studied the portrait miniatures.

"My wife," he murmured. "And myself. We gave them to each other for Christmas the year Bart was born. I gave them both to him when his mother died.

He was away at Eton then, and I could no longer bear to look at what I had lost."

He barely glanced at the marriage certificate, appearing to be lost in thought. His hand strayed often to the pictures and he looked at them, but only out of the corners of his eyes, as if afraid he would show an unseemly emotion if he gazed for long at his dead wife's portrait.

"I am glad you came of your own free will, boy," he said at last to Nicholas. "Glad you wanted to see me, that I did not have to send for you."

"I am not sure I would have come in answer to a summons, sir," Nicholas said. He was touched by his grandfather's grief for his lost wife and son, but he wanted the old man to be aware that Nicholas was not there to become a permanent part of his household. "I came because my parents wanted to mend the breach between your family and theirs. My mother felt particularly strongly after my father died."

"Ah, yes, a true Colonial." The marquis smiled benignly. "Independent to a fault!"

"We stopped being a colony eighty years ago, sir," Nicholas said between gritted teeth. It was bad enough that his grandfather patronized him, but to be treated like an uncouth rustic was beyond maddening!

"I take it you are determined to welcome this unknown American as Bart's son," Granville said. He had observed the scene, nodding his head from time to time as if this was all exactly what he might have expected. "Those pictures might be of anyone, you know, my lord."

"The one is the spitting image of your mother, and you know it," the marquis said. "And you can see the lad here is the image of Bart as well. Give it up, Granville. Your chance to pass the title on is gone. Young Nicholas will take over at your death."

"I am not dead yet!" Granville all but spat the words at his father. Anger radiated from his face.

"You soon will be if you continue to tap the brandy bottle the way you have been," the marquis shot back. "They are gone, Granville, and he is here."

"And I say again I am not dead yet. And until I am, I am capable of begetting sons. The young claimant had better not forget that!" Granville swung around to confront Nicholas head on. His face was a mottled red and the whites of his eyes showed yellow, but anger seemed to burn away the alcohol from his system and he spoke more clearly than he had since Nicholas had arrived.

"I do not want—" Nicholas began, but Granville held up a hand to stop him.

"Do not bother to try to convince me you're happy in some log cabin in the new world and wouldn't trade it for the chance to be a marquis of England."

"Very well," Nicholas said, giving up the attempt. "I won't. But 'tis true nonetheless."

The marquis gave a cackle of laughter, and even Dalton smiled as Granville stamped out of the room.

"Nicely done," he said. "That stopped him. Log cabin, indeed. I happen to know you've done rather well for yourself and are able to keep your mother and brother and sister in reasonable comfort—as much as anything in your primitive country can be said to be comfortable."

Nicholas gritted his teeth. Anything that wasn't English, any wealth that wasn't old, inherited acres simply didn't register on his grandfather's consciousness. Well, he was only going to be here for a few weeks.

His business would not permit him to stay away much longer than that. The thought gave him considerable comfort.

When his grandfather leaned back and closed his eyes, Nicholas decided, with some relief, that it was time to go. He wondered if his grandfather would insist that he move into one of the guest rooms in the house. He hoped not. From what he could see, Claridge's Hotel offered much more in the way of comfort. Not to mention safety. He wouldn't put it past his Uncle Granville to put poison in his morning coffee—assuming, that is, that coffee was available in this benighted place!

"I'll be taking my leave, sir," said Nicholas after a moment. "Perhaps I could stop and pay my respects again before I leave for home."

The marquis's eyelids snapped open. "What! What do you mean, leave for home? I've told you you are my heir, and your response is that you must leave. Impossible! You can't leave now!"

"I am afraid I must, sir." Nicholas tried to sound regretful. Indeed, as he looked at his grandfather and saw the baffled anger in his eyes, he did regret having to disappoint the old man. But he did not for one moment regret not staying in England to learn to be the kind of stubborn, difficult autocrat his grandfather exemplified. Or, worse yet, a snobbish drunk like his uncle.

"Why? What can possibly be more important than learning about your heritage, learning to be a British nobleman?"

The marquis's face was beginning to look bright red. Dalton, who had stood in the background up until now, went to the chest near the bed and poured a yellowish liquid from a small vial into a glass of water, turning it cloudy. He came to the bed and bent over his master, offering him the medicine. The marquis shook his head impatiently.

"I am afraid I must ask you to leave, Mr. Nicholas," the butler said, ignoring the marquis's clutch on his arm. "The doctor has strictly forbidden his lordship to excite himself. You can see the results of ignoring his orders."

With relief at his escape, Nicholas smiled at his grandfather. "I will come again tomorrow, sir, if that is all right with the doctor and Dalton."

"No, wait!" The marquis contrived to push himself upright in the bed. "I want you to promise to stay at least for Christmas. Come to Bellingham Place for the holidays. See what your heritage is before you decide you don't want it. Bring anyone you want. I want you to be happy and feel at home."

Nicholas doubted he would ever feel at home in his grandfather's house or wearing his grandfather's honors, should that day ever arrive. "Thank you, sir. We will talk more about it tomorrow. Good day now."

And with that he made his escape from the sick-room, only to find himself facing Granville in the lower hall, as he waited to retrieve his long astrakhan overcoat and tall beaver hat.

"So you managed to convince the old man you're Bart's beloved son," he sneered.

The brandy fumes were stronger than ever, and Nicholas backed away from them. "I came to make peace. I have done that, I think, at least with the marquis. I am sorry you cannot see your way clear to do the same."

"You are not going to take my place as Marquis of Bellingham," Granville said. "I won't permit it."

"As I understand it," Nicholas responded mildly as he drew on his gloves, "even English aristocrats die. So it would seem someone must take your place eventually. Why do you care who it is?"

"It should be my son, not Bart's." His voice was almost tearful, like a small child denied a treat.

Nicholas lost patience with this pathetic sot. "Then for God's sake, marry again and beget one! No one will be happier than I if you do."

Granville's response was to make a rude noise of disbelief and turn away. Nicholas shrugged and nodded to the footman, who opened the door for him.

What a family!

"So you see my problem," he said later that evening to Jeffrey and Lucinda as they stood conversing in the midst of a reception at the home of friends of the Bancrofts. "I feel as if I must go to spend Christmas at Bellingham Place. I could be home in time if I took one of the new steamships, but I know my mother would want me to stay."

"It does not sound as if you are going to have a very pleasant time, with your grandfather sick and your uncle so ill-disposed toward you." Lucinda accepted a glass of champagne from a passing waiter and sipped. She turned to smile at Priscilla, who had come up to the group in time to hear her words.

"The marquis did say I could invite anyone I wanted to come, too. I don't suppose you and Jeffrey . . ." Nicholas allowed his words to trail off as he looked at his friends with a hopeful smile.

"I don't know. We had planned on a quiet time, with just ourselves," Lucinda said, biting her lip and looking at Jeffrey with a question in her eyes. "What do you think?" she asked him.

"Well, I don't suppose we can leave him to wander about the estate all alone," he said with a smile. "I think we must rescue the man from his relations. Which will in turn rescue us from yours, my dear."

At Lucinda's horrified look, Jeffrey appeared to notice Priscilla for the first time. "Oh, hello, Cilla," he said, with no visible apology.

Nicholas was embarrassed for his friend. He saw Priscilla's painful flush, and as he looked into her china blue eyes, he thought he saw a lonely look, as if she were used to being left out, but she did not like it. She smiled, but Nicholas could see it was forced and he could not help but feel sorry for her—and a little angry at Jeffrey.

"Miss Harrowby," he said, smiling at Priscilla. "I don't suppose you could persuade your mama to let you spend Christmas at a house party at my grandfather's estate, could you? Bellingham Place, it is called. Your cousin will be there to lend propriety."

"Bellingham Place?" Priscilla whispered, her eyes as large as saucers. "Your grandfather is the Marquis of Bellingham?"

There was a pause. Then Jeffrey said, his voice sardonic, "I think we can assume Mama will have no objections."

Four

"That young American at Lucinda's is related to the Marquis of Bellingham?" Edwina Harrowby's voice was a squeal of joy. "And he has invited us to visit for Christmas?"

Priscilla set down her fork very carefully and held her breath. "I—I believe he asked just me, Mama," she said with a smile meant to placate. Opposition could set her mother off on one of the tirades Priscilla spent her life trying to avoid.

"Of course, he meant for your mama to come with you, Cilla, dearest," Edwina said with a complacent smile. "No well-brought-up young lady of marriageable age could be expected to attend such a party without her mama." Edwina leaned back in her seat and patted her mouth with her napkin.

Her father was sitting at the head of the table. While Priscilla hated the kind of scene her mother could make at any time, she hated them most of all when her father was present. He would sit and stare at his wife and daughter as if they were exhibits in the zoological gardens. Then he would shake his head and sigh, and Priscilla knew he was wishing her cousin, Lucinda, still lived with them.

This time, however, her father surprised her. "Do not be absurd, Edwina," he said. "Lucinda is a married woman now. She will be a perfectly adequate chaperone. Besides, the Connaughts are a large family. There will no doubt be a number of matrons in attendance for the holidays."

Her father had spoken in a voice that brooked no argument. Ordinarily, that would have been enough. But, to Priscilla's surprise, her mother did not bow her head in the submission a wife was expected to show. Apparently, the hope of a visit to one of the great seats of the aristocracy for a Christmas house party was too much for her mother to give up without an argument.

"Nonsense, Mr. Harrowby," his wife said. "A mama is a requirement. I must go."

"So I am to spend Christmas by myself in this house while you gallivant around some country house trying to marry off our daughter!" Mr. Harrowby threw down his napkin and glared at his wife. "Is that your idea of your duty, madam?"

Priscilla could feel her stomach turn to ice. She had never heard her father speak so bitterly. Now that she looked at him closely, she had never seen him look so haggard and old.

It was a shock. She had never thought of her father as old. Or as young, either, for that matter. He was her father, the unacknowledged pillar of her life. Always in awe of him, certain he looked down on her, she had never considered his human qualities. Now she looked at him as if seeing him for the first time.

He looked worried, and the thought made her afraid. Her father was the bulwark of their family, the source of their security and strength. If he despised Priscilla as foolish and silly and a little bit stupid, she had always thought he had a right to do so.

But he had no right to be worried. She might be as

silly as he thought, but that only meant she depended
even more upon him. She viewed him now through
eyes suddenly much clearer than they had ever been
before.

What she saw frightened her. His skin was pasty
and his eyes had deep circles under them. She noticed
his hand shook, and he clasped and released the heavy
linen napkin by his plate.

"Ooooh," her mother began to wail. "Noooo! You
cannot do this, Mr. Harrowby! It may be our girl's last
chance! There is an earl, the son, a widower. Think!
Just think!" Edwina's face turned a shade of red that
was almost purple. If Priscilla had not seen this same
scene enacted almost daily over the years, she might
have been alarmed.

Instead of rushing to her mother's side, murmuring
and fanning her flushed face, Priscilla sat and watched
her father. The weariness in his face increased and she
found herself for once not wanting to flee from the
grown-ups' arguments. She wanted it to stop as much
as ever, but now her sympathies were with her father.
He still intimidated her as much as ever, but she somehow felt sympathy for him.

Her father passed a hand over his forehead, then
looked wearily at her mother. "I want you to stay
home, Edwina. Priscilla may go, but you will stay
here."

Priscilla watched as her mother's eyes filled with
tears and her small, full-lipped mouth begin to tremble.
Edwina turned a piteous face to her husband, but her
dramatics left Barnabas unmoved.

"You have my permission to tell Mr. Cannon you
will be pleased to accompany him to the Connaughts',"
he said to Priscilla. "I will speak to Lucinda myself."

"But—but," Edwina sobbed. "A mother's care . . . at such a time . . ." She dabbed at her eyes with a lace-edged handkerchief and looked at her husband out of the corner of her eye.

"A mother would simply get in the way. You have no idea of how to conduct yourself, Edwina. You would make it absolutely clear in the first five minutes that you were hoping for the widower earl for your daughter. Nothing could be better calculated to drive the man away." He held up his hand for silence when Edwina opened her mouth to remonstrate with him. "No, I have quite decided. Priscilla is to go with Lucinda. You had better ask Lucinda to see to your wardrobe, daughter. She will know what to wear. And if she doesn't, at least you will both look alike and that will make it seem as if perhaps you are in the vanguard of fashion."

Having given Priscilla exactly what she wanted, her father retreated behind his food and said nothing else until he excused himself some ten minutes later. He refused the pudding course, asked that he not be disturbed, and left for his study.

"Oh, my dear, we must look at your wardrobe right away," said her mother. "Never mind what your father said about Lucinda. She knows nothing about fashion." Tears filled Edwina's eyes. "I did so want to go. To see a famous seat of the nobility! I don't know why your father had to be so disobliging!"

With a shuddering sigh, she rose from the table. "I have the most dreadful headache, thanks to him. I must retire for the night. Your wardrobe will have to wait." And with her wrist held to her forehead and another dramatic sigh, she left the room.

Priscilla almost smiled, but she was afraid that somehow rejoicing at this early stage might jinx her chance to spend time with Nicholas Cannon without her mother's presence. Tomorrow she would go to visit Lucinda and ask about simpler fashions. She had a feeling Nicholas would appreciate them.

Her steps were light as she left the dining room, but on her way upstairs she paused for a minute in front of the closed door to her father's study. The door, made of heavy dark carved oak, seemed always to shut her out. She remembered Lucinda was often allowed into this inner sanctum of her father's, but she never was. She had heard the murmur of voices coming from inside the room when Lucinda was there, and sometimes even the sound of laughter.

Now her father was alone. For a moment, remembering how sad and old he had looked at dinner, Priscilla actually contemplated knocking and asking if he wanted company. She could read to him, she thought vaguely. The newspapers or something.

The very thought frightened her. Her father would be seated at his huge walnut desk, reading some important-looking papers. He would look at her over the rims of the spectacles he wore for reading and raise his eyebrows, as if she had suggested something outlandish. No, she could never be her father's companion. She was too foolish, too much like her mother. She turned away and proceeded up the stairs.

The next day, when she went to Lucinda's to begin her wardrobe replenishment, Priscilla found her plans thwarted. Lucinda was not at home. Unfortunately, Jeffrey, who frightened Priscilla almost as much as her father did, was there and received his wife's cousin with his customary sardonic smile.

"So, Priscilla, are you looking forward to meeting a marquis and an earl?" he said.

Priscilla was surprised to find she had given the Connaughts scarcely a thought, focused as she had been on seeing Nicholas and on keeping her mother from suspecting her motives. Now she found she wanted to keep Jeffrey in the dark as much as she did her mother. Her mother would scold and Jeffrey would laugh at her. She wanted to prevent both.

"I am looking forward to it, of course," she said, suppressing her usual nervous giggle. "Do you expect Lucinda back soon, Jeffrey?"

"Do sit down, Priscilla," he replied with exaggerated politeness. His smile told her he was about to make fun of her. Priscilla clasped her hands together and swore to herself she would not giggle.

She perched on the edge of a chair, ready to flee at a moment's notice. "Where has Lucinda gone?" she asked.

"She is nursing at St. Luke's Hospital today," Jeffrey responded.

"Nursing? Now that she's married? You do not object?" Priscilla was amazed. Most men would be horrified if their wives even suggested working. It would look to society as if they could not support their families. It had never occurred to her that such a thing might be done. Surely one of the rewards of marriage was to take your ease, ordering servants about and entertaining your friends at tea, relying upon your husband to support you.

"No, I do not object. Do you? Lucinda is a gifted nurse as well as an administrator. I knew when we married she would find it difficult to do nothing. Don't you get bored?" He looked at her as if he truly wondered. "Don't you get tired of doing nothing? Would you like to be a nurse, Priscilla? Wash dirty people and clean up their slops and feed them?"

"No!" She shuddered. Sick people had always horrified her. She didn't know what to do around them, how to act, or what to say. "No, I could not."

"No," Jeffrey said, looking at her with a sarcastic smile. "I don't suppose you could."

Priscilla had endured enough. She rose to her feet and gathered her things. "Please tell Lucinda I will send around a note this afternoon to see when it would be convenient for me to call."

"Of course. She will be sorry to have missed you."

Priscilla had almost reached the door to the drawing room and freedom from Jeffrey Bancroft's palpable dislike of her when the door opened and Nicholas came in.

"Miss Harrowby," he said, but the smile of welcome on his face died as she hurried by him, biting her lip and refusing to look at him.

"I must go. I must." Priscilla knew if she listened to any more sarcastic remarks, she might very well cry. She would rather die than let Nicholas see her cry. Her nose always got red and her eyes became puffy.

"Let me see you home, then," Nicholas replied, casting a reproachful glance at Jeffrey, who had picked up his newspaper and sat looking bland and blameless.

"No, no, I can easily—" She hated the way her voice wobbled. She was pretty, her father was rich. Why then did she melt into a puddle of insecurity whenever someone disapproved of her? Especially someone like Jeffrey Bancroft, who was, after all, no one at all—even if he was handsome as sin and rich as Christmas cake.

"Nonsense, I insist." Nicholas took her arm and led

her gently out to where her carriage awaited her. "I have not yet managed to buy a carriage and pair but am forever borrowing Bancroft's. Otherwise I would offer you a ride."

The groom helped Priscilla into the carriage, while Nicholas entered without help. He looked around at the maroon velvet upholstery and thought how becoming the dark color was to Priscilla's fair hair and strawberries and cream complexion.

"I am so pleased you will accompany the Bancrofts to my grandfather's." He gave her a reassuring smile. "I have only just met the old gentleman, and I confess he is a little difficult. I need friends around me, particularly since it will be Christmas soon and I will miss my own family in America. It is kind of you to agree to be away from yours at this time of year."

"Yes, of course. Mama was pleased to let me come."

He noticed her voice was mechanical and she cast her eyes down. Those china blue eyes were the most revealing things about her. When she hid them she looked like a little girl's doll, all golden ringlets and pastel ruffles. Even her long, fitted coat was pale blue with ruffles at the hem and the collar. Nicholas had a sudden desire to sweep her hair straight back from her face and gaze into her eyes with nothing to interfere with the truth he thought he would see there.

"I would love to see you in a dark dress," he blurted without thought. "One made of this dark red, perhaps," he blundered on.

"What?" She was clearly bewildered. What other man had ever told her what to wear, he thought. No one. Of course. No one in his right senses would do such an unmannerly thing.

Well, in for a penny, in for a pound, as Jeffrey would

say, he thought. "When you lean back against the upholstery, your hair looks as if it had been spun from gold. And your skin is ivory and glows."

She was blushing and looking confused and adorable. But she was not slapping his face, or turning away in disgust. Perhaps he hadn't done anything irreparable. And he did want to see her in a dark red dress this Christmas. She would light up his grandfather's gloomy castle like a flame.

"Mama says light colors are best on blondes," she said. She did not say she agreed with her mama, he was happy to note.

"But Mama is not going to be at Bellingham Place," he murmured.

"No, she is not." Priscilla smiled at him, and for the first time he saw a hint of mischief in her face as her dimples deepened.

"I hope you are attending the reception at the Bancrofts' friends the Blankenships this evening," he said, thinking he had better change the subject.

"I do not know. There is a musicale at one of Mama's friends, but I am not sure." Priscilla's brow puckered for a moment.

"I will continue to hope to see you there," he said as the carriage drew to a halt in front of the Harrowbys' house, only two streets over from the Bancrofts'.

"I will hope so too." Priscilla smiled at him and extended her hand to him as the groom opened the door. "I will tell the coachman to take you wherever you have to go. Good-bye, Mr. Cannon."

"Good-bye, Miss Harrowby," he said gravely, bowing over her hand.

* * *

Priscilla was prepared to be devious that evening in order to avoid the musicale and attend the Blankenships' party. She knew her mother did not care for Henry Blankenship, a self-made man who made no attempt to be more genteel than he was. Mrs. Harrowby especially did not approve of the new Mrs. Blankenship, a woman no one had ever heard of. She had heard the most astonishing rumors—that the new Mrs. Blankenship had been a ladies' maid or perhaps a laundress before she married the wealthy industrialist.

Whatever she had been, it had not been genteel, and Mrs. Harrowby did not want to know Mrs. Blankenship. But Mr. Harrowby did. So when Priscilla, the picture of innocence, inquired as to whether they were to attend the Blankenship party at dinner that evening, her mother had immediately said no.

"I cannot conceive of how we came to be invited," she said, helping herself lavishly to a dish of turbot stewed in butter.

"We were invited because I do a great deal of business with Blankenship," Mr. Harrowby had interrupted. "And we will attend, if you please."

"Mr. Harrowby!" Edwina's eyes filled with tears. "I don't know what has come over you! Last night you insisted my darling girl go off to a house party by herself, without her mother. And tonight we must go to that coarse and vulgar man's house when Mildred's musicale is going to be the event of the season."

"Yes, my dear, I do insist." Mr. Harrowby ignored his wife's tears and continued to eat his meal. "Henry Blankenship is a very good man. Mildred Lamington's musicales are dreary beyond measure. Besides, her suppers are terrible, while Blankenship has the best food in London."

"Food!" Mrs. Harrowby shuddered, showing her contempt for anything so vulgar. "Please! I already feel another of my sick headaches coming on. You go ahead if you must see Mr. Blankenship. Priscilla can stay and put lavender water on my poor forehead."

"Nonsense! Priscilla must go to the Blankenships, whether you come or not. There are any number of eligible young men for her to meet there. Substantial young men with prospects, rather than the useless sprigs of the nobility that congregate at your friend's boring musicales." Heedless of his wife's gasp of outrage, Mr. Harrowby threw his napkin down on the table and rose. "I will expect you to be ready in exactly thirty minutes, Priscilla. So no dawdling, if you please."

"But what about me? Who will see to me?" Mrs. Harrowby's voice rose to a plaintive wail.

"You should be thinking of your daughter and of her chances! Your maid can do all that is required," Mr. Harrowby snapped as he strode toward the door. "Come, Priscilla."

"Yes, Papa."

Priscilla's voice was meek and she cast her eyes down as she hurried past her mother. She did not want anyone to see the glint of anticipation or the tiny smile of triumph she could feel lifting the corners of her mouth.

If she had thought for a moment that her mother was truly ill, she would have felt obliged to stay with her. But she knew Edwina's constant headaches and fainting spells were not serious but were bids for attention. They were her mother's method of getting her own way.

Well, not this time. This time her father, using stronger words than Priscilla had ever heard him aim at her mother, had ordered her to go with him. A small, subterranean glow lighted her soul. Her father wanted her with him.

She rang for her maid and rushed through her wardrobe in a frenzy. Every dress she saw was covered with ruffles and bows. Every one was a pale pastel color. Remembering Nicholas's words, she longed for a dress in a deep jewel tone, but, of course, there were none.

She could do nothing about that, but she could perhaps do something about the style. She pulled a blue silk dress out and looked at it as the maid she shared with her mother entered. Priscilla hoped she could rely on her not to tell Edwina what she was about to do.

"We must hurry, Clara," Priscilla said. "Is there something we can do with these ruffles? Can we cut them off, or something?"

Clara, who was interested in fashion, smiled. "Yes, indeed, miss. I have some small scissors right here and we can have them off in a trice."

Her words proved true. Priscilla descended the stairs to meet her father in a far simpler dress than any she had worn before. The neckline and small, puffed sleeves were unadorned. There was only a single deep flounce along the hem of the dress. Her curls were drawn back from her face and held with a simple blue velvet ribbon. A matching ribbon was around her slender neck and an ivory cameo held its ends together.

Her father gave her a preoccupied glance, then looked at her again. "I don't know what you've done to yourself, Cilla," he said with a puzzled frown, "but you look different. Very pretty," he added hastily, "but different."

Priscilla swelled with pride, and beamed at her father. "Thank you, Papa," she said, and shrugged on the white evening cape the butler held out to her. "Shall we go?"

Priscilla could not remember attending another party like the one at the Blankenships'. Everyone wore evening dress, and the ladies' costumes were as elaborate and colorful as those at the parties Priscilla was used to. The men were, if anything, more distinguished looking than those at the parties her mother favored.

But here there was so much laughter and camaraderie, so much delicious food and so many smiles and such pleasant conversation that it almost felt enjoyable. Priscilla was startled by the thought. Surely she had enjoyed all the parties she'd gone to in the past. Hadn't she?

Absently, she accepted a glass of lemonade and pondered the idea. It seemed to her she had viewed those other gatherings as work. She was charged with the task of finding a suitable husband. Everything else had been subordinate to that. And Priscilla realized, with a shock, that she had really no idea of how to go about finding a good husband. She only knew how to meet eligible young men at parties.

She was beginning to think flirting and giggling and saying "oh, really" at suitable intervals had nothing to do with finding a good husband.

She looked around her. This gathering radiated good cheer and friendliness. It didn't matter if you could find anyone suitable or not. It only mattered that you smile and laugh and enjoy yourself. Why, even Jeffrey had smiled at her for a moment before he remembered who she was. Priscilla found herself smiling back, not fearing his censure for just this moment in time.

She looked around her, pretending her interest was in the company in general, knowing she was looking for Nicholas. There he was, just across the room. She felt her heart give a tiny little skip as he looked up and smiled at her. His brown eyes seemed to her to hold a special light.

"You are looking particularly pretty tonight, Cilla," said a voice beside her.

She looked around in surprise to see Lucinda smiling at her. She had been concentrating on Nicholas so intently that she had not seen or heard her cousin approach. She noted Lucinda herself was wearing a simply cut dress of deep emerald green that matched a pendant and ear bobs of square cut emeralds set with tiny diamonds. Priscilla flushed. Her simple cameo and blue silk dress did not hold a candle to her cousin's toilette. Surely Lucinda was making fun of her.

"Thank you," she forced herself to say.

Lucinda shook her head. "I am not being sarcastic, Cilla. You do look pretty. I like your hair pulled back like that, and the ribbon around your neck is very becoming."

Priscilla gave her a searching look. Lucinda's eyes were free from malice. Her compliments were sincere.

"Thank you," Priscilla said again, this time with an answering smile. "I cut off some of the ruffles Mama had the dressmaker put on."

Lucinda smiled. "I used to do that with your dresses when Aunt Edwina gave them to me."

"I wondered why my clothes looked so much better when you wore them."

The two girls smiled at each other, for once in perfect understanding.

"Papa has said I must have some new clothes for the house party," Priscilla said after a brief hesitation. "I wondered if you would—that is, I would like you to help—if you wouldn't mind?"

Lucinda grinned. "I would love to. I have longed to see you in richer colors and simpler lines. You are such a pretty girl, Cilla, but I think those pastels and fluffy dresses your mama favors hide your looks." She held out a hand and Priscilla grasped it. "Thank you for asking me. Why not come to my house at around eleven tomorrow, and we can spend the day at my dressmaker's."

For the first time, Priscilla felt she and Lucinda might truly become friends. It was a strange thought. She had spent most of her girlhood detesting her cousin. If she were truthful, she envied Lucinda her looks and cleverness. Most of all, she envied Lucinda's relationship with Priscilla's own father. Perhaps because her father had reached out to her tonight, perhaps because she agreed with Lucinda about her mother's taste in clothes—whatever the reason, Priscilla felt a stirring of what she thought must be friendship toward her beautiful, accomplished cousin.

Just as she was contemplating the fact that she wasn't sure exactly what friendship felt like, never having felt it before, a familiar, deep voice sent shivers down her spine, though all it said was, "Good evening, Miss Harrowby."

Nicholas.

Mr. Cannon, she corrected herself.

"Good evening, sir." She meant to cast her eyes down as she so often did, to signify meekness and acquiescence to a man's greater knowledge. But somehow she couldn't. She didn't feel like playing games with Nicholas. She wanted to look at him. She raised her eyes and feasted them on his hawk-like face and sparkling brown eyes.

His gaze tangled with hers and for both of them, no one else existed. Priscilla smiled, her lips curving in a welcome she had never before extended. Nicholas reached out a hand and Priscilla put hers in his and they moved off across the room, leaving Lucinda smiling behind them.

"He is bewitched," Jeffrey said from behind her. He held out a glass of champagne and Lucinda took it.

"So is she. Do not interfere, Jeffrey. Priscilla is changing because of your friend, and I do not want that interfered with."

"Changing? Your cousin? It is difficult to change a porcelain head and a wooden heart," he said, shaking his head. "You are much too kind, Lucy, my dearest. Your cousin is as heartless as the animated doll she resembles."

"Nevertheless, let it be, dearest. People can change. Look at your sisters. They were taught to despise you, and now they are your staunchest friends. They are forever singing the praises of their 'dear brother Jeffrey.'"

"True, but remember, I am worthy of their praise," he said, his smile glinting over the champagne glass.

She grinned at him. "Such conceit! So is Priscilla. Your relatives are not the only ones who can mellow like wine." Lucinda gave him a saucy smile, and they both turned to look at Priscilla and Nicholas as they strolled about the room.

Priscilla could feel her hand tingle with awareness as it rested lightly, politely on Nicholas's arm. She was so filled with Nicholas she scarcely noticed anyone else until Nicholas looked down at her and smiled.

"You have met Mrs. Blankenship, I'm sure," he said.

Startled, Priscilla looked up to find herself being observed by a plain but kindly looking woman, dressed with elegance if not in the first stare of fashion in a gown of dark green brocade trimmed discreetly with gold. She had a warm smile, and Priscilla felt herself responding to the force of her personality by smiling wholeheartedly back at her.

"Yes, indeed. It was so good of you to invite my father and me this evening, Mrs. Blankenship." Priscilla infused the banal words with the sincerity of her feelings. This evening was one of the nicest she could remember spending, and she instinctively knew Mary Ann Blankenship was the reason the room was suffused with warmth and good feeling.

"Your father has charged me to tell you he will be closeted with my husband for a few minutes longer and you are to enjoy yourself until he returns." She nodded to them and said, "If I can do anything to make your visit more pleasurable, do let me know, Miss Harrowby." Then, with a polite bow, she resumed her trip around the room.

"What a nice woman," Priscilla said.

"You know, of course, she was the widow of a com-

mon soldier before Henry Blankenship married her."
She could sense Nicholas observing her closely.

"Some of the story I knew. Lucinda is a great friend
of Mrs. Blankenship's, so I knew she worked at the
same hospital Lucinda does. She is a lovely person,
isn't she?" There was wonder in Priscilla's tone, and
a faint pucker on her forehead. She was grappling with
a new idea, one her mother never believed. To Edwina,
virtue was equivalent to money or titles. Poor people
were to be useful and deferential. Poor people who
became rich, like Mr. Blankenship or Jeffrey, were to
be respected, but they were never quite the equal of
those who had been born into affluence.

Priscilla had never questioned this assumption, but
now she realized she did not share it. She knew instinctively that Mary Ann Blankenship was a lovely
person, warm and charming to everyone. She had not
become conceited because she had married well, nor
did she try to impress anyone with how genteel she
was. Mary Ann simply was who she was. Priscilla also
suspected most people would find the combination of
Mary Ann's charm and her husband's money totally
acceptable.

Her mother was wrong. Priscilla felt somehow dis-
loyal. She had found herself disagreeing with her
mother more and more these days, and it made her
uncomfortable. At the same time, it was liberating, and
that was a little frightening. Priscilla had never had
any desire to be free, or to disagree with her mother.
Not until these past few days.

Not until she had met Nicholas.

She looked up. His eyes held a teasing smile and
she responded to it with one of her own.

"What has had you so preoccupied?" he asked.

"Surprised to find some of the members of the Great Unwashed are really people just like you?"

Priscilla could feel her face turn a painful red. She began to count from one hundred backward—not that easy to do, she found—hoping not to cry. Despite her efforts, she could feel her eyes fill. She hated it when people made fun of her. Not, as Lucinda had always thought, because she felt herself so superior but because she always reacted like this and she hated it.

"Priscilla? Miss Harrowby?" Nicholas's face was a picture of consternation. "I did not mean to upset you, truly I didn't. I was teasing you, the way I do my sister. I am sorry."

"Don't be silly, Mr. Cannon." Priscilla giggled. She couldn't help it. "Your opinion means nothing to me. Nothing you could possibly say would upset me. Excuse me, I must find my father. It is growing late."

Blindly, she made her way to the nearest door. Anything to escape before she did something truly stupid and socially inexcusable, like bursting into tears in front of an entire room full of people. The hall was lit, but Priscilla stumbled as she hurried down toward some place to hide. She heard voices behind her, laughing and talking, people she could not afford to meet until she had composed herself. She slipped into the first room she came to and leaned against the door, breathing heavily, trying to control herself.

Ever since she could remember, she had fled from disapproval. Unable to take teasing, she had resorted to hiding pain with giggles and returning unkindness for unkindness. Until tonight she had never quite realized how high a price she paid for hiding her misery. She moved away from the door and went to stand in front of a long window that seemed to look out over the back garden. In the dark it was hard to see, and Priscilla didn't much care what it looked like. She only wanted to get control of herself.

Nicholas Cannon had teased her, and she had felt so crushed that she had struck out at him and fled. *Really, Priscilla,* she scolded herself, *you have to stop this.*

There was a gentle knock at the door and she heard Mrs. Blankenship's soft voice asking to come in. Priscilla was sure her own voice would wobble, and besides this was Mary Ann's house. She murmured something incomprehensible.

When Mary Ann entered, she stopped for a moment, then hurried over to the window where Priscilla stood. "Are you all right, my dear?" she said. "I saw you leave and thought you looked a bit upset. Is there something I can do to help?"

No one had ever spoken in quite such a kindly way to her before. To her horror, Priscilla found that kindness did what teasing could not. She broke down and, with a little sob, threw herself into Mary Ann's open arms.

"There, there, my dear. It's quite all right. You go ahead and cry. You'll feel better in a little while. There, there."

Priscilla sobbed harder for a few moments. Then, with a gulp, she swallowed hard and managed to control herself.

"I don't know what came over me, Mrs. Blankenship. Look, I have ruined your beautiful dress." Priscilla was mortified, but somehow she no longer felt so alone and foolish. Mary Ann's soothing presence and ministrations had calmed her.

"Nonsense, my dear. I learned how to clean brocade

long ago and will have this as right as rain in a trice."
Mary Ann's matter-of-fact tone eased Priscilla's mind.
"Now, just let me pat a little cologne onto your temples
and you will be fine. Your father is looking for you."

"Thank you," Priscilla murmured. She did not want
to leave Mary Ann's soothing presence, but duty
called. "I will go and find my father. He hates to be
kept waiting."

"As what man does not?" Mary Ann said with a
chuckle. "Come with me, my dear, and I will take you
right to him."

As she passed the door to the large reception room,
Priscilla looked in and saw Nicholas searching the
door. When he saw her, he started to move toward her,
but Mary Ann swept her along and Priscilla left without saying a word to Nicholas, about the house party
or anything else.

Five

The Bancrofts' elegant traveling coach swung around the bend of the gravel driveway and Bellingham Place, ancestral home of the Connaught family, came into view.

"Oh, my," Priscilla breathed. It was enormous. She had read in Burke's that the estate consisted of over ten thousand acres, and the mansion—or castle or abbey or whatever it was—certainly looked large and imposing enough to preside over such a huge swathe of land.

"Impressed?" Jeffrey said in his usual sardonic tone.

"I hope they give us breadcrumbs so we can find our way to our rooms," Lucinda said with a grin.

"Looks almost as big as some of the sultan's palaces we visited in Constantinople," Jeffrey said. His grin was every bit as impudent as hers. "Remember?"

"Of course. Meeting the sultan was the high point of my visits." Lucinda frowned at her husband. Priscilla knew it was on her account. Lucinda didn't want to reminisce about the time she and Jeffrey had spent in Turkey when Priscilla was around.

Feeling left out as usual when Jeffrey and Lucinda were together, Priscilla gazed out of the window. Nicholas was not with them. He had gone down the day before at his grandfather's insistence, having delayed his departure as long as he could. She was not sure whether she was glad or sorry he was not with them. He had hurt her feelings at the Blankenships' party, and she had not forgiven him yet.

She had seen him twice in the ten days since, and both times Nicholas had behaved as if nothing had happened. He hadn't apologized again or said he understood how he had hurt her feelings. Priscilla had been nursing her hurt feelings for several days, even though it was hard to feel terrible when you had just bought five new dresses, all of them more becoming than any you had owned before.

Priscilla couldn't help but smile at the memory of the day she'd spent shopping with Lucinda. It reminded her of the first few times she had been taken shopping by her mother. The excitement, the sense of being a grown-up at last were the same, only this time she also had the delicious feeling that she had escaped her mother for a few hours. She could choose what she liked, without Edwina's veto, Edwina's disapproval of whatever didn't meet her stringent standards of what became a little girl or a young lady.

Priscilla had accepted those standards without thinking for a long time. Now she found she herself questioning them, just as she was beginning to question her mother's standards and opinions on a number of topics.

"Are you all right, Cilla?" Her cousin's voice intruded on her thoughts.

"Yes, of course, I am fine. Just looking at how green everything is."

"Grass and trees have a tendency to be that color." Jeffrey's sarcastic tones.

"But it is almost Christmas," Priscilla protested.

"The trees are evergreens and the grass stays green this far south and close to the coast." Jeffrey sounded as if he were lecturing a five year old.

"Yes, of course." Priscilla heard her own nervous titter and hated it. Why was she so afraid of Jeffrey's censure? He had no hold over her. She, thank heaven, was not married to him. Imagine hearing that tone every day! Besides, she thought, falling back on her mother's reasoning, her father was rich and her hair was thick and curly!

Somehow, this time, the thought of her father's money and her own golden prettiness did not give her spirits a lift.

Priscilla sighed as the horses drew to a stop in front of the sweep of mellow stone steps leading to the massive front door of Bellingham Place. The sight of such magnificence drove all thoughts of Jeffrey out of her mind. Instead, she found herself wondering how Nicholas was finding life as a member of the family that owned this enormous, formal pile.

She did not have long to wonder. As the groom helped Lucinda and her down from the carriage, Jeffrey himself strode up the steps and raised the brass knocker. Almost before it could fall onto the plate, the door was flung open and Nicholas bounded out, his hand outstretched to Jeffrey, a smile of welcome lighting his saturnine features. After greeting Jeffrey, Nicholas looked down at the two young women who were still standing by the carriage, looking up at the imposing edifice that was to be their temporary home for the next several weeks.

"Welcome," Nicholas said, taking the shallow steps two at a time. His hand was extended to Lucinda, but his eyes were smiling into Priscilla's. "I realize this mausoleum lacks a certain cozy charm, but I trust you will enjoy yourselves anyway."

His hand found Priscilla's. "I am so glad you have come."

Priscilla found her heart beating faster than she could ever remember. Absurd, really. She hardly knew this man. Here she was at the seat of an enormously wealthy peer of the realm, and her heart was thudding in her chest because of a pair of brown eyes and a warm hand that clasped hers. She should be following her mother's advice and looking about, hoping to catch the eye of the earl.

"There are going to be all sorts of people here," Nicholas murmured, his lips near her ear. Priscilla shivered and she could hear his low, secret chuckle.

"There are?" she said, her voice high and a little breathless.

"Yes, but I hope you will find some time for me. It is difficult being a visiting colonial, you know." He grinned at her.

"America isn't a colony any more," she said. Sudden doubt assailed her. She really knew practically nothing about history. "Is it?" she added in a small voice.

"No, love, not any more." Nicholas chuckled again.

Priscilla gasped. "What did you call me?" She tried to sound indignant.

They had been standing in the huge entrance hall while servants bustled about getting luggage from the carriage. They now waited impatiently to conduct the guests to their rooms.

Nicholas suddenly noticed he had been engaging in flirtation in a most inappropriate spot. Just as he turned to beckon to the housekeeper, a clatter of heels sounded on the marble stairs.

"Oh, lord, and I haven't had time to warn you," Nicholas groaned.

"Warn me? About what?"

"The Connaught family. There are thousands of them, and they all descend on Bellingham Place for Christmas." Nicholas gestured to the stairs. "Here comes the first battalion now."

Priscilla looked up to see three young ladies hurrying down the stairs. Two of them were quite pretty, she noted. Their eyes were fixed on her. The third, who looked to be somewhat younger than the others, also looked at Priscilla, but she could see *her* eyes were curious rather than cold.

"Nicky, dear," the prettiest of the three trilled as she hurried up to him and laid a proprietary hand on his arm. She was a brunette whose coloring and features resembled his, though Priscilla thought the somewhat aquiline look was more becoming in men than women.

"Remember, I promised to show you all over Bellingham Place," the brunette said. "I have been spending Christmas here since I was a baby, so I know every inch. I am a Connaught, you see," she said to Priscilla. "One of Nicholas's cousins."

"How nice." Priscilla smiled and tried to look interested.

"Priscilla and Lucinda and Jeffrey are here at my express invitation," Nicholas said. "They are my guests."

"Oh." The young lady seemed a bit crestfallen, but her pretty companion was less easily cowed. No matter that two young women were already known to Nicholas although he had only lately arrived from America.

They were Connaughts, and Priscilla thought they felt that made up for any lack he might find in them. They bestowed two chilly smiles on Priscilla and all but turned their backs on her.

"These are my extremely rude third cousins, Annabelle, Susan and"——he gave the youngest girl, who hung back and looked a little discomfited by her relatives' rudeness, a smile—"this is my cousin Elinor."

Elinor, a somewhat plump young lady with a wealth of chestnut ringlets, seemed to shrink as the other two glared at her, their brown eyes icy. She rallied quickly, however. "I am pleased to meet you."

Nicholas ignored the other two and spoke only to the youngest. "Allow me to present Mr. and Mrs. Jeffrey Bancroft and Miss Priscilla Harrowby."

Susan and Annabelle pouted and turned away, but Elinor smiled again and curtsied politely. Then, when the housekeeper bustled forward in response to Nicholas's summons, Elinor excused herself. The housekeeper, Mrs. Sandles, escorted the three arrivals to the rooms that had been assigned to them.

On the way, she told them there were thirty guests. Priscilla knew the house was enormous, but thirty guests!

"How do you take care of so many?" she said, before she had time to censure her thoughts. Her mama would have been horrified had she heard Priscilla encouraging a mere servant to be so familiar. But her curiosity overcame any sense that she was behaving badly. And the housekeeper, Mrs. Sandles, seemed happy to explain. It kept them engrossed until they came at last to Priscilla's room.

"What a lovely room!" Priscilla exclaimed. The

hangings were of rose and cream, and while light and feminine there was not a ruffle in sight.

Mrs. Sandles beamed and told Priscilla that tea would be served in both the game room for the gentlemen and in the morning room for the ladies in half an hour. After the housekeeper left, Priscilla was horrified to find she had not the least idea of how to find the morning room! The house was so huge and there were so many twists and turns, new wings thrown out at odd angles and rooms tucked away in strange places, that she was totally lost.

As she combed her curls and washed the travel dust from her face and hands, she decided she would not worry about it. She was not going to give in to her silly fears. This trip, in her new, more elegant gowns, she was going to behave like a new, more elegant Priscilla. She looked at herself in her new tea gown of soft deep blue silk. It gave her a thrill as she looked at it. In this dress, she could do anything. She would simply find her way to the central part of the house and ask the first person she saw.

Nevertheless, she was very happy when a knock sounded on her door just as she was about to put her plan into action. She was even happier when she discovered Nicholas standing before her.

"I thought you might get lost trying to find your way around this gigantic pile," he said with a grin as he extended his arm. "It has taken me some time and a great deal of help from Dalton, my grandfather's butler, but I think I have now mastered the labyrinth."

Priscilla could feel the huge smile light her face. Relief mingled with delight at seeing Nicholas and made her feel lighter than air.

"Why, thank you, sir." She sketched a curtsey. "You are most kind."

They walked down the shadowy hall in companionable silence for a few moments. Then Nicholas spoke. "That dress is the color I have always wanted to see you wear."

"Lucinda helped me pick it out."

"Not your mama?"

"No, this time Papa insisted Lucinda help me."

"Do you need help? Do you not know what becomes you? My sister was picking out her clothes by the time she was ten. And you should have heard the tantrums she would throw if our mother disagreed with her choices!" Nicholas chuckled and shook his head as he remembered those days.

Priscilla felt her happy mood begin to seep away, like air from a punctured balloon. She was not as decisive as his sister. When she'd been ten, she'd had ideas, true, of what she would like to wear or say or do. But her mother had other ideas, and for all her die-away airs, Edwina was a very determined lady. Priscilla was no match for her. She had found it easier to bow to the inevitable and wear or say or do what her mother wanted.

Now she found Nicholas's questions caused a little iron to enter her soul. She *did* know what she wanted. On their shopping trip, Lucinda hadn't told her what to buy. Lucinda had offered suggestions and then agreed with Priscilla's choices. And the dresses Priscilla had bought that delightful day were the most becoming she had ever owned.

Lucinda had said so. Now Nicholas said so. But most important, Priscilla found she thought so too. Her buoyant mood restored, she smiled up at Nicholas.

"Yes, I know what I like. I have always known, I think. I have just not always been able to get it."

His hand tightened on her arm. "I hope from now on you will always be able to have exactly what you want. Whatever will make you smile like that."

Priscilla decided she would wear this dress at every opportunity! She rested her hand on Nicholas's arm and shivered a little. She was happier than she could remember being in a very long time. Perhaps ever.

That was a daunting thought.

Nicholas Cannon was a visitor to England, and though he had an aristocratic family, he didn't seem at all interested in staying and becoming part of the aristocracy himself. He would leave and go back to America. Priscilla loved her travel books, and she longed to travel herself—or she thought she did. But the idea of living in another country, one thousands of miles away from her family and everything she knew and understood, frightened her.

"Have you ever thought of staying here in England?" she asked.

"Not for a moment," he said promptly, his smile glinting at her. "My Uncle Granville would be very upset if I stayed here. For some reason, he is afraid my grandfather will favor me if I do. I will have to explain to him I have a business in New York which I must return to."

"You must?" Priscilla looked up at him.

"Yes, love, at least for a while. I know my mother wants to come over next spring and bring my sister and brother. I'll come back then, but my home is in America."

They were stepping together down the wide staircase to the second floor, where the main reception rooms were located. Nicholas turned and smiled down at her.

"Do you think you might be happy in New York? With the right company, of course."

Priscilla's breath caught in her throat. What was he saying?

"I—I—" She was so unnerved she could feel a giggle fight its way to her lips. She clamped them shut and was relieved to see, through an open door, a group of women gathered. This must be the morning room.

"I have frightened you, haven't I?" Nicholas said ruefully. "I always seem to rush at things. Never want to wait. I see things so clearly it's difficult to wait while others catch up to me." He smiled down at her, warmth lighting his eyes. He patted her hand where it still rested on his sleeve, then said, "You'd best go in. I must find the gentlemen and allow them to bore me about foxes and hounds and British politics."

Priscilla looked after him, drinking in the sight of his broad shoulders and the free and easy way he strode down the corridor. Then she entered the room full of female strangers and prepared to defend herself against what she was sure would be any number of veiled insults and smiling knife thrusts.

She should be used to it by now. She had never been able to make a friend among the other debutantes. Every girl had been on the hunt for a husband and so every other girl was a threat and a potential rival. Priscilla, with her blonde curls, china blue eyes, and large dowry was a bigger threat than most, and consequently aroused more enmity than the others.

Somehow, though, she had always felt a vague longing for someone to talk to, some other girl who shared her sense of the tedium of spending one's days and nights husband hunting. What did you do once you got him? she longed to ask another girl.

Now she looked around and, as she had suspected, she encountered frosty stares and false smiles. Lucinda was nowhere in sight, so Priscilla resigned herself to smiling politely and pretending she did not hear, or understand, the giggling insults. She sighed and prepared to defend herself as best she could.

"Would you like a cup of tea?" a soft voice ventured from beside her.

Priscilla turned and looked down at the girl Nicholas had called Elinor. Dressed in a simple frock of pale blue, she was gazing apprehensively at Priscilla, as if she feared a severe set down. There was a faint frown between her brows.

"I should love one," Priscilla said with a smile that was broader than usual out of relief.

"Good." Elinor smiled back. "Come right this way." She led Priscilla to a table set in front of the windows. "For some reason, we always help ourselves to tea when the gentlemen are not present. I think it is because the footmen are all busy getting ready to serve dinner and a lot of females do not merit servants. At any rate, here you are." Elinor handed her a cup.

"Thank you. I'm afraid I would have waited for someone to offer the cups round and gotten very thirsty."

Elinor looked at her out of narrowed eyes. "You are very pretty. I'm not, but I wonder if we could perhaps be friends anyway." She blushed painfully and looked down at the floor. "I shouldn't have said that, I suppose. You wouldn't want me for a friend. I'm young and I don't know anything except what I read."

"Then you know more than I do," Priscilla re-

86   *Martha Schroeder*

sponded. "I'm afraid I've never read very much. Never had a great deal of time for it and just never got started. So, you see, you have a great deal to teach me."

"Oh." It was clearly a new idea for Elinor. "And you could show me how to dress and—" She broke off in obvious confusion when Priscilla started to laugh.

"No, no, I wasn't laughing at you," Priscilla hastened to reassure her. "I was laughing because this dress is one of the first ones I was ever allowed to pick out for myself. So I am just learning how to dress as well."

Elinor gave a relieved smile. "You look so wonderful, I was afraid to talk to you, afraid you would be conceited and full of yourself and would not want to talk to someone like me."

"Oh, I'm not all that splendid," Priscilla replied. "My cousin Lucinda—now there is someone who can make you feel you have no business being in the same room with such perfection."

"Now, really, Cilla, I am not a gorgon!" Lucinda laughed as she tapped Priscilla on the shoulder. "I couldn't help overhearing you, and I must protest. You never thought I was splendid when we were living in the same house."

"Of course I did," Priscilla replied. "And I hated you for it, though I didn't recognize it. But for some reason now that you are gone I can see you more clearly. You are very daunting and I am glad I do not have to face you every day."

Elinor, who had been staring at the two cousins as they bantered half seriously, now spoke up. "But you are both so beautiful. You look like the opposites of each other. One so blonde and the other so dark. I can't imagine anything more wonderful than to be related to either of you. I can't imagine that you weren't as happy as queens to be together. Both so different and so wonderful."

"Wonderful?" It was not the word Priscilla would have chosen to describe the years she and Lucinda inhabited the same household. Nor did it bear any resemblance to her view of herself. Pretty and silly and useless—the words she was sure Lucinda and Mr. Harrowby both would use to describe her.

"Beautiful?" Lucinda said. "I would say pretty. Passably pretty. Both of us."

Priscilla grinned. She couldn't help it. Was it possible her cousin Lucy truly didn't know what she looked like? "Don't be absurd, Lucy. 'Passably pretty' might do for me, but you are truly beautiful. Everyone knows it. You must know it too. Surely you look in the mirror."

"Of course. And it tells me I am well enough." Lucinda shrugged. "Why are we wasting time discussing this? Pray let me know who this very kind young lady is. One of Nicholas's cousins, I presume." Lucinda greeted Elinor with a dazzling smile. Priscilla noted that, as usual, Lucy had made a conquest.

As she performed the introductions, Priscilla found her mind wandering, as it so often did, to Nicholas. What was he doing in the company of all these strangers who were members of his family?

At that moment, Nicholas was longing to be almost anywhere else but Bellingham Place. The male Connaughts were almost to a man the kind of people Nicholas detested—stuffy, snobbish, small-minded, and dull as ditch water. For a moment he considered excusing himself and going for a tramp around the manicured lawns or the carefully tended copses.

"Must be gratifying to be here at last," one of the cousins near him in age was saying. "Nice to be in a civilized country, I daresay."

"I grew up in a civilized country," Nicholas responded. "I have lived in a civilized country all my life." He tried to sound cordial.

"Well, to be sure," the man laughed heartily and clapped Nicholas on the shoulder as if he had made a good joke. "You haven't lived among the Hottentots, I know that. But still . . ."

His voice was a little uncertain, and he drifted away from Nicholas, who stood alone near the window, wishing he were outside, or in the library looking at the vast collection of books. Or, indeed, anywhere other than where he was.

The sight of his Uncle Granville did not make him any happier to be where he was. Granville's disdainful expression reminded Nicholas of someone who had a bad smell in his nostrils.

"My father wishes to speak with you," Granville said, his expression grudging.

"I will go over to my grandfather at once," Nicholas responded and felt a sharp stab of pleasure at the pinched look on Granville's face at the words *my grandfather.*

Nicholas strode over to the fireplace where the marquis was seated in a deep wing chair, his feet on a footstool placed near the flames. He had made the effort to come down to greet the family and was dressed in conventional dark clothing, his linen snowy white. The shirt gapped a little at the old man's thin neck.

Nicholas was surprised to feel a pang of concern at his grandfather's appearance. Dressed like every other man, the old man's fragility was even more apparent.

"You wished to speak to me, sir?" Nicholas said. He had developed a fondness for his grandfather in the few days he had known him. He knew his departure for America would disappoint the marquis, who found it impossible to believe anyone would wish to leave Bellingham Place when he could stay.

His grandfather made an impatient gesture and frowned up at him. "Oh, sit down. I hate craning my neck to see you."

Nicholas drew up a dark oak corner chair that stood by the fireplace and seated himself. "Yes, sir?" he said with a smile.

"I want to discover what you think of your home, Nicholas." He might be old and frail, but his voice was still strong.

"It is a beautiful spot, sir. My father often said it was the loveliest place in England."

He spoke only the truth, yet there must have been a hint of reserve in his manner, for the marquis frowned again. "Yet you are not happy here."

"I have not said so." Nicholas knew his mother would be disappointed in him if he left his English relations on an unhappy note.

"But I can tell. You have the same look Bart had before he left. What is it you both seek that you cannot find here?"

The marquis looked around him, clearly baffled at the attitude of his grandson, as he had been by that of his younger son. He himself had found everything he could desire in this place. He belonged here. It belonged to him. Perhaps that was the difference, Nicholas thought. Perhaps that was the reason.

"I need a place that belongs to me. So did my father, I think."

"But you are Connaughts. You belong at Bellingham Place. Bart belonged here, too." The old man spoke as if he were voicing a truth universally acknowledged.

But Nicholas did not acknowledge it. In the kindest way he knew, he said, "Perhaps, sir. But Bellingham Place did not belong to my father and will not belong to me." As he said the words, Nicholas knew they were true, both for his father and for himself.

"He is right, Father," said Granville. Nicholas was not surprised he had been unable to resist joining the conversation, though the marquis had clearly wanted a private word with his grandson. "He and Bart are the same. Both want no part of their heritage—or their family."

Granville's pale brown eyes glittered with malice. Nicholas was weary of his uncle's dislike and fear. He had told him every way he knew how that he did not want Granville's inheritance. Granville was welcome to marry and beget as many heirs as he could to stand between Nicholas and Bellingham Place. The more the better.

"It is not our family my father and I reject, uncle. We simply wanted to make our own way in the world." Nicholas tried to be patient with the stubborn old man, whom he had grown fond of in the short time he had known him. But patience was becoming difficult. How was he to explain to these people that what they regarded as of supreme importance and value was of no interest to him whatsoever? He had tried, but to no avail.

"And have you?" Granville could scarcely refrain from sneering.

Nicholas took a deep breath. He was sorely tempted to reveal just how well Bartholomew and Nicholas Cannon had done, but some innate sense of caution held him back. "Well enough," was all he said.

Granville's lip curled, but he said nothing.

"If you would leave us, Granville," the marquis said. "I wish to have a few words with my grandson privately."

It was not a request but an order, and Granville heeded it. So did all the other gentlemen, though Nicholas was ready to wager fifty guineas they were all perishing of curiosity to know what the marquis was going to say. Still, they all stayed away from the fireplace and left the two alone. Apparently, being head of the family still counted for something when the family were Connaughts.

The marquis drew his bushy white eyebrows together in a formidable frown. "What must I do to convince you that your place is here?"

"Why, nothing, sir." Nicholas smiled at his grandfather. "You have been everything that is kind. I know you will welcome my mother and brother and sister when they come as well."

"If that is what it will take to keep you here."

Nicholas shook his head. "I thought you understood. We will visit. We are family, and we acknowledge it gratefully. But I do not belong here, grandfather. I am an American, and my home is there."

"Granville is almost fifty years old," the marquis said.

"That is right. My father said his brother was two years older than he. And my father died last year, at forty-seven." Nicholas still found it difficult to believe his vital, handsome father, with his infectious laugh and zest for life, was no more. It seemed impossible.

The marquis's face clouded. "Bart was the liveliest, most mischievous child. I suppose I tried to keep him on too short a leash and it drove him away."

"To be honest, he always said it was the family's attitude toward my mother that was the final straw. But he had thought of emigrating long before he met her." Nicholas smiled a little, remembering the many times his father had told him the familiar tale.

"I'm sure she is a fine woman," the marquis said, and if his words were lukewarm and halfhearted, they connoted acceptance. Nicholas knew it would be enough for his mother.

"The finest in all the world, to her husband and children." Nicholas smiled. He held no grudge toward his grandfather for forbidding his parents' marriage. He was delighted his parents had left this land and sailed for a wider, newer, and to his mind, better place.

"I will accept your mother and the rest of your family gladly, Nicholas," the marquis said. "But I cannot and will not accept your attitude toward your home and your family here."

"I am sorry for that." Nicholas laid his hand for a moment over his grandfather's. "I did not come here to cause you pain, sir."

"You won't," the marquis said with complete assurance. "I will find a way to keep you here in England where you belong." He set his jaw and, for a moment, Nicholas could see a strong resemblance to his own father.

Two stubborn men, his mother had called them. Well, he could be stubborn too. He shook his head and smiled down at the old marquis. "I will send Dalton to you, sir. It must be almost time to dress for dinner."

"Yes, so it is. Come to me tomorrow in my upstairs study. I have something to discuss with you that may be of interest." The marquis gave Nicholas a thin smile, but there was triumph in his eyes, and Nicholas felt a pang of apprehension.

Six

Priscilla dressed with unusual care for dinner that evening. If her mother had been there, Priscilla would have said it was because a marquis and an earl—both unmarried—would be in attendance. That would be of overwhelming importance to Edwina. The fact that the marquis must be close to seventy and the earl over forty did not matter in the least!

In fact, she probably would have said, "All the better, Priscilla, for then you will be a young and titled widow and can have a most amusing life!"

But Edwina was not at Bellingham Place, and her daughter could admit to herself she was happy to be dressed in a beautiful gown because Nicholas was going to be there. She hoped his eyes would take on that sparkle that told her he thought her beautiful.

The dress was of deep rose pink, rather than the pastel shade she usually wore. There were no ruffles and very little trimming. The material itself, a rich satin brocade, was decoration enough, Lucinda's dressmaker had assured her. The neckline was a bit lower than she usually wore, but a look in the pier glass assured her she could carry it off.

"Oh, miss, you do look a treat!" said the young maid assigned to help Priscilla and several of the other young ladies. She had just finished arranging Priscilla's curls into an elaborate evening hairdo and now stood back to admire the result. "Just let me fasten these pearls around your neck and you'll be perfect."

Priscilla smiled. At home, she shared the services of her mother's overworked maid, Clara, and had always felt as if she were a burden. Now Priscilla, who had never come first with anyone or been admired for anything other than her marriageability, basked in the pleasure of having people think she was worth something. Nicholas, Elinor, and now this little person.

"What is your name?" she asked.

"Gillie, miss."

"Well, Gillie, thank you for helping me."

Priscilla astonished herself. Thanking servants was not something that was done in the Harrowby household. Edwina did not believe in giving servants praise. It made them conceited, she said. Mr. Harrowby simply took all services for granted. Now, as she saw the grateful smile on Gillie's face, Priscilla wondered if perhaps treating servants as people might not make them work harder. At any rate, it made her feel good, and Gillie seemed to like it, too.

There was a knock on the door. Expecting Lucinda, come to inspect her protégée, Priscilla gave herself a last look. For the first time since she had been a little girl, she felt right in her clothes and ready for a party.

When Gillie opened the door, however, Elinor stood there, smiling shyly. As a young girl not yet formally "out" in society, Elinor was dressed in white, but someone had made sure that the dress was a soft shade of ivory and was trimmed with peach ribbons, setting off the girl's creamy skin and light brown hair.

"I've come to show you downstairs," Elinor said, "in case you don't remember the way. We are in the east wing," she added when Priscilla joined her. "It is complicated. When I was little, I would regularly get lost on the way. I'm sure you wouldn't, but I thought you might be glad of a guide." She gave Priscilla a doubtful look, as if she were not sure of her welcome.

Priscilla's heart swelled a little. She had never been admired, not the way this girl so transparently did. Girls in her social set had envied her money and her looks and had, she was sure, secretly rejoiced when her twentieth birthday came and went and she was still unmarried, without even one serious suitor. Lucinda had despised her.

But now, someone thought she was charming and sophisticated and wonderful. She smiled at Elinor. "I would most certainly have gotten lost. Thank you very much for coming to get me."

They had arrived at the doorway to the family drawing room on the second floor, where all the Connaughts had gathered. Thus, Elinor's blinding smile of gratitude, meant for Priscilla, beamed upon the entire family.

Only one was close enough to comment.

"Whatever are you grinning about?" said Granville Connaught, Earl of Ashden, fixing the two girls with a look of icy disdain.

Under ordinary circumstances, Priscilla might have retreated into uncertain giggles in the face of such a look. But she was here at Nicholas's invitation, and she had made a friend. She was armored in newfound self-confidence, so she fixed the earl with a look as disdainful as his own. She was helped in her resolve by the strong smell of brandy that emanated from him. He might be an earl but he was no gentleman, to be drunk in front of ladies—and before dinner, too.

"Sir," she said and inclined her head the millimeter required for bare politeness. She rose to her full height and raised her eyebrows in a look she copied from Jeffrey Bancroft. She had seen it aimed at her often enough. She knew exactly how to do it.

Beside her, Elinor gasped. "G-good evening, Cousin Granville," the young girl managed to whisper.

Granville ignored her, and stared at Priscilla. "You are a pretty one," he said, with a smile that might have been charming if it had not been so full of sly innuendo. "Who are you? What moldy branch of the family tree do you hang from, m'dear?"

With a tiny grimace of distaste, Priscilla replied, "I am not related to you, sir." Her tone implied strongly that she was very glad of the fact.

"Really?" It was a chilly drawl. "Then you must be my dear nevvy's friend."

There was a wealth of sarcasm in his tone, and Priscilla flushed to the roots of her hair. She squared her shoulders and looked the earl straight in the eyes. "Yes, I am here at your nephew's invitation. He told me I would enjoy the hospitality of a true nobleman at Christmas. Until this moment, I would say he was right."

The earl threw back his head and gave a sharp crack of laughter. When he again looked at Priscilla, it was to see Nicholas standing at her back. He had entered the room in time to hear her words and his uncle's laughter.

His frown was formidable. "I hope my uncle has given you no cause to change your mind, Miss Harrowby."

There was a short, uncomfortable silence as Nicholas's dark brown gaze bored into his uncle. Finally,

Granville shrugged in surrender. "Very well, nevvy. I shall do nothing to disturb the peace of your visitor. I do hope you have no plans to marry him, Miss Harrowby," he said, malice dripping from his words as he bowed in her direction. "He will never succeed my father. I will forever stand in his way. I and my sons."

With that, he turned on his heel and left them. Priscilla would not allow a moment's silence to contemplate Granville's words. "Well," she said, "your uncle has a gift for conversation, doesn't he, Mr. Cannon?"

Elinor gave a gasp of laughter, and Priscilla smiled at her gratefully. "Do your relatives always say the first thing that comes into their heads, dear Elinor? I confess it will take me some time to grow used to it."

By this time Nicholas had recovered his temper. He smiled down at Priscilla. "Do you know, I had not thought to find my grandfather's relatives this entertaining. Pray tell us who each of them is, Cousin Elinor, and what conversational bricks each may drop on us."

Elinor laughed again. When she did, Priscilla noticed she lost the diffident, somewhat apologetic look that marred her looks and became a very pretty girl.

"I will be glad to share what I know, but I have not yet been presented to society, so I am not admitted to the adult conversations." Elinor shrugged and her face took on that apologetic frown again.

"I'll wager you know a great deal about everyone here. Remember"—and Nicholas smiled warmly at his young cousin—"we know absolutely no one and are at a loss in this throng. You must help us."

Elinor's face lost its worried expression. Priscilla hastened to add, "Yes, indeed. I am quaking in my slippers at the sight of all these strangers."

As she looked around the room, she thought she hadn't exaggerated by much. Though years of attending social gatherings of all sorts in the capital had given Priscilla the sort of social skills others envied, she still became uneasy at the sight of a number of strangers. Now, after the unpleasant encounter with Granville, she felt as if the ground were very uncertain under her feet.

What were these Connaughts like? Surely not all like Granville!

"I will be glad to do what I can," said Elinor. "Come with me. You are the one everyone wishes to meet, Cousin Nicholas. And Miss Harrowby is the prettiest woman here. I will be the envy of all if you are both seen with me."

"First tell me who they are." Nicholas's brown eyes gleamed with interest. "Who is that corpulent gentleman over in the corner, surrounded by younger men?"

"That is Edgar Connaught. His father was the marquis's younger brother, who died while jumping a horse over a banquet table after drinking all night. Cousin Edgar is very rich, unlike most of the others, so he always has a group of men around him."

"Hmm. Rich, is he? How did he make his money?"

"Make?" Elinor was clearly puzzled. "He did not *make* money, cousin. He has a large estate. He is rich, but he does not work. He doesn't make money. No one in the family *makes* money. They *have* money."

Nicholas grimaced. There was a wealth of innocent snobbery in Elinor's remarks. No one in this room would dream of soiling his hands with work, even if "work" consisted of moving money from one investment to another. He sighed, longing for home. Then he looked at Priscilla and thought staying in England for a little while longer might not be such an altogether terrible ordeal. At least he could stay long enough to persuade a certain blonde beauty to come back to America with him, perhaps.

He looked more closely at her. Would she go with him, leave her family and her country to embark on a life that far away? His mother had the strength to do it, but Priscilla was such a pampered darling, with no knowledge of the real world outside her life of parties and dresses and domestic rituals.

"Who is that beautiful woman standing next to Edgar?" she was asking Elinor as Nicholas once again began to listen to the conversation. "The one in the ice blue satin gown, wearing the diamond necklace."

Nicholas turned to regard Edgar's companion with a smile. A somewhat hard looking woman of about thirty-five, he thought, wearing at least a hundred carats of brilliantly cut stones. A fortune around a woman's neck.

"That is Edgar's second wife," Elinor explained. "They met at Brighton or Bath or some such place. She was a widow and before the family even heard of her, they were married. Quite a scandal! There was some talk that the marquis would not receive her, but in the end he decided to swallow his pride. She is not very well born, you see."

Then, remembering the family story about Nicholas's Scottish mother, Elinor turned red and clamped her teeth over her lower lip. She looked as if she might cry. "I—I'm sorry, Cousin Nicholas," she managed to murmur.

Before he could say anything, Priscilla spoke up with a chuckle. "Oh, pish and tush, Elinor. Nicholas knows you didn't have anything to do with the family's behavior. That was due to the marquis! And, after all, he asked for gossip!"

"So I did," said Nicholas, smiling down at his mortified cousin. "And you seem to know a great deal more than you let on, cousin."

Elinor blushed, but she smiled as well. Priscilla had put her at her ease, Nicholas noted. "Well, children are to be seen and not heard in this household, and that means we get to hear most of what goes on."

"I think that's true in most households." Nicholas was thinking of what he and his brother and sister had managed to glean about their parents' lives from what they had overheard. Of course, there were no other relatives to learn things from, and that made it less interesting than Elinor's surfeit of aunts and uncles.

"Not mine," said Priscilla. "I am an only child. Lucinda didn't come to live with us until we were twelve—much too late to conspire to find out any secrets. If my parents had any." She shook her head, clearly doubtful Edwina and Barnabas Harrowby ever had anything interesting enough to hide from their child.

"Would you like to meet some of your relations?" Elinor asked. "They all want to meet you. They are all looking at us."

"I suppose it would be a good idea. My mother will want to know what they are like. Come along, then, let's beard the lions and lionesses in their den."

He noticed immediately that Priscilla held back and would have slipped away if he had not held fast to her. "Where do you think you are going?"

"I thought you and Elinor—being family—it would be more seemly."

She looked down in confusion and Nicholas felt his

heart lurch in his chest. It was not a feeling he was familiar with, but he recognized it. "I am not going anywhere without you."

"What?" She looked up, straight into his eyes. Something she read there must have told her what she needed to know, for she said nothing further, just put her hand on his arm and proceeded to go meet the Connaughts.

A half hour later, when dinner was at last announced, Nicholas was more than grateful she had not refused to stay with him. He noticed that when faced with cross-looking older Connaught—about two-thirds of the family—she became a charming young girl. Her voice was higher pitched and she smiled and giggled. All the elderly cousins responded despite themselves, he noticed. With the younger cousins, she became a sophisticated older woman, one who showed an interest in them, thus insuring their competition for her attention. To him, all the relatives were sullen and almost rude. Priscilla pretended not to notice, but every now and then she would squeeze his arm as if to let him know they were there together.

At dinner, he was seated next to the hard-featured blonde in the ice blue satin. Edgar's second wife, if he recalled Elinor's explanation correctly. Priscilla was halfway down the long table, seated between a young sprig of fashion whose muttonchop whiskers were too sparse to be attractive and an older gentleman with a perpetual scowl.

So far no one had actually accused him of not being who he said he was. His grandfather's acceptance had stilled their tongues to a degree. But Granville did not believe him, and the herd was willing to follow him. The marquis had been seen with him only this afternoon during a brief teatime conversation. While that was enough to keep them polite, it was not enough to ensure cordiality.

Consequently, the conversation swirled around him this evening. He was not one of the inner circle of the family, at least not yet—not until the marquis publically announced that Nicholas Cannon from America was his grandson and, next to Granville, his heir.

The lack of acceptance bothered Nicholas not at all. He had only disdain for this motley group of snobs and hangers-on. Except for his grandfather, only Elinor escaped his judgment. She seemed like a nice enough girl. As for the rest, they only added to his desire to be gone, back to America. They all obviously thought he was hanging about, dying to be accepted as a "real" Connaught, given an allowance and the opportunity to become the kind of useless drone they all were.

The ladies left the dining room at last. The gentlemen passed the port and told slightly off-color stories and exchanged political gossip of the kind anyone could read in the newspapers if they chose to waste their time. Nicholas was thoroughly bored. Stifling a yawn, he began to go over some of his appointments in his head.

"Excuse me, sir," said one of the younger cousins, "but Granville has addressed a question to you."

"Sorry, Uncle," said Nicholas. "My mind was elsewhere."

"Really, nevvy? We would not wish to bore you. What is it you find so much more interesting?"

Nicholas decided not to lie. "Stephenson's new steam engine."

"A railroad engine?" Granville's eyebrows shot up to his forehead. "You were drinking port aged in oak, laid down thirty years ago, and thinking of steam engines?" His laugh was more of a malicious snicker. "You colonials will never be civilized! You must learn to appreciate the finer things now that you are in England and have left the frontier behind."

"You should learn to appreciate the beauty of a perfect machine." Nicholas wouldn't tell them what a collection of useless fools he found his relations, but he would stick up for his chosen life. "You have men here who build the most astonishing machines. The Germans have better workmen, and we can make things cheaper and quicker, but you English—"

The looks on the faces of his father's family would have been comical if they had not been so unkind. "Really, my dear fellow." Granville raised a languid hand to his mouth as if to hide a smile. "You are as English as we are. Or at least, you are as British. Your mother is Scots, as I recall, but your father was a Connaught. Or so you say."

"So your father says, as well." Nicholas rose to his feet. "I think it is time we joined the ladies."

Granville looked startled at the break in protocol. As his father's son, he was the host, and it was his privilege to end the after-dinner ritual. But he made no protest, and the men all rose and prepared to join the ladies in the drawing room.

"Well done, Nicholas." Jeffrey Bancroft's murmur reached his ears alone. "I was wondering how much of their heavy-handed patronage you were going to take."

"I have an open ticket on one of the new steamship vessels. If I want, I can be on board in a day and back in New York in two weeks."

Jeffrey smiled. "It must be a great temptation to

take a train to London tomorrow morning and be gone, but I beg you will not. I have been able to arrange a visit for you to Stephenson's factory. It is a great honor," he added.

"Yes, I know and I am grateful," Nicholas said. But his attention was riveted across the room, where Priscilla was engaged in conversation with his uncle, Granville. "Excuse me."

He left Jeffrey without another word. He felt almost as if he were being pulled across the room by invisible strings held by Priscilla. He had to go to her side. When he reached her, she looked up at him and he recognized the relief and gratitude he saw in her eyes.

"Why, nevvy, the way you hastened to Miss Harrowby's side, one would think you felt she needed rescue." His uncle's affected drawl scraped along Nicholas's nerve endings like sandpaper.

"Does she, uncle?" Nicholas kept his voice and expression neutral, but only with an effort. "Does a guest in your home need rescue from your unwanted attentions?"

Granville flushed. "Of course not. We were merely engaging in the social conversation that is usual in polite society. I feel I must explain such usages to you, nevvy, coming from the wilds of America as you do." His smile was poisonous.

"America is quite civilized now, my lord." Priscilla's voice was small but determined. "I have read New York has over half a million people in residence now. That is your home, Mr. Cannon, is it not?"

Nicholas could have hugged her. Small but valiant, she would defend him against an earl, in his own drawing room.

"Yes, my family lives in New York." Nicholas

smiled down at Priscilla and moved a little closer to her. He did not touch her, remembering how her mother had objected to the lightest contact.

"Ah, yes. There are such colorful neighborhoods there. One has heard of Five Points and the Tenderloin. Which do you inhabit, nevvy?" Granville smiled as he considered his nephew smugly, having named two of the most notorious slums in New York.

"Actually, uncle, my home is on Fifth Avenue. You may have heard of it." Nicholas knew that even in England, Fifth Avenue was synonymous with wealth and style.

Granville's eyebrows lifted, and he gave his new nephew an appraising glance. Nicholas could have kicked himself. Up to now he had kept his financial status a secret, but the revelation of his address had awakened his uncle's suspicions. Whatever Granville was, he was not stupid about society, and Nicholas had learned that society was concerned above everything with money.

Priscilla's reading about New York had apparently not concerned the niceties of addresses. She looked up at Nicholas, her expression the same as before. He breathed easier. He wanted Priscilla to care for him for himself. Knowing her mother, knowing Jeffrey's opinion of Priscilla herself, Nicholas longed to prove to his friend—and, just a little, to himself as well—that the woman he had come to care for so much cared for him, too. Priscilla's father's money meant nothing to him and he wanted to be certain her feelings were equally pure.

"Shall we stroll about for a few minutes, Miss Harrowby," he said, bowing slightly. "I am sure my uncle will excuse us."

Granville's expression grew a little more sour. He, too, bowed to Priscilla. "Miss Harrowby, do not forget our ride tomorrow. I am eager to show you over my estate."

"Really, Uncle? I was not aware you had an estate near here. Where is it?" Nicholas smiled blandly and tried to look innocent.

"Bellingham Place is my home," Granville said between gritted teeth.

"But not your estate. Not while my grandfather lives."

Nicholas turned away and, with Priscilla on his arm, made his way slowly toward the door.

"I thought we might look at the conservatory," Nicholas said. He had been careful to locate it during the day, with a tête-à-tête with Priscilla in mind.

She nodded and he said, without looking at her, "Is my uncle courting you?"

Priscilla gave a little gasp. "That is a very personal question, Mr. Cannon. Ordinarily, gentlemen do not ask young ladies about their suitors."

"But, you know, I am an American, not a gentleman," he said, and drew her arm a little closer to his side. "So I am asking you. Is Granville courting you?"

"Yes, I believe so." Priscilla looked down at the floor, old oak, polished to a golden gleam. "He attempted to tell me you were not a good match for me because you will never be a marquis."

"While he will be, of course." For a moment Nicholas struggled against a tide of anger so strong it left him shaken. "And must you be a marchioness?" He almost dreaded the answer. Helen, the girl he had thought himself in love with, had needed money as others need air and would have loved winning a title as well. But Priscilla was nothing like Helen, no matter what Jeffrey said about her.

Unaware she was being judged, Priscilla said, "No, Nicholas. I could never marry your uncle. There is something about him I cannot like. I am a little afraid of him, I think." Her voice got smaller and smaller as this speech continued.

"What did he say to you? Did he threaten you?"

He hadn't been aware of how he must have sounded until he looked into Priscilla's shocked and frightened face. "I'm sorry. I don't want anyone to frighten you and now here I am, frightening you! What was it about Granville that upset you?"

"I cannot explain it. There is a look in his eyes. Wild and yet cold. He sounds so civilized and yet—"

"It is the alcohol speaking, I think," Nicholas said. He was not being altogether honest. He believed it was also Granville's hatred for Nicholas that led him to woo the woman Nicholas had brought to the family party.

Priscilla shivered. "Whatever it is, I find I cannot like to be around him. He seems to be about to devour me."

Nicholas laughed. They had strolled along through corridors and rooms that now had led them to the conservatory. Like the rest of the enormous castle, it was lit with candles and oil lamps. The soft light cast a romantic glow over the trees and flowering plants that were arranged for show. There were large succession houses in the back where fruits and vegetables were grown in the winter, but this area was just to be enjoyed. Wrought iron benches were set here and there, but Nicholas noted no one else had come to the secluded spot.

Perfect. He was going to do what he had longed to do since the first moment he saw her. But not if she didn't want it, too. He would know the moment he looked into those clear blue eyes. He thought they would never lie to him.

But Priscilla's eyes remained stubbornly fixed on the floor. Her shining hair, worn smoothly tonight and gleaming golden in the warm light of the nearby candles, was all he could see.

"Look at me, Priscilla," he said, his voice hoarse with strain.

Slowly, she raised her eyes. In them, Nicholas saw everything he'd dreamed of. Slowly, still giving her time to change her mind, he drew her into his arms and fitted her against him. Her full rose-silk skirts belled out behind her, and she looked at him with honesty and love shining from her eyes.

"I am going to kiss you, Priscilla," he said, gazing at her full pink lips.

Her mouth trembled, and for a moment he thought fear and all the admonitions her mother had no doubt drummed into her head would take control of her response and she would turn and flee.

"Oh, yes, please," she whispered.

His heart pounding with mingled triumph and love, Nicholas bent his head and took her mouth with his. It was ravishment and seduction, fierce and gentle at the same time. And Priscilla was a revelation. He could tell she had not been kissed before, yet her response was everything he could have desired. It was as if she had been made for him. Her lips opened under his and she welcomed him as freely as if they were already married.

His head reeling, he lifted his lips from hers and

drew back a little. But Priscilla clung, her arms reaching up to hold him, her mouth reaching for his. He resisted for a moment, but when her lips pursed in a disappointed pout and her tongue reached out to moisten them, he was lost.

It could have been minutes or hours before he came to his senses again. This time he knew he had to be the strong one. Priscilla was not wise enough to know what she risked in giving herself so freely to him.

"My love," he murmured, as his fingers traced her features and the rose petal softness of her cheeks. "My dearest Priscilla, it is time for us to go back. In fact, it is past time."

"You are worried about my reputation," she said.

"I am worried about your chastity," he replied bluntly. "Now come along."

"If you will call me your dearest Priscilla once more," she said.

"You drive a hard bargain, my dearest love."

She laughed, a soft, triumphant sound, and they left the conservatory hand in hand.

Seven

Priscilla came to her senses as they walked back down the dimly lit corridors toward the drawing room. Slowly the warmth and sense of communion she had shared with Nicholas seeped away and awareness of the world and its rules trickled back into her head. What would people say if they came back together? What would they say if she came back alone? Should she go to her room?

Yes, that was the answer. The devious, socially acceptable answer. She would say she had the headache and retire to her room without saying anything.

"I'll go to the smoking room and say you've suddenly developed the headache," Nicholas said before she could speak. "You can get to your room before they miss you."

Then he smiled down at her, and Priscilla could feel the warmth rush back. Her heart expanded to fill her throat. At the same time, it felt as light as a balloon in her chest.

"You look thoroughly kissed, Priscilla, love."

She smiled mistily up at him. As usual when emotion filled her, she could think of nothing to say, so she turned reluctantly away. She floated down the corridor toward the central staircase. Her mind wasn't working, but the image of Nicholas rose in her brain and champagne flowed in her veins. She had never actually tasted champagne—her mother would not permit it—but she was absolutely certain it would taste exactly the way she felt at this moment.

Nicholas! Nicholas had kissed her and her heart had exploded, her knees wobbled, her head whirled. Absolutely everything she had ever heard about love from her friends was true—thrillingly, marvelously, totally true! Her feet seemed to float above the floorboards as she picked up her skirts and began to ascend the stairs.

Nicholas! The name rang in her heart like bells.

Nicholas! The most wonderful, handsome—

"Leaving us so early, Miss Harrowby?"

The earl of Ashden's cold, insinuating voice seemed to slither along her skin like a snake. She shivered.

"I—I have the headache," she said, fighting back a nervous giggle.

"Really?" His smile was as cold as his voice. "I would have said you look like a woman who has just been kissed." His keen gaze must have seen the heat she could feel in her cheeks.

He pounced on her guilt. "My dear nephew, I assume?"

She said nothing for a moment. Then, for the first time in her life, she decided to attack a tormentor. "Why do you hate Nicholas?" she said, trying to sound innocently curious. "Is it because he is your heir and is younger and likely to outlive you?"

Her words had an effect far greater than she had bargained for. The earl's expression darkened and his eyes flashed with an icy fire. He took a menacing step toward her. "It is because he is an uneducated colonial lout and may succeed to one of the great titles in England through a piece of totally undeserved good fortune."

"Why do you care so much?" she persisted, despite the fear his anger aroused in her. "You will be dead, after all, when the dreaded event occurs."

He raised his hand, as if he intended to strike her. Instead, he brought it down on the bannister. She managed not to flinch, but she had to tighten every muscle in her body to prevent herself from fleeing as fast as her little kid evening slippers could carry her.

"You understand nothing. You are enamored of a handsome face. You do not understand what a real man, a nobleman, could give you." He advanced another step.

She could feel the heat of his body and smell the overpowering scent of brandy that emanated from him. Gritting her teeth, she stood her ground, but instinctively wrinkled her nose in distaste. The gesture seemed to inflame him further.

"I would not gamble on the young lout ascending to the title, my dear," he said. "Far better to place your wager on me and your own ability to give me a son. Better an earl in the hand than a possible marquis in the bush." He grinned down at her. "What do you say? Cast your lot with me, and with your father's money and my birth we will have everything!"

"No!" Her answer was instinctive, as immediate and honest as the shudder she gave as she recoiled from him.

"Ah, he has been wooing you with kisses, has he not?"

Before she could speak, the earl clamped one arm behind her head and swept her into his embrace with the other. His mouth descended on hers in a kiss that was wet and devouring. She all but gagged in response and fought to free herself. She beat her hands on his back and raised one foot to try to give his leg a kick. That threw her off balance and she felt herself falling backward, over the bannister. Fear clawed at her, but she did not reach out to the earl. Instead she took advantage of the fact that he too had stumbled a little and loosened his hold a fraction of an inch. She drew back both arms and shoved him as hard as she could.

But despite his slender build, the earl was strong enough to withstand her onslaught. Anger had given him additional strength, and he did not let her go. Instead, his bruising grip tightened again, and Priscilla began to feel a kind of paralyzing fear that sapped the power from her body. Just as she began to give up and allow the conviction something dreadful was about to happen to overpower her, a voice like that of an angel came from below.

"Priscilla, are you all right? Cousin Nicholas said you had the headache and I thought—" Elinor's clear voice carried up the stairs, getting louder as she approached. "Why, how are you, Cousin Granville? Are you helping Priscilla to her room? How thoughtful of you, but I can perfectly well help her now. Another woman, you know. So much more acceptable."

And with those foolish-sounding words, spoken in a high, fluting voice, Elinor took Priscilla out of the earl's arms and, placing her own arm around Priscilla's waist, led her away toward her bedchamber.

Without a word, she opened the door and ushered Priscilla inside and over to the chaise longue in front of the window. "Oh, my lord, Priscilla, what was he doing to you?"

"I—I—he kissed me and he wouldn't stop! He

asked me to marry him, but in the most objectionable way!" Priscilla could hear her voice begin to break. "It was beginning to be very—very—"

She couldn't continue. Reaction to the scene and to her own helplessness overcame her. She bowed her head and began to cry. She could feel hysteria begin to bubble up within her. Before it could take control of her, however, Elinor hurried over to her. Kneeling in front of her, she took Priscilla's hands in hers and began to gently chafe them.

"It will be all right." Her clear brown eyes, with the perpetual frown between the eyebrows, looked deeply into Priscilla's. "You are not the only one he has done this to, but you are the first within the family."

"I am not one of your family." For the first time, Priscilla was glad not to be one of the aristocracy. If this was how earls behaved when they were at home, she did not want to know any.

"But you are a guest at a family house party. He usually reserves his attacks for the maids."

Priscilla shuddered. "He is an awful man."

"All the women in the family would agree with you. We learn early on to stay out of his reach."

Elinor's brisk, commonsense voice and wry humor steadied Priscilla's nerves. The world seemed to right itself. She lifted her head.

"Thank you for getting me away from him without a fuss." Priscilla did not think she could have faced a crowd or the gossip and laughter that would have inevitably followed such a juicy scandal. She was also well aware that whatever the truth of the situation— even if everyone who heard the story knew of the earl's reputation—it would be her reputation that would suffer.

Elinor frowned. "Sometime, somebody *should* make a fuss when Granville puts his hands where they have no business being."

Priscilla gave her a wan smile. "I am afraid that brave lady could never be me."

"Oh, I am not so sure of that. You are very courageous."

"No, I am not. He terrified me."

"You were fighting him very bravely when I came up."

Priscilla thought for a moment. Elinor was right. She *had* hit the earl. She had even kicked him. Perhaps she was not the sniveling coward she had always thought she was.

"Thank you, Elinor." She braced her hunched shoulders, raised her head, and smiled at the younger girl.

"It is you who fought. I only told you what you had done, but you are very welcome." Elinor smiled back.

Elinor rose to her feet and went to the large wardrobe that stood in the corner of the room. She opened it, rummaged inside, and drew out Priscilla's dressing gown, a fluffy confection of ice blue silk and swansdown trim.

"This does not look very warm." Elinor held it up and regarded it doubtfully. "I thought you should change out of that beautiful dress and put on a cozy dressing gown and sit down by the fire. I will ring for some hot milk and biscuits."

Priscilla shrugged. "My mother picked that out. I meant to ask one of the maids if she could run up a simple flannel wrap, but somehow I never did."

"Your mama must think you very beautiful, to give you such a lovely thing." Elinor sounded wistful. "My mama died when I was just a little girl. My aunt inherited me along with mama's jewelry, which she much prefers. She does not think there is any hope for me." Elinor rubbed the spot between her eyes where Priscilla had noticed the habitual frown.

"I think she is wrong. You looked very pretty tonight."

Elinor glanced over at Priscilla with a wry smile. "Do not think you have to be polite."

"I am seldom polite. That is one of my great sins. Ask my cousin Lucinda." Priscilla looked at her new friend. With sudden insight, she asked, "You are nearsighted, are you not?"

Elinor's face turned a bright red and she bit her lip. "You noticed. My aunt says if I do not wear my spectacles I will attract young men and that I will soon grow used to not being able to see. But I have not—neither attracted young men nor gotten used to seeing the world as if through chiffon." Elinor's shoulders drooped as she lay the blue silk dressing gown on the bed.

Priscilla was not used to comforting anyone. She could put cologne-soaked handkerchiefs on her mother's aching forehead or mix a dose of sal volatile for her, but she was not used to being of help to a friend. She didn't know how to talk to someone who needed reassurance.

But she liked Elinor, and she could at least try. After all, Elinor had rescued her and, even better, had made her believe she might have been able to rescue herself.

So she rose and went over to Elinor. "You are still very young to be worrying about young men, aren't you? I think you are pretty and will grow to be even prettier in a few months. As for your eyes, I should think you could wear your glasses except in the evening. Would your aunt not agree to that? So you could go about in the day, be outdoors or play cards or whatever and be comfortable. It is the headache that makes you frown, isn't it?"

Elinor brightened. "Yes. And it's true, I am young. So the fact no one interests me that way is not proof I will never be interested. Or that no one will ever be interested in me. Is it?"

She sounded brighter, and Priscilla hastened to reassure her further. "Of course not. It is just a matter of time, really. It is foolish to try to rush into society. You are not even out yet, are you?"

"No, but my aunt would like me married and off her hands as soon as possible. She has my cousins to marry off and I think she doesn't want me around after her own girls have married and left home."

"Those two disagreeable girls Nicholas introduced me to this afternoon?"

"Annabelle and Susan, yes. And you are right, they are disagreeable. In fact, they're horrid. I'm an orphan, and they let me know I don't belong." Elinor shook her head. "But now you and I are friends, so I do not have to envy them any longer."

Priscilla was uncomfortable all of a sudden. Elinor's description of her life with her cousins sounded very much the way Lucinda would describe her life with Priscilla. Ashamed, Priscilla turned away and began to untie the tapes at the neck of her rose silk dress.

"Here, let me help you." Elinor hurried over. "This is fun. This is what Annabelle and Susan do for each other. I hear them laughing sometimes late at night." Her voice was wistful.

"You are much brighter than your cousins." Priscilla was sure she was right in making it a statement rather than a question. Elinor had quick wits and a keen eye for the foibles of her elders.

Elinor shrugged, but she looked a bit uncomfortable. "So I am told. My aunt does not regard it as an advantage."

"Oh, but it is!" Priscilla blurted out. "Lucinda is very clever and my father adores her. Jeffrey adores her, too. And neither of them think I can button my own boots or read a book all the way through."

"Why, Priscilla, I am sure you are wrong. I think you are very clever too, in your own way."

"You do?" Priscilla was pleased that her new friend did not find her silly and stupid. Of course, she had managed not to giggle since she had arrived at Bellingham Place. That must help her seem sensible.

As she stepped out of her dress and unfastened her crinoline, she noticed Elinor hastened to pick up her petticoats and hang her rose silk dress carefully in the wardrobe. Ashamed, Priscilla took the undergarments from Elinor's hand.

"Here, let me do that. I imagine the little maid is busy with your cousins."

"And several others who need help with everything." Elinor smiled. "I'll ring for the hot milk now."

"Very well. I'll just get in bed. Then we can have a lovely time. You can tell me what we are going to do tomorrow so I will know what to wear."

"Oh, dress warmly for tomorrow. We are to go out and gather holly to decorate the hall." She frowned a little. "Somehow, no matter how hard we try, it never looks very festive, but we do it anyway. Then if it is cold enough, we can skate on the lake."

Priscilla had never had much opportunity for outdoor sports, living in London. But she was willing to try. As long as Nicholas and Elinor stayed close beside her and the earl stayed far, far away. Priscilla shivered. Yes, that was all that mattered.

The next morning, Nicholas awoke early, as he always did. He made his way to the breakfast room and, finding himself alone, looked around at his ancestral home. The very phrase made him smile. He had no need of ancestors, had enough living relations and a large enough home in America to satisfy any normal man.

As he looked about for food and found none, he frowned. At home, his servants knew he never stayed in bed past six o'clock and consequently had his breakfast ready when he needed it. He always found the rest of the world hopelessly slow. They all seemed to need more than the five hours' sleep he enjoyed. Finding no bellpull to summon the servants, Nicholas wasted no time repining, but went in search of them.

It was easier said than done. His ancestral home—he grinned to himself every time he thought that anyone could see this enormous, cold, and formal castle as home—was a rabbit warren of corridors and stairs with no logical arrangement. Why someone hadn't pulled down the drafty old pile and started over sometime in the past hundred years he could not understand.

After several false turns, he managed to find the back stairs that led to the kitchens. Once there, he was appalled. Dark, dank, hopelessly old fashioned, the kitchen of Bellingham Place was as different from the modern, sunny room his mother had designed for their home as it was possible to imagine.

He had noticed that parts of "the Place," as the Connaughts called it, were not in the best repair, but he had assumed it was because they preferred the look of old, frayed fabrics and dark, smoke-stained walls. Now he wondered if they ever thought about repair and modernization at all. Who could work in such a place?

Apparently, a good many people. Under the flickering light of oil lamps set in the walls and on tables, he could see a good many people were bustling about. A few sat in their shirtsleeves at a large oak table set in an alcove. They were eating what smelled and looked to Nicholas's hungry eyes like a feast.

"Excuse me," he said. "Do you mind if I join you?"

His voice was polite and his smile pleasant, but it was a rhetorical question. He had every intention of sitting down at the kitchen table and enjoying a hearty repast. He had often done so in New York.

The reaction here was not the welcoming "Of course, Mister Nicholas" he was used to. Instead, the butler-valet, Dalton, rose to his feet and said, "Oh, no, sir!"

Nicholas could feel his eyebrows draw together in an expression that had made him apprehensive when he saw it on his own father's face. He had seen it again yesterday when he had displeased his grandfather.

"I beg your pardon." His voice was icy.

But Dalton only smiled fondly at him. "I'd know you anywhere just from the frown, sir. Exactly like your father. And the marquis, too." The old man looked positively misty.

But Nicholas was not feeling misty. "Breakfast, Dalton, if you please." He moved over to the table and looked around for a chair.

"Upstairs, please, sir. We are trying to prepare breakfast, as you see. But we have not yet got anything fit to eat. The stove takes a bit of getting ready." Dalton looked embarrassed.

Nicholas hastened to reassure him. "I will be perfectly happy with whatever you are having." Seeing the look of consternation deepen on Dalton's face, he said with a smile, "I have done so often at home, I assure you."

Dalton actually blushed. "I do not doubt you, sir. But here, you see, it is usual for the family to eat above-stairs."

Nicholas smothered a laugh. Dalton clearly thought Nicholas ate in the kitchen at home because there was no place else to eat. He sighed. He did not want to take the time to explain, and he did not yet wish to reveal his financial circumstances. He was beginning to regret he hadn't told the truth to begin with.

Then he thought of the state of the kitchens and the threadbare look of several of the minor drawing rooms. No, this place would swallow all the money he could spare, and the marquis would be ruthless in extracting every groat from his well-heeled grandson. Best to get away clean, if he could.

He looked around the dark kitchen again. There were no signs of anything edible, only the preparations for cooking, nothing finished.

"Have you all had anything to eat?" he demanded. His servants always had a decent, if sketchy, breakfast of bread and cheese and coffee before they began on the family's meal.

"We will eat when everyone upstairs has partaken," said Dalton.

Nicholas thought of all the female cousins, who would no doubt want chocolate in their rooms—not to mention Granville, who, he was sure, breakfasted at noon. These people would not eat until luncheon was served.

"That won't do, Dalton," he said, before he thought. "You should all have something to eat before you begin all this work. Bread and cheese, at least, and a hot drink. Coffee. You should all have coffee."

"Coffee, sir?" Dalton sounded baffled and he looked at Nicholas as if the young heir were certifiably mad.

Nicholas wished he had never started this conversation. It was none of his business if his grandfather's servants never had a chance to eat and had to work in this dungeon of a room.

"Tea, then," he said, with a careless gesture. "No one can do his best work with a cold and empty stomach."

"No, sir," Dalton said, in a voice that could soothe a fractious child. "I will take it up with the marquis."

Nicholas grinned. "In a pig's eye you will, Dalton! Never mind. I will mention it myself."

"Yes, sir, Mister Nicholas." Dalton began to move toward the door. "Now if I could persuade you to wait upstairs in the breakfast parlor, I will see to it that tea and toast are brought to you directly."

Nicholas could see he was holding up the morning's work. With a shrug, he allowed himself to be ushered out. He would take this up with his grandfather in the interview the marquis had demanded later in the morning. The first thing an employer did was look after the welfare of his workers. And no matter that the marquis had servants and workers who had been in his service for generations, he was still an employer. The days of feudal overlords and serfdom had ended, even in this corner of England.

Nicholas decided to take a walk rather than cool his heels in the breakfast parlor. He had to get his own coat—there was not a footman or other servant to be found. His grandfather needed to augment his staff if he was going to hold many house parties like this one. The servants he had seen were stretched to the utmost.

He walked about the gardens for a while, but their tame regularity did nothing to sweeten his temper. He looked around and began to tramp toward a line of trees he had been told was the beginning of the "home wood," whatever that meant.

As it turned out, it meant he wandered through a carefully cared for stand of trees. Whatever the deficiencies of the interior, the outdoors at Bellingham Place was well maintained. After a half hour or so, Nicholas returned to the house, his temper restored by the exercise and the sight and smell of the outdoors.

He entered the breakfast parlor and stopped, unwilling to disturb the two who had preceded him. They seemed to be having a very intimate discussion.

Priscilla stood with her back against the black marble fireplace while Granville leaned over her, his hand placed on her arm in what to Nicholas seemed like a possessive gesture. She did not break free.

"You must listen to me," Granville said, his voice low and passionate.

"My lord, please—"

Was it his imagination, or did Priscilla sound more flirtatious than upset? He scarcely had time to form the thought before she jerked her arm from Granville's grasp and rushed past both men and out the door.

Granville raised his eyebrows and gazed haughtily at Nicholas. "I cannot understand what makes women think they are more desirable when they pretend disinterest." He shrugged with apparent unconcern, but Nicholas was aware Granville's eyes were sharp and that he studied his nephew closely, gauging his reaction.

"I would have said Miss Harrowby was not pretending. She looked as if she wanted to be somewhere else—anywhere you weren't from the look of it, Uncle." Nicholas grinned at the older man, though he was conscious of a burning desire to strike that smug, arrogant face.

Something of his feelings must have been apparent to Granville, for he turned away from the sideboard, with its chafing dishes and covered tureens.

"I find I am not hungry after all," he said. "If you will excuse me . . ." Without waiting for Nicholas to reply, he walked quickly out of the room.

"I'd stay away from Priscilla Harrowby if I were you," Nicholas called after him. It was only when his uncle's footsteps had died away that he gave vent to his feelings by crashing the top of a silver dish onto the table.

"Damn him, damn him!" He would give anything to be able to leave this place, filled with the likes of Granville Connaught. He couldn't eat. Perhaps he could find Priscilla, talk to her. Surely she hadn't been listening to Granville—whatever he'd been saying.

But Jeffrey had told him Priscilla's aim in life was to marry well. And on the face of it, Granville was a catch—an earl who would in the not too distant future be a marquis. Any girl would like that, wouldn't she?

In Nicholas's experience, that was what girls would like most of all. Doubt, a dark worm, began to eat at his peace of mind.

He left the breakfast room just as Dalton entered

with a platter of sauteed trout. Dalton was dismayed. "But, Mister Nicholas," he said, "you haven't eaten a bite!"

"Later, Dalton. I'll eat twice as much at luncheon!"

Eight

Priscilla leaned against the door of the library, a room she had given only a nervous glance when being shown around the castle the previous day. An enormous, gloomy room, it was paneled in wood so darkened by time it was almost black, its windows swathed in hunter green velvet draperies. Lined with books from floor to ceiling, adorned here and there with marble busts on tall pilasters, it was not a room where Priscilla would ever feel at home.

But now it was a place of refuge. She had slipped inside when she heard Granville's steps hurry by. She breathed a sigh of relief when they continued on by and faded away. She didn't care where he went, so long as it was nowhere near her.

He had accosted her as soon as she had entered the breakfast room. Last night had not affected him at all. He was not embarrassed or apologetic. He gave her a lazy smile. Intended to be intimate and seductive, it had made her flesh crawl. She could almost feel once again that suffocating, wet, monstrous kiss. Thank heaven Nicholas knew nothing of what had happened.

If he had seen her, he might have thought she was leading his uncle on. Or, worse, that she was the kind of girl a member of the peerage like Granville Connaught—and his nephew, Nicholas Cannon—would not marry, but only maul at a party.

Priscilla's eyes filled, but she refused to give way to nerves or fear. No one but Elinor knew of Granville's behavior, and no one ever would! If her mother were ever to learn of the earl's kiss and subsequent behavior this morning, Priscilla would be on her way to the altar before she could draw her next breath.

Just as she was beginning to relax and think perhaps she could open her eyes and even consider leaving her temporary sanctuary, there was a knock at the door she was leaning against. Startled, she took an involuntary step forward into the room and the door opened.

"Nicholas!" she breathed, for all the world as if she were a maiden chained to a rock and had just seen a knight approach. "It is you!"

"You seem happy to see me," he noted as he deftly entered, closed the door, and took her into his arms, all in one fluid motion.

"I am," she admitted, knowing full well no well-brought-up young woman ever told a man she was happy to see him. Well, perhaps in a drawing room filled with other people, when it was a mere polite pleasantry. But not when she stood in his embrace, alone with him in a dim room with far too many deep, comfortable chairs and sofas. And certainly not with the look she knew must be in her eyes.

Adoration. Infatuation.

Love.

Love? Frightened of the thought, she tried to pull away, but Nicholas's arms held her fast.

"I am equally happy to be here with you," he murmured, and took her mouth with his.

Bliss. It was absolute heaven to feel his lips, firm

and warm, on hers. A strange, new warmth seemed to pervade her limbs and she sank against him, molding herself to him as closely as her restrictive clothing would permit. She slid her arms up to encircle his neck, without even thinking whether this was acceptable behavior or not. She didn't care what was acceptable!

She could tell it was acceptable to Nicholas. His arms tightened around her waist and pressed her closer to him, while his lips moved provocatively over hers. Instead of clamping his mouth to hers, as Granville had done, Nicholas kissed first her upper lip then her lower. Gently, he urged her to open her mouth to him. When she did, he took his time before his tongue began to explore.

Priscilla sighed. This kiss was even more wonderful than the kiss they had shared last evening. She was in heaven, floating on a cloud of warm sensations she had never felt before. But, wonderful as it was, she wanted more. Without conscious thought, she twined her arms tighter around his neck and began to kiss his lips as he had kissed hers. Nicholas growled deep in his throat. Priscilla knew that meant he liked what she was doing.

She didn't know how she knew that, any more than she had known Nicholas's kiss was special, even though it was the first one she had ever had. Some things you did not need experience to know. Some things were so wonderful you knew right away they were perfect and nothing else would ever be as good.

Now, just as she was beginning to know there was more she could experience with Nicholas, though she wasn't sure what it would feel like, only that it would be wonderful, he pulled away from her. He was breathing hard, as if he had just been running. His eyes, as he looked down at her upturned face, were glowing.

"Priscilla, love, we have to stop this now."

"Why?" She was disappointed. She had only begun to enjoy herself. She knew there was much more to be experienced.

"Because if we do not, soon I will not be able to." He pulled farther away from her, but Priscilla leaned toward him.

"I am not sure I want you to."

There, that was honest. How she dared say these impossible things to him, she did not know. They were not the things a well-brought-up young lady should ever, ever say. They were probably not even the sort of things a wife should say to her husband! Priscilla was shocked at herself, but her blood was warm and racing through her veins and her body hummed with desire and the shock she felt was delightful. She had never been so daring, and she liked the feeling of power it gave her. She stepped closer to him.

But Nicholas was determined. He took her arms and set her away from him. "I have to see my grandfather this morning, love. I promised him, and if I don't appear, Dalton will come and hunt me down. So I must go. You wait here for a few minutes. Go and pick out a book and sit in the window seat." He looked around at the dark room. "It's the only spot in here where you can see well enough to read. They really should do something about getting decent lamps in here."

Priscilla pouted. She did not want to be dismissed. Had she been wrong about Nicholas? Was he just taking her kisses and disregarding her? That was what her mother would think, if she were ever to discover what Priscilla had been doing.

"Do you love me?" She needed to know the answer.

Nicholas looked startled. Then thoughtful. This was not good. Priscilla was sure of that. He should have immediately said yes and fallen to his knees to propose. That much she had learned from listening to other girls and reading novels.

"Yes, I believe I may," he said at last, just as Priscilla felt tears prickle at the back of her eyes. "I suppose we'll have to do something about that, won't we?"

"Do not tease me, Nicholas." Priscilla took a step away from him. Her blood was cooling rapidly, and she was beginning to wonder if her mother didn't have the right of it after all. Men had to be manipulated and brought up to scratch. You could not treat them in a straightforward fashion. Look at what had just happened when she had asked for an honest answer to the most important question in the world. "This is serious."

"I know it is, love."

"Do not call me that if you do not mean it."

Nicholas sighed. "I am not going to stay in England, Priscilla. If we marry, you will have to come to America with me. To live."

She stared up at him. "Is it awful there? Are you afraid to take me there?" She twisted her hands in front of her. She realized she had not the faintest idea of what Nicholas's family's status was, but her heart told her she had to be brave and fling herself into the future. She raised her chin and smiled. "I have always thought I would like New York. From the pictures, you know."

He grinned at her. "Well, we drove the Indians out a few years ago. It's safe now—for the most part."

Priscilla had read a number of travel books. She

knew her leg was being pulled, and she did not appreciate it. Looking at Nicholas with a cold eye and a disdainful shrug, she turned away from him and walked over to one of the bookcases, where she pretended to examine the titles with what she hoped looked like cool unconcern.

She had not acted a moment too soon. There was a discreet knock on the door, followed by a loud cough and the rattle of the doorknob. Then Dalton's face appeared. A worried frown was replaced by a relieved smile once he saw their relative positions, across the room from each other.

"Mr. Nicholas," he said, "the marquis wishes to see you now. If it is completely convenient, of course," he added as an obvious afterthought.

"Of course. You have found the volume you were looking for, Miss Harrowby?" Nicholas spoke in a voice that was almost a parody of Dalton's polite tones.

"Yes." Priscilla's voice was subdued and her head was bent over whatever book she had picked at random from the shelves. A stray sunbeam lit her hair and turned it to gold. The only light in the dusty old room was concentrated on her, Nicholas thought as he turned and followed Dalton out the door.

"My grandfather is up early this morning," Nicholas said. "It can't be much past eight o'clock. He said yesterday he would see me after luncheon, in his study."

"He wakes early most days," Dalton replied. "Most old men do. His joints ache and he cannot sleep."

"Does he usually conduct business this early in the day?"

"No, Mr. Nicholas. I told him you were up, along

with Mr. Granville and Miss Harrowby, and he wanted to keep you out of trouble."

Here was plain speaking with a vengeance, Nicholas thought. "So he thinks I can't take care of myself, does he?"

Dalton hastened to smooth Nicholas's ruffled feathers. "I don't think it was you so much as Mr. Granville. Your grandfather knows how much the earl hates the idea you may inherit one day in place of his son."

Nicholas felt a surge of impatience. "Is he incapable of understanding that I have no wish to inherit the title or the estate? He is welcome to do both. I wish he would marry tomorrow and produce a son nine months to the day after the wedding." He began to walk faster. "And one a year every year thereafter!"

He realized he was striding down the corridor in an attempt to outrun his anger. Dalton was panting, trying to keep up with Nicholas's younger, stronger legs. "Sorry, Dalton," he said, slowing down and walking alongside the old servant. "I'm afraid my uncle gets my goat." He grinned in apology.

"Your goat, sir? I was not aware . . . but, of course, in America I'm told everyone keeps animals. Somewhat like Ireland and other of the less civilized provinces."

Nicholas stared at Dalton, trying to gauge if he was being laughed at. But the old man's serious expression tended to make him think Dalton was merely ignorant, as so many seemed to be, of life in America—or, indeed, anywhere that was not England.

"It is merely an expression, Dalton. A bit of slang."

"Oh. Oh, thank you, sir. I do like to try to keep up with all the modern ideas."

They had reached the marquis's suite of rooms by

this time and, after a discreet knock, Dalton opened the door and peered in.

"Oh, for heaven's sake, man, do stop creeping about as if I were already dead! Bring the boy in!"

The marquis's querulous voice seemed stronger this morning. Nicholas entered behind Dalton and immediately went over to his grandfather's bedside.

"Good morning, sir," he said. "I hope you are feeling well this morning. You look lively, I must say." He couldn't help but grin at his grandfather's exasperated look.

"Do not try to turn me up sweet, you young rascal," the marquis answered. "I may be old, but I am not yet in my dotage. I know I look like something the cat dragged in from the graveyard."

"Nonsense, sir. You are fishing for compliments." Nicholas looked around the room, finding it as cheerless and barren as it had been before. He recalled the slightly shabby, uncared for look of the library and wondered if there was less money in the Bellingham purse than he had supposed.

"Pull a chair over and sit down."

The only chairs were straight-backed and hard, but Nicholas obediently moved one to the bedside and sat.

"You wanted to see me, grandfather?" he said.

The old man reached out a paper-thin hand and grasped Nicholas's. "What do you think of your home now you have had an opportunity to see it?"

His glance was eager, and Nicholas hastened to reassure him. "It is beautiful, sir, as you must know."

"Impressive, is it not?" There was a wealth of family pride in his voice.

"Indeed it is." Thus far, Nicholas was having no

difficulty agreeing with the marquis. But he knew that would shortly become much more difficult.

"A prize worth fighting to maintain." The grasp on Nicholas's hand became tighter and more demanding. "An inheritance worth learning about."

"But not my prize or my inheritance, sir."

The marquis ignored the interruption. "You could manage all the properties, Nicholas. You could bring them back to where they were before I became ill. They have not been truly cared for since then."

"I am not the person you should be having this conversation with," Nicholas said, keeping his voice in the same neutral tone. He did not wish to argue with this frail old man. "Granville is your heir."

"Granville!" The old man positively snorted with disdain. "He cares for nothing but the money the property brings in. Gives not a single thought to the land or the people on it. He simply wants to wring every last penny out of it so he can pursue his pleasure in London."

Nicholas refrained from shrugging, but it was an effort. "Surely you control his income. There must be a limit to what he can spend."

"Ha! Little you know, my boy. Runs up debts, and of course everyone looks to me for payment." He held up his hand to forestall comment. "I know I need not pay them, but I am an old man. They know they need only wait until I die and they can distrain estate funds, if need be. Worse than that, he gambles."

"How much has he lost?"

"Two hundred thousand in the last year."

"My God! I had no idea one could lose that much at a gentleman's pastime." Nicholas never gambled at cards. His business was a gamble, and that was excitement enough for him.

"Oh, no, he does not play cards or vingt-et-un." The marquis stirred restlessly, his head against the pile of pillows. "I wish he did. It would be less disastrous."

Nicholas had the distinct feeling his grandfather was playing up the drama of the situation for his own purposes. He frowned, resisting the marquis's ploy.

"What then?" If he sounded impatient, he was sorry, but in some strange way he could feel the tentacles of the Connaught family closing around him.

"The 'Change!"

"My uncle attempts to win buying and selling shares?" Nicholas hoped he did not sound as incredulous as he felt. He did not want to anger his grandfather by saying what he really thought of his uncle's business skills. "He does not seem like someone who knows much about the business world."

"You are too kind." The marquis grinned. It gave him the look of a mischievous boy—an odd sight in his wrinkled old face. "He is a babe in the woods. He knows nothing of business and does not care to learn."

"A sure way to lose."

The marquis nodded. "I want to prevent him from beggaring the estate after I die."

"I am not a solicitor, sir. I wouldn't know how to protect it."

The marquis waved his hand in dismissal of such talk. "I do not need a solicitor. I have one, and I know as much as he about wills and trusts. No, I need you for another purpose."

Nicholas eyed his grandfather with growing unease. It was as if the old man had shed twenty years in the past few minutes. Talk of the estate, the family, and how to protect them had galvanized the marquis's energies and focused his formidable will and intelligence. If he had thought it would be easy to stand fast against his grandfather's demands, Nicholas was beginning to change his mind.

"And what purpose might that be?"

"Do not sound so suspicious, my boy." The marquis tried an ingratiating grin.

It might have worked with others, for it radiated charm, but Nicholas was not buying charm from this old fox. He tried again for information. "What is it you would like me to do for you?"

"Most of the property is not entailed," the marquis said. "I would like to leave it to you, to manage and control for the next generation. Once Granville and his creditors learn he will not have unlimited funds to draw upon, his credit will dry up. I will settle his bills this last time and tell him of my new intention. That should do it," he finished with satisfaction.

"No." Nicholas could feel the entire weight of the Connaught family descend on his shoulders, and he hastened to shrug it off. "I know nothing of estates or the responsibilities of English aristocrats to their lazy family members. I come from America, where everyone earns his way. And I know nothing of this family, of who anyone is or what they can do. No," he repeated, warming to the idea. "I cannot do it. You cannot ask it of me."

"I am not asking." There was steel in the marquis's voice, and he raised himself from his pillows to stare his grandson in the face. As his eyes met those of his grandfather, Nicholas had the oddest sense he was encountering his own father. That same implacable will, hidden behind charm and warmth, but always there when needed.

"You cannot force me to become the trustee for your family, sir." Nicholas was angry, but anger had never deflected his father. He had a sinking feeling he wouldn't fare any better with his grandfather.

"Yes, in fact, I can. A will is a gift from beyond the grave. A gift and a demand. I will give you the money and the land—vast quantities of both, my boy—and demand you take care of it." A smile played around the marquis's mouth. "You are your father's son and my grandson. I know you will not fail his family, for it is yours as well."

Stubbornly, Nicholas shook his head. He could see his life in New York, so rich and full of what he loved, fading away, like the sight of it when his ship sailed. He would fight to keep it. "Gifts can be refused, sir."

"You won't refuse this one. Not if I leave the estate to Granville as default legatee if you do." The smile blossomed. It seemed to Nicholas intolerably smug. "You know what he will do with it. Liquidate everything, sell everything that isn't entailed and spend the money on his dreams of glory. He has always wanted to prove he deserved his good fortune, that he should be the heir."

"But he has always been your heir. What was there for him to prove?"

"That what people said was not true. Everyone thought Bart should have inherited. He was so clever, so charming, with such skills at managing people and money. Granville heard those whispers and resented them."

"My father had no desire to take his brother's inheritance." Nicholas felt annoyed at Granville for his resentment of someone who had no such feelings toward him. "My father wanted exactly the life he had. He wanted to make his own way. That is why he went to America. He could have stayed in Britain, but here he would always be a Connaught, the younger son of a fabulously wealthy marquis. Nobody would have believed he was making his way without your help."

"I know." The marquis sighed. "But if Bart had known the threat Granville posed to the family, he would not have stood by and let the Connaughts founder and fail."

"There are at least ten men here who are members of your family. Not all of them are like Granville. Most must understand estate management far better than I ever could. Any one of them would be glad of the chance. Let one of them do it."

The marquis shook his head. Again, he reached out and grasped Nicholas's hand. "I do not want them. I want you. I know you can do the job. You have the skill. Better yet, you have the steel to see it through. I want you," he repeated. His hand tightened to a vise-like grip for a moment. Then he leaned back against the pillows. Now he looked exhausted. "Go now, my boy. We will talk again later."

Nicholas looked down at the frail old man and clamped his teeth together. It was on the tip of his tongue to say he was not only refusing the gift of the Connaught family fortune but he was leaving on the next ship for New York. Instead, he bent and kissed the old man on his forehead.

It wasn't until he had left the room and stood with his back to the door that he muttered, "Well, I am sorry, but you cannot have me, grandfather."

Nine

To her surprise, Priscilla found herself interested in the Bellingham Place library. She discovered several books of engravings of cities in the Far East, and she began to pore over them, as she did every book of travel to far-off places. She stayed in her niche by the window, as it remained the spot in the room where it was bright enough to read.

The sun rose higher in the sky. Even though it was December, the little nook became uncomfortably warm. Priscilla looked around and found a long stick with a hook on the end. With some fiddling, she was able to find the corresponding spot on the window frame and inch it open a crack.

The crunch of shoes on gravel announced that someone was taking a walk. To her surprise, the footsteps stopped just under her window. Voices carried on the thin, crisp air. Not very interested in whatever two nameless members of the high and mighty Connaughts might have to say, Priscilla turned back to her book.

"Nicholas actually might inherit all this?" It was Lucinda's voice.

"If Granville manages to drink himself to death or lose all his money and put a bullet through his brain." Jeffrey, judging others as harshly as he did Priscilla.

"Jeffrey!" Lucinda scolded. "I do not suppose

Nicholas is looking forward to that eventuality any more than Granville is."

"I fear it may happen. Rumor has it Granville has sunk what is left of his money into a new railroad venture in Wales that is very unlikely to succeed."

"Oh, dear. Then I suppose he will have to find an heiress to marry very quickly." Lucinda added, "Just so it isn't my cousin, I wish him well."

"Why not Priscilla?" Jeffrey chuckled.

It will most certainly not be me, Priscilla thought indignantly. How could Jeffrey even think it!

"They deserve each other," he continued. "Both of them are as selfish as they are stupid. A match made in heaven—or hell, if you prefer. The only difficulty I see is that Priscilla's father has invested in the same Welsh rail scheme. I don't know how much he's sunk in it, but whatever amount it is, it is as good as gone."

At his first words, Priscilla had gone stiff with anger. She had opened her mouth on an instinctive protest. She was *not* stupid. True, she could not hold a candle to Lucinda, but who could?

And she was not selfish—or at least not very. Less so than her mother, surely, if a little more than her father. Even Lucinda had stopped at nothing to try to snare wealthy beaux, no matter if they had been interested in another girl first. Of course, she had changed once she met Jeffrey, but still . . .

At his words about her father, however, she sank back against the cushions. For a moment fear made her cold. Then she shook her head. It could not be. Her father was rich. That was as certain as the sun in the sky.

"Jeffrey, I wish you would stop sniping at Priscilla," Lucinda was saying. "I think she truly cares for Nicholas and he for her, and I do not want you trying to talk him out of his feelings for her."

At that, Priscilla sat up again, her eyes wide with surprise. Lucinda was taking her part. More important, Lucinda thought Nicholas cared for her. Priscilla smiled and hugged herself. Lucinda was Nicholas's friend. She would know if he cared for Priscilla.

"Very well," Jeffrey said. "I will simply tell him I agree with his plan to renounce the title and return permanently to America. That should put an end to Priscilla's attachment. She wants nothing as much as a title and a fortune. Nicholas's affection—if you are right and he is foolish enough to feel any—will mean little once she learns he's given up both."

"Is that what he intends to do?"

"So he tells me. Come. You are beginning to look a bit chilled, my love. Let us walk on."

The footsteps began again and faded away.

Priscilla sat up began to think. Was Jeffrey right? Would she sacrifice everything for a title? No, not if the title went with Granville Connaught. The thought of being married to the earl made Priscilla's flesh creep. There was something dark and violent in his eyes, hidden deep behind layers of boredom and cynicism. Others might doubt its existence, thinking Granville just a useless aristocrat, but she had seen it, felt it, when he had forced his kiss upon her.

So that was settled to her satisfaction: a title and a fortune did not mean everything to her. But would she marry despite those things, marry a man who had both within his grasp and had thrown them away? Would she marry Nicholas Cannon and go to a country she had never seen? Would she risk poverty—perhaps even danger?

The answer was clear almost before the question formed in her mind.

Of course she would!

She loved Nicholas, and she would go with him anywhere. In fact, part of his fascination was that he came from a land she had always associated with adventure, chances taken, and dangers dared. Of course, all she knew of America was contained in the somewhat fanciful and lurid newspaper stories she managed to read from time to time if she could sneak them out of the kitchen, where the maids read them avidly.

Yes, she was ready to go to New York City with Nicholas and live no matter how. She quaked a little as she thought of telling her parents—especially her mother—what she intended. But somehow she had recently come to believe that in matters of her own happiness, she knew better than her mother. Like the clothes that became her, the people she liked—she had learned she could trust her own instincts where the man she loved was concerned.

Now there was only one little matter waiting to be seen to.

Did Nicholas love her?

Where was she?

Where was Priscilla—the only person Nicholas wanted to see at this moment? Somehow her presence would soothe and relieve him. She would understand with her heart, even though he was sure she had no idea what an entail was. Priscilla didn't need to know things. She believed in him and she knew him. She was ready, he was sure, to take a chance on him.

Priscilla did not know or care about his family. She

would not believe he was deserting them, leaving them to flounder on as best they could—a lot of lazy good-for-nothing aristocrats who never would have been able to do what his father had done.

Nicholas continued to fume, to insist that returning permanently to America was the best thing. It would teach the Connaughts to fend for themselves. Perhaps some of them would amount to something, figure out how to earn money, how to live a life on their own terms, instead of as prisoners of their name.

Priscilla would understand how trapped he felt, like a fox that would rather gnaw its own foot off than remain ensnared. Priscilla would see and understand. She would tell him he was right. She would go with him.

Where was she?

He had looked in the library, but she had left. It was once more just a drab chamber in need of a good cleaning. His random strides at last led him to his cousin Elinor.

"Where is Priscilla?" he demanded.

"Good morning, Cousin Nicholas," she replied with undiminished good humor. "Priscilla has gone out with the group that is looking for holly and mistletoe to decorate the—" She did not bother to finish, for Nicholas had gone.

Without stopping to don an overcoat or scarf, he strode out into the crisp air. One of the rare footmen was on duty in the hall and told him where the group was going. There was a grove not far from the house where the holly trees grew to great height and mistletoe could be found growing on the oaks as well. It was where the Connaughts always went to find holiday garlands.

It took only a few minutes' walk to find the group. He spotted Priscilla immediately. She wore a sapphire blue velvet cloak trimmed in swansdown, and she looked like a winter princess. Several of the Connaught cousins were standing near her, and his Uncle Granville was not far away, glowering at Nicholas as he approached.

At another time, he might have been amused, perhaps even jealous. Now all he could think of was Priscilla, talking to Priscilla, getting Priscilla's answer to the most important question he had ever asked.

"So then Lucinda and I—" Priscilla was saying with a chuckle when he took her arm and turned her to face him. "Nicholas! Good heavens, what are you doing?"

"I must speak to you," he muttered and began to hurry her off deeper into the woods.

"I say, old chap, this is hardly fair!" The voices were friendly, but he knew his conduct was boorish. He didn't care.

As the trees closed around them, he stopped suddenly and drew her against him. "Come to New York with me. Come now, Priscilla!"

"Wha-what—"

He did not want to take the time to explain, but he tried, in a headlong fashion. "I love you. Come to New York with me. Let us leave now, right away! We'll go first to London to tell your parents and then we'll go to Southampton or Liverpool, wherever there is a ship leaving immediately, and we'll—"

"Wait, wait!" Laughing, breathless, she held up her hands and placed them firmly against his chest. "What is all this about? What do you mean?"

"My grandfather wants to force me to stay in England forever. He wants me to give up my business, my life in America, and stay here as a sort of servant to the Connaught family!" Nicholas ran a hand through his thick, brown hair. "I can't do it, Priscilla! I won't!"

"But I do not understand. You have always said you were leaving in January to return to New York. Why the sudden urgency? The marquis cannot force you to stay here, can he?"

"No, not really." How could he explain the sense of dread that came over him whenever his grandfather spoke of Family, Land, Tradition—as if a great weight were descending on his shoulders and he was helpless to avoid it.

"Then why would you disrupt the party and cause a scandal, when you are leaving anyway?"

She had a point. He didn't want his grandfather to be embarrassed by him. His mother would never approve of that!

He relented. "Very well, then. I'll stay at least until after Christmas and that silly thing you Brits do the next day. What do they call it?"

"Boxing Day," Priscilla said. "And good, that will make it easier. Then you can claim you have been called back to New York sooner than you expected—a family illness or some other lame excuse. People will not believe it, but it will serve."

"And you will come with me?" He began to stamp his feet. It was beginning to seem cold to him, and he realized he had run out without a coat or boots.

Priscilla looked at him, noting he had come to seek her without an overcoat. It gave her a thrill to think he would pursue her so recklessly.

"Just like that?" she said, the thrill she had felt giving way to a slight pout. He had not yet told her he wanted to marry her. She thought he did. Lucinda had said so, and Lucinda was very intelligent. Jeffrey seemed to think so too, though of course he was not very happy about it.

Nicholas had asked her to go with him to New York. Surely that meant marriage. But she wanted—needed—to know he loved her, to be asked to marry him on bended knee, with an engagement ring, no matter how paltry. She was more than happy to give up her mother's dream for her, but she still had her own dream: to be the love of Nicholas's life, the person he would give up everything for.

"You ask a great deal of a girl," she said.

There was fear in his eyes. "I know, but I need you to come with me, to be with me, to understand why I have to go."

"Because you will lose your American life if you stay," she responded.

"Exactly! The life I love, the life I want you to share!" He took her hands in his and pulled her, unresisting, into his arms.

The sapphire blue hood on her cloak fell back, revealing her bright blonde curls. Nicholas hugged her to him even tighter and Priscilla lifted her face to his, inviting his kiss.

Slowly, his head bent over hers, blotting out the sun. When their lips met, all Priscilla's doubts melted in the fire of that kiss. She loved him. He loved her. He must. He could not kiss her, ask her to go home with him if he did not.

Her lips became soft, pliant, and instinctively they opened under his. Once again she felt the magic Nicholas brought to her. Once again, she felt excited, seized with a strange feeling that her skin was on fire, her nerves flaring with a need to be touched.

"Priscilla." Nicholas drew back, only far enough to look into her eyes. "You will come with me, won't you?"

Priscilla gave a brief, shuddering thought to her mother's reaction when she told her. But it would be all right. Nicholas would be with her.

"All right. Where will we be married? Can you get a special license?"

"On board ship," Nicholas replied. "We will go straight to board the first steamer to New York. The captain can marry us."

It sounded reckless and romantic to Priscilla. She would throw in her lot with the man she loved. She, who had never thought to love anyone, never thought love should be even mentioned in the same breath with marriage—that very girl was going to toss aside a chance to be a countess and later a marchioness to go to an unknown country with a man she had known for a few weeks!

Priscilla laughed. "Yes," she said.

Nicholas's smile was wide and victorious. "Good girl!"

It was not what she wanted to hear, but it would do for the time being. What she really wanted was another of those wonderful kisses. She tilted her face and tightened her arms around his waist.

"You have got to stop enticing me like this," he murmured. "I can't resist you!"

"Good. Then kiss me."

He did, and for another few minutes the world stepped back and left the two lovers alone. A soft cough brought them back to earth. Priscilla, far more embarrassed than Nicholas seemed to be, tried to step away from him and face the intruder, but Nicholas would not let her go. He kept his arm firmly around her and faced the embarrassment with a smile.

It was Elinor. "I am very sorry to—to interrupt," she said with a worried frown. "But you have been missed, and if you do not return to the house now, there will be the most awful gossip and fuss." She looked at Priscilla, rather than Nicholas. "You know what I mean."

She certainly did. She had participated in just the kind of scandalmongering that would take place if she stayed alone with Nicholas one moment longer.

"I will come back and help with the decorations," she said, looking up at Nicholas with a silent plea for understanding. Nicholas had no patience with the social strictures of the British upper class, but nevertheless he would not want Priscilla made the object of unwelcome talk. He released her.

While Priscilla and Elinor made their way back to Bellingham Place, with the garlands of ivy and sprays of holly Elinor had gathered in their arms, Nicholas remained behind for a moment.

Chilled though he was without a hat or coat, his blood ran hot in his veins, and he could think of nothing but Priscilla. He wanted her, he loved her, and nobody was going to prevent him from having her in his life forever!

"Thank you, Elinor," Priscilla was saying at that same moment. "I know you must think me terribly fast. A veritable loose woman."

"Pooh," said the young girl. "You are in love. I hope

someday I fall in love with someone as handsome and exciting as Nicholas. And I hope he looks at me the way Nicholas looks at you."

Priscilla could feel the blood heat her cheeks. "But my behavior was not what anyone could approve—" She stopped. Her behavior had been exactly what she had wanted it to be. She had acted on her feelings. Now she was letting the rules of society tell her she was wrong and should be ashamed.

"I love Nicholas," she said. "And it was wonderful! And I will do it again the very first chance I get!"

Elinor laughed and squeezed her arm. "Good. Just do not get caught. That is the only true rule, in my observation. Do not let anyone catch you!"

Laughing together, the two entered the great entrance hall and followed the sound of raised voices up the stairs to the largest reception room in the main part of the house. There four or five women stood facing each other in what was obviously an argument. The holly boughs they had brought in lay in discarded heaps while several footmen stood frozen, trying to pretend they could not hear anything that was being said at the top of several voices.

"Good afternoon," said Priscilla, smiling at everyone as if she were coming in on a scene of the greatest amity. "Are we going to put these around and about before tea?" She went over to the enormous fireplace at one end of the room. "Would not the ivy look attractive here, Susan?" she said, singling out Elinor's nemesis, who was one of the most vociferous of the combatants.

"Where?" Susan asked, her face a thundercloud.

"Draped along the mantel, perhaps with red velvet ribbons and red candles." Priscilla proceeded to hand the ivy to a footman and demonstrate what she meant. "If you like," she said, still smiling at the angry-looking Susan, "you could show this footman—James, isn't it?—how to make the holly into garlands and put it above the draperies. And then you could use some more for the windowsills."

James smiled sheepishly at being remembered by one of the guests, and Susan soon became interested in just how to arrange the holly to show to best advantage when the red velvet draperies were pulled back as she directed them to be.

Priscilla was soon summoned by another of the ladies to see to her placement of the mistletoe in the doorway. When the reception room had been decorated to everyone's satisfaction, the ladies moved on to the dining room and from there to some of the smaller apartments.

"The Yule log is going to be brought in to the great hall downstairs. It is one of the earliest parts of the house." One of the male cousins spoke to Priscilla, as if she were in charge of the decorating. Embarrassed at having put herself forward more than was seemly for an unmarried woman who was not even a member of the family, Priscilla disclaimed any authority. She was horrified to feel a giggle force its way up her throat for the first time in days. She was struggling to keep her composure in a situation she was sure her mother would never condone, when Lucinda strolled into the room and came to her rescue.

She seemed to take in the situation at a glance. "Yes," she said, smiling at her scarlet-faced cousin, "best let Priscilla tell you where to put things. She has a positive gift for all the elements that go into entertaining." And the newly married Mrs. Bancroft, whose husband was known to be worth at least a million pounds and was thus completely acceptable, put her arm around her cousin and, standing shoulder to shoulder with Priscilla, dared anyone to question her cousin's authority.

Priscilla swelled with pride. Lucinda seldom complimented her. But today Lucinda's support had given her the authority she needed.

"The Yule log," she said, "will lend this a very festive air once it is lit, and candles have been placed around the room. Could we have the candles in the chandeliers lit as well?" She had not seen any of the elaborate ceiling fixtures lit, and was not sure why this was so, but hesitated to take the responsibility for ordering them to be used.

"Why, of course. That will make all the difference, Miss Harrowby." Susan Connaught was positively smiling at her.

Priscilla had to work to keep her jaw from dropping.

"We will ask Dalton to see to it."

Within minutes, the room glowed with light from both candles and a snapping, crackling fire. As she stood looking at it, Priscilla could not help but smile at the festive faces around her. It looked more and more like Christmas, and she couldn't prevent a small glow of satisfaction. She had something to do with it!

Indeed, most of the Connaughts were more than willing to give Priscilla the credit for the decorations and the consequent good cheer. They had even asked if she would consult with the housekeeper and the cook to see if the food could be improved, as well.

Priscilla was very loath to put herself forward that way. She had dealt with servants all her life, not very successfully for the most part. She had followed her mother's example and had treated servants as if they were not very important—not quite human, in fact. She had never considered whether they were cold or tired or overworked. She simply told them what she wanted, and expected them to do it. But recently, she found herself looking at the people employed by her family the way Lucinda did—as human beings who worked better if they were rested and well fed and praised.

She brought that attitude to the kitchens of Bellingham Place. As she looked around, she saw very much what Nicholas had seen that morning, a sad and sorry place where work was difficult and good work all but impossible. An air of discouragement hung about the place like a pall.

There was not a great deal she could do about it, being only a guest, but Priscilla thought she would try. She began with a smile and then assumed an air of deferring to the wisdom and experience of the cook and the housekeeper, Mrs. Bennett and Mrs. Sandles. Both were pleased to be consulted and to have their expert knowledge appreciated. Without demanding anything, or even really suggesting a great deal, Priscilla left with every member of the staff looking a great deal more alert and energetic.

Tea proved the value of Priscilla's visit. The tea cakes were covered with mounds of icing dusted with red and green sugar, and the savory sandwiches provided the gentlemen were fresh and succulent.

At dinner, where the food was hot and unusually well-prepared, everyone commented on Priscilla's efforts. For the first time, she was the center of attention because of something she had done rather than what she wore or how she styled her hair. It was a novel sensation, and Priscilla found she liked it very much.

There was to be a dance the night after Christmas, which was just three days from tonight, and the younger Connaughts pleaded for an impromptu hop after dinner. So they could practice their steps, they said, when the earl raised his eyebrows and frowned.

"Oh, do let's have a little dancing," Susan pleaded. "Do you not think it would be delightful, Miss Harrowby?"

The earl's cold brown eyes stared at her as if, Priscilla thought, she were a bug. A giggle wormed its way toward her throat, but she fought it down.

"Yes," she said defiantly, meeting the earl's gaze with her own, "I think it would be lovely. Surely among all of us we can find enough pianists to keep us going for a half hour at least."

As the young people hastened toward the ballroom, the earl caught Priscilla's arm. "A little early to be playing lady of the manor, is it not, Priscilla? Though I confess you play it very well for a little middle-class miss. I congratulate you, but I think you have backed the wrong horse. If that is the role you seek, you would do better to listen to my suit. My nephew——"

"Your nephew is very tired of hearing your ideas about the succession, uncle. And so, I am sure, is Miss Harrowby. Come, Priscilla, let's go and dance."

And, to Priscilla's relief, Nicholas took her arm and led her out of the room.

Ten

Waltzing with Nicholas was the most wonderful feeling in the world, Priscilla decided the night of the ball. The informal dance had shown her that she would love dancing with Nicholas in full formal regalia. She couldn't wait until he saw her in her new, deep blue ball gown. She had been dancing in the ballrooms of some of the most elegant mansions in London ever since she turned sixteen. At that age, Edwina had decreed her daughter ready to be liberated from the schoolroom—never more than a pretext in any case—to go into society and seek a husband.

And now she had found one! The perfect one. A handsome, clever man and related to one of the great families of England, as well. Her society friends would envy her. A man who was about to introduce her to the adventure of travel and life in another country, far across the sea. One who was handsome and kissed in a fashion guaranteed to weaken the knees. One who waltzed divinely.

But more important than all of those things was the fact that she was sure Nicholas loved her and would protect her from the likes of the earl of Ashden and from her own weakness and stupidity.

She did not giggle when she was with Nicholas!

Christmas had been wonderful. Everyone had complimented her on the decorations. Even the marquis had been kind, keeping her beside him for almost ten minutes at the elaborate Christmas tea.

The only problem had been that she and Nicholas had not had one moment together. Elinor's Aunt Margaret had made sure they did not dance with each other more than twice even at the family dance. Christmas festivities had kept her busy and Nicholas surrounded by his family. She was sure all the Connaught ladies would try their best to be certain the two of them did not make a spectacle of themselves this evening, either.

Her gaze found him almost immediately. He stood with others of the family. They were all tall and good looking, in an aquiline sort of way, with dark hair and brown eyes, but none of them had Nicholas's vitality, his charm and good looks. In his stark black and white evening clothes, he was the handsomest man she had ever seen. A passing glance at Jeffrey Bancroft showed her that he was taller and some people might find him more conventionally handsome, but to Priscilla's mind he lacked the crackling energy that made Nicholas so exciting.

"Isn't Jeffrey the most handsome man you have ever seen?" said Lucinda, who was standing beside her.

"Umm." Priscilla did not want to start an argument.

Lucinda chuckled. "You do not need to say it. I know what you are thinking. We will simply agree to disagree on who the best looking man in the room is."

Priscilla smiled. "Very well. Look, here they come."

The two men approached and bowed. Priscilla curtseyed and looked up into Nicholas's smiling eyes.

He led her to the floor for the first dance, a waltz of course, and as he whirled her around the enormous Bellingham Place ballroom, he laughed down at her and pulled her scandalously close. Priscilla didn't care. That was another thing Nicholas gave her, the sense that life was more—a great deal more—than what you could get by obeying all the rules and regulations and being a good girl.

"Happy?" he asked as he whirled her around.

"Oh, yes." She felt as if she were flying in her satin slippers. "Very, very happy."

"So am I. I haven't seen you in weeks." He whirled her in a reverse and her deep sapphire skirt belled out around her. "I love waltzing with you. I promise we will waltz at least once a week in New York." He grinned down at her.

"With an orchestra?" she demanded with a pout and an upward flash of her eyelashes. It was a look she had practiced for hours in front of her mirror.

He laughed down at her. "Little flirt! Of course. Though my sister, Melinda, plays the piano admirably. Almost as well as Elinor played for us the other evening."

Priscilla glanced around at the other couples circling the room. "It is too bad Elinor is not allowed to dance, being not yet out. It seems like such a silly rule when it is just the family and neighbors."

The music ended with a flourish, and Nicholas led her from the floor. Almost at once, they were surrounded by young Connaught men eager to dance with an unmarried lady they knew and to whom they were not related. Most of them viewed the neighboring squires' daughters as beneath their notice. Priscilla laughed and danced and enjoyed the sensation of being the belle of the ball. And if it was a very small ball, well, no matter.

She had always had partners for dances in London,

though sometimes she had to sit out a dance or two with her mother, which was a humiliation. Edwina never let such an occasion pass without a reminder of what her task was in going to parties and balls. And failure to dance meant a failure to marry. It was as simple as that in Edwina's mind. One danced and flirted and giggled and then a man proposed. It was Priscilla's job to do the former so as to achieve the latter.

Now she found she was at last dancing every dance with men who showed every sign of wanting to be with her. The secret, she decided, was that she no longer cared, if indeed she ever truly had. Perhaps her failure to attach a young sprig of fashion or scion of nobility during the four years she had been trotted out and about by Edwina like a horse trainer showing off a pony's paces before prospective buyers was because, at heart, she had not wished to do so.

She had been, she decided as she whirled about the floor with one of the young Connaughts, waiting for Nicholas. Now that she had found him, she did not care whether she charmed anyone else or not. Paradoxically, because she no longer appeared desperate to do so, she seemed to enchant them effortlessly.

After four or five dances, Nicholas apparently decided he'd had enough of dancing with young ladies who were desperate to charm him. He returned to Priscilla and, ignoring protocol, he ruthlessly cut in on her current partner and whirled her away.

"You are not dancing with anyone but me for the rest of the evening," he growled into her hair. "Lord, you smell good. I have had enough of seeing you happy and being bored to death myself!"

"Your cousins and all the neighboring ladies were

doing their best to see to it you were amused." Priscilla laughed up at him, pleased to see the frown on his face and what she thought was a jealous gleam in his eye.

"My cousins and all the unmarried neighboring ladies are only interested in being the next marchioness of Bellingham," he said, his voice steely. "I could have horns and a tail and it wouldn't matter a jot to any of them! They'd tell me they found horns delightful and that all the best men had tails!"

"Oh, surely not everybody," Priscilla said, a laugh in her voice. "Some of the men must merely want to be on good terms with the marquis."

"Good enough to warrant receiving an allowance out of estate revenues." Nicholas was clearly disgusted. "Though I acquit the neighbors of wanting anything more than to purchase a horse or a field or some such. But everyone wants something!"

"But surely all your cousins get allowances now." It was the accepted way of doing things among the wealthy aristocrats and some of the newly rich middle class. It was a mark of distinction to be able to live without gainful employment.

Nicholas answered by whirling her around the floor so fast her head spun as quickly as her heels. "Well, they wouldn't get a penny if I had anything to say about it. Which, of course, I don't. And I don't want to," he added, as if Priscilla had said something.

"Goodness, you are prickly tonight, Mr. Cannon." Priscilla smiled at him, sure he would not take offense. It was wonderful to be with a man and not have to watch every word to be sure it did not offend. She could tease Nicholas, and he would merely grin and whirl her a little faster around the room.

When the dance ended, Priscilla was breathless. She

stood, fanning herself, and looked around for her next partner. Nicholas took her arm and said, "I don't think you should dance with anyone else this evening. I want to spend all my time with you."

"Oh, but we cannot. The rules—"

"What rules?" Nicholas inquired with a bland look.

"Oh, Nicholas, you know the rules. Surely they are the same in America. One simply cannot dance all evening with the same lady. Even if she were your wife, it would be improper." Priscilla tried to look stern.

"I suppose we do have such silly ideas in America. We borrow a lot of foolishness and folderol from you folks."

"Did you not borrow your government from us?" Priscilla said. "Do you not have a parliament, or something?"

"Not a parliament. More 'something,' " Nicholas said, grinning down at her.

"I have said something foolish again."

Priscilla knew she should feel ashamed of having tried to say a single intelligent word about politics. She would have with any other man. But she could not, absolutely could not. Nicholas was grinning at her, as if he found her forays into American history charming.

"No, it is not what you say, it is the way you say it that makes you such a delight," he responded, sending her heart soaring.

"You mean I sound like an earnest idiot," said Priscilla, with sudden clarity.

"No, that's not it. It's that you don't try to sound as if you know more than you do. Your remarks are usually very intelligent, but you say them in this soft, apologetic way. That's why it's funny." He took her hands in his. Priscilla gave a fleeting thought to the gossip this was going to cause and then dismissed it.

She didn't care. No excuses, no attempts at self-justification. She was breaking some of society's most sacred taboos, established to protect the reputations of young ladies just like her. She knew it, and she just plain didn't care. She clasped Nicholas's hands in hers and beamed up at him.

"No one has ever, ever thought I was intelligent. I am so grateful."

But they were not as isolated as she had thought. The earl had come upon them while they were talking and now stood smiling sardonically at them both.

"Good for you, nevvy," he said, clapping his hands in soft, sardonic applause. "Tell a bluestocking like little Elinor that she's beautiful and a lovely ninny, er, lovely young thing like Miss Harrowby here that she's intelligent. That's the way to win 'em."

Priscilla felt both revulsion at the leer the earl directed at her and the familiar sinking feeling that she had been found out. Silly, foolish Priscilla. A giggle caught in her throat.

Then Nicholas squeezed her hand and suddenly all her self-doubts fled. Nicholas thought she was clever and amusing. He loved her, she knew he did. She was able to smile at the earl with charm and a certain cheeky confidence. She was wise enough to say nothing in the face of the earl's veiled insult.

"And when they are both beautiful and clever, uncle?" Nicholas said with a grin. "As Priscilla is, as Elinor will be. What do you say then?"

"The same thing?" Priscilla hazarded a guess before Granville could speak.

"Exactly." Nicholas's grin changed to a warm smile

as he gazed down at her. "So who is to know when a man is telling the truth as he sees it? Might as well accept all compliments as sincere."

Priscilla was amazed. How easy her social life would have been if she had been able to do that instead of doubting and giggling and becoming flustered. Even obviously sardonic compliments, like those her cousin's husband, Jeffrey, gave her could be accepted at face value, thus saving all sorts of emotional difficulties. And leaving Jeffrey speechless as well, no doubt. She couldn't wait to try out Nicholas's idea.

"Thank you," she said.

Nicholas looked into her eyes and she could see he understood exactly what she meant. "Think nothing of it," he said. "It's about time someone told you that little secret."

They managed two more dances together before society, in the person of Elinor's aunt, came up to them with partners for each of them. Every bit as self-important and overbearing as her daughters, she got her way. Even Nicholas could do nothing in the face of her determination to separate them.

The rest of the evening was a blur. The manners that had been instilled in her from childhood helped her to act as if she were having a wonderful time, even though she longed to spend every moment with Nicholas. The dance ended at last. As she made her way toward the staircase, Nicholas pulled her aside.

"Thanks to that silly aunt of mine I haven't had a minute alone with you." He drew her back into the shadows and held her close.

"I told you about the rules." Priscilla's heart was thundering. Just being near him, smelling the scent of starched linen, soap, and sandalwood that was Nicholas's alone, made her dizzy.

"Damn the rules. We leave tomorrow. Come with me now."

"Yes." It never occurred to her to say anything else.

"Get your cloak and meet me at the summerhouse. It's on top of the hill in back of the formal garden. No one will look for us there in the winter." He stroked her cheek for a moment. "Hurry. Promise me."

Her heart sang. "I promise."

It was easy enough to escape the other girls, who wanted to chatter, by pleading fatigue. "I have danced my slippers to pieces. I need to rest," she said, trying to look tired. She waited for a few minutes until everyone had retired to their rooms or found some other occupation. Then she swung her blue cloak around her shoulders and tiptoed down the stairs.

The weather had turned colder, and a sharp wind sent her skirts swirling around her ankles as she made her way down the gravel path past the bare rosebushes and neatly mulched flower beds toward the hill, the summerhouse, and Nicholas. A few flurries of snow began to fall as she hurried along, and the wind seemed to blow harder.

She saw the little building rise before her, ghostly white in the fitful moonlight. She picked up her pace. It was either round or octagonal; she couldn't tell in the dark. She hoped it would not be too cold, for it was a summery looking place, all white wooden lace and large windows. There were columns and a little porch wrapped around the entire circumference. She hoped no one else was out, for the windows would provide no privacy. For a moment she wondered about the wisdom of her actions. Then the snow seemed to spit at her, sent rushing at her by the erratic wind. Nicholas was waiting for her. She hurried on.

As she reached the porch, the door swung open and Nicholas reached out to pull her inside. Without a pause he swept her into his arms and laid his lips on hers.

"You came," he said. "I thought you might not risk coming out when I saw it had begun to snow."

"Pish and tush," she said. "A little snow could never stop me."

"Good." He put his arm around her and led her into the little room. "I've built a fire so we'll be nice and cozy." He kissed her ear and she melted against him.

Priscilla looked around. There was a white rattan settee with puffy blue cushions pulled up close to the white brick fireplace, where a fire snapped and blazed. She hadn't seen the smoke in the swirl of snow in the dark. She hoped no one else would notice it, either.

"In a few minutes it will be warm," he assured her.

"It's warm now as long as you keep your arm around me." Priscilla smiled up at him and flirted with her lashes. She liked to practice her old tricks now that she no longer needed them. And they seemed to amuse Nicholas, who was not taken in by them. He smiled and his deep brown eyes sparkled.

"I'll hold you as close as you like." He pulled her to his side, and she rested her head on his shoulder.

How happy she was! All the years of wondering if she would ever find anyone to love, anyone who would love her were past. Now, in the light of Nicholas's love, it was as if she had never worried, never doubted. She was as certain and happy as if she had known all along that a man named Nicholas Cannon was going to come into her life and transform it.

"I feel as if you were made for me," Nicholas said, echoing her thought. "Designed to be perfect just for me." He took her face in his hands and stroked her cheeks. "Perfect. I'm so glad you waited for me and didn't go marrying someone else before I had a chance to come along."

"I couldn't marry anyone else. I was waiting for you."

He kissed her then, and once again she felt the familiar heat rise up and weaken her knees and set her heart racing. This time he began exploring her mouth with leisurely thoroughness. Of its own volition, her mouth opened and she relaxed into his kiss. When he drew back, she whimpered a little in instinctive protest and reached up to pull his head down once again.

Now it was her turn, and she returned the favor with interest. Where had she learned to nibble on his lower lip and swirl her own tongue around his? Nowhere. She was born knowing how to please Nicholas—and herself. She gave no thought to any of the lectures her mother had given her through the years. Indeed, she was doing everything Edwina had warned her against, and a few things Edwina had never thought of.

His hands now were moving over her neck and shoulders and she leaned into the movement, wanting his touch, the warm shivers his hands sent over the bare skin above her dress. His fingers moved over her bodice and cupped her breasts. Priscilla gasped and Nicholas stopped immediately.

He looked down at her and thought he had never seen such a beautiful face. All the artifice that occasionally marred her expressions had been wiped away by passion. She wasn't pulling away from him, slapping his hands and warning him off. No, his Priscilla was breathing deeply, trembling slightly, but not repulsing him. On the contrary, she smiled a little, her eyes closed, and leaned toward him, as if inviting whatever he wanted to do. Her vulnerability made him want to protect her. He was afraid she didn't know what came next, what would happen if they didn't stop now.

"Priscilla," he said, "we should be getting back to the house. I don't want you to get in trouble with that dragon of an aunt or cousin or whatever she is to me."

Priscilla's china blue eyes opened wide at his words, and her mouth drooped in disappointment. "Oh," was all she said, but it conveyed a world of bewilderment and hurt.

"It's not that I want to let you go," he hastened to assure her. "But if I don't stop now I won't be able to later."

"You won't? Why not?" She ran her finger down his cheek and over his lips. He caught her hand and kissed it, relishing the little tremor that ran over her skin at the touch of his lips.

Could anyone be that innocent? Was she teasing him, pretending to be without guile or ulterior motives? He looked deep into her eyes. The love he saw there humbled him. No, Priscilla wasn't playing a game. She was completely in earnest.

"It is the way men are made, love."

She smiled shyly at him. "I don't want to stop, either. I know we should. We must. But——" She reached out for him and twined her fingers around one of the buttons on his vest that had come loose.

"But we don't want to. I know. I don't want to stop. Your kisses are like a drug. A few more of them and

I won't want to stop until I have taken your clothes off and laid you down on that rug there and—" He gestured to the fluffy white rug that lay on the hearth in front of the fire.

Priscilla's eyes were wide and her lips parted. For a moment, Nicholas thought he had frightened her away, but then she smiled. "Oh," she whispered. "Oh, yes, Nicholas. Do all that. Don't send me away."

He shook his head and held her away from him. "You don't know what you are saying."

He thought her stubborn pout was adorable. "Yes, I do. Stop treating me as if I were some silly little schoolgirl who doesn't know what she wants."

"Do you, love? Do you know what you want?"

"Of course I do." She began to fiddle with the buttons of his shirt. "I want you."

Still, he couldn't quite believe she knew what she was asking for. "Do you know what that means?"

She looked him square in the eye. "You are the most unromantic man I have ever met, Nicholas Cannon. Instead of kissing me and making love to me, you are asking me questions about how much I know. As if this were a science experiment, or an arithmetic problem, or something. My cousin and her friends are nurses. Of course I know." She turned away from him and went to stare out one of the wide, many-paned windows. "Now you've spoiled it! I might as well go back to the house."

Nicholas knew he had behaved badly. He wanted to explain that because he loved her, he wanted to be sure she knew what she was doing. He could never forgive himself if he made her unhappy or frightened her. He came to stand behind her, putting his arms around her waist.

"Look carefully outside, love. I don't think we can go back yet."

The snow, which was coming down heavily, swirled around as if stirred by a giant hand. It was like a constantly moving curtain of opaque white.

"I can walk in the snow," Priscilla said, pulling away from him. When she turned to go toward the door, he could see her eyes were filled with tears.

"It's so thick and blowing so hard that you'll lose your way. People have gotten lost and died in freak storms like this one."

"I don't care." Her voice broke and she turned away so he couldn't see her face. But he could see her shoulders shake, and he cursed himself for a clumsy oaf.

"I'm sorry, love. I just didn't want to take advantage of you, of your innocence. I wanted to be sure that you were sure." His voice was coaxing, and he again went to where she was standing, this time irresolute before the door.

Ignoring his words, she braced her shoulders and opened the door. "I'm leaving."

The wind carried the snow whirling into the room and blew her back toward him. In the few seconds it took him to slam the door, snow covered her feet and dusted her face and dress. She shivered.

"You can't go out in that storm. I won't let you." He took her into his arms. "I've heard about storms like this in the south of England. They come roaring in, last for a few hours, and then blow out to sea. We'll be alone for a while, love. Let me love you."

She shrugged and turned her face away from him. "I threw myself at you, and all you could do was talk to me like a schoolteacher or a minister!"

He grinned at her tone of angry accusation. How

many young, unmarried women would be angry because a man *didn't* try to seduce them? Most would
cry and scream if he did. "I'm sorry, love." He tried
to sound humble while he slipped her cloak off her
shoulders and brushed at her dress. "You're all wet. If
you take off this lovely dress and stand in front of the
fire, it should dry off in just a few minutes."

"But I'll be cold in just my petticoat." She frowned
at him.

"No, you won't. I'll hold you. You'll be warm as
toast." He pulled her into his arms and began untying
the tapes at the back of her dress. "I promise you."

There was doubt in Priscilla's eyes, and Nicholas
cursed himself for putting it there. He had known all
along this girl—woman—did not have a great deal of
confidence in herself. His success in giving her a little
well-deserved faith in her own power and charm had
pleased him enormously. Yet he had pulled away from
her and questioned her motives and knowledge. He
had seen the doubt return to her eyes, and he despised
himself for it.

"I am in love with you," he said, seeing it clearly.
It was not just need, not just desire. It was love he felt.
"That is why I behave like such a consummate jackass
where you are concerned. I have never felt this before,
and I don't know what to do."

She gave him one of her wide, blindingly glorious
smiles. He sighed with relief. He had said the right
thing at last. Just then, the last of the tapes at her back
gave way and her dress slithered to the floor. He gave
her no time to feel embarrassed or frightened. Instead,
he swept her into his arms and began to kiss her and
caress her. He felt her knees buckle as he slipped her

chemise down to her waist and cupped her breasts in his hands.

In only a few moments, all their clothes had seemed to melt away and they lay naked, their limbs entwined, on the rug in front of the fire. At last Nicholas could gaze his fill at his beautiful love. Her curves were voluptuous and her skin glowed in the firelight, a warm ivory, touched with peach and coral. Reverently, he stroked her nipples and bent to take each one in his mouth, flicking them with his tongue, smiling as she moaned deep in her throat.

He began to stroke her skin—long, gentle strokes that had her writhing in his arms. "Nicholas," she breathed. "I don't know what you are doing to me, but it is wonderful."

He began to trail his lips where his hands had been, and Priscilla responded by pressing closer to him and moving her body in instinctive invitation. His own body was tight and hot. He had wanted her from the first moment he had seen her in the Bancrofts' drawing room. Now that she lay open and willing beneath him, he hesitated on the brink of an experience he knew would be greater than any he had known. His emotions were all on the surface. He felt as if he could laugh in triumph or perhaps even cry at the enormity of what he felt for her.

But Priscilla would not let him wait. "Please, Nicholas," she murmured as he again began to stroke her, this time more intimately than before.

"This may hurt," he began.

"I know," she said. "But only this one time."

He entered her as slowly and gently as he knew how. She gave one sharp gasp as he felt the barrier of her virginity give way but then began to move with him as together they were swept up in a storm as fierce as that raging outside the summerhouse windows above them.

He shuddered and cried out as his climax overtook him. Priscilla's cry was drowned out in his, but he could feel her body's response to his and his happiness spiraled even higher.

They lay together, basking in the afterglow of love until Nicholas glanced up and saw that the snow was beginning to slack off.

"It is time to go, love," he said.

"Must we?" Priscilla lay languid and boneless, smiling at him.

"Yes, love. I don't want to do any more damage to your reputation, or your parents may not think me a fit husband."

"Would that stop you from marrying me?" she asked as she rose gracefully to her feet.

Nicholas could feel desire rise in him again as he looked at her naked perfection. He tried to concentrate on her question. "No, but it would be easier if they agreed so we could be married before we leave for New York."

"Will your family be angry if you marry without them?"

He felt a twinge of guilt. His mother would be disappointed, but he had no doubt he could talk her around. "No. Marcus and Melinda can be married at Trinity Church if Mother likes. I want you with me."

Priscilla was dressed, and he quickly pulled on his own clothes and went to tie the tapes she could not reach. He lent her his comb so she could tidy her curls, and then inspected her to be sure there were no telltale signs of what they had been doing.

Priscilla put her arms around his neck and kissed him softly. "I am looking forward to a long ride in the carriage when I can look at you and think about doing this again," she said with a smile.

"Minx." He took her hand and raised it to his lips. "Just this little time to be with other people and pretend we don't care. After that, we will be together forever."

Eleven

Priscilla's dreams that night were filled with waltzes and kisses and the most exquisite lovemaking. As a consequence, she overslept and had to scurry around with Gillie, the maid's, help and pack as quickly as she could, so as not to keep Jeffrey and Lucinda—and most importantly, Nicholas—waiting.

Gillie snuffled as she packed. "I'll be that sorry to be saying good-bye to you, Miss Harrowby," she said. "The other ladies aren't half so nice. And when they leave I'll like as not be sent back to the farm. And it won't be long now. The ladies will leave once they learn the earl left for London this morning, early like." She sighed. "I don't suppose you'd be needing a maid in London, would you?"

Priscilla sighed. Her mother would never allow her to have a maid of her own. She shared an overworked girl who had aspirations of becoming maid to a truly fashionable lady. "I am sorry, Gillie. You have done very well, and if I hear of a position in London I will write and tell you."

Gillie looked disappointed, but shrugged philosophically. "Yes, ma'am," she said.

When Priscilla arrived, she found Lucinda and Jeffrey waiting for her, Jeffrey with ill-concealed annoyance. She sighed. The day was off to a bad start. But

with Nicholas with her, she was sure she could withstand even Jeffrey's heavy disapproval.

Then she discovered that instead of waiting for her,
brown eyes sparkling with mischief and love only she
could see, Nicholas had gone on ahead of them. Like
the earl, he had left early that morning. Her heart sank
to her shoes.

She had counted on hours of closeness, stolen looks,
and smiles. It was all that would have made a long trip
with Jeffrey sneering sardonically at her every word
bearable. Now she was to face it alone, without Nicholas's constant belief in her to give her backbone, and
she would have to hide just how disappointed she was.
Underneath the disappointment was a spurt of anger
and below that, down where she almost did not recognize it, was a tiny flicker of fear.

She took a deep breath. She could do it by herself.
She would simply imagine Nicholas was there with
her. "Good morning, Lucy. Good morning, Cousin Jeffrey." She smiled and took a perverse pleasure in seeing Jeffrey frown as she reminded him of their
relationship.

Lucinda, as always, stepped into the breach. "You
are looking lovely this morning, Cilla."

Priscilla tried to look appreciative. She had dressed
with special care, for Nicholas's sake, in a new traveling dress and matching fitted coat of deep cobalt
blue. Now there was no one but Lucinda to be impressed. Concerned neither Lucinda nor Jeffrey guess
how fragile her peace was, she smiled again. "You told
me this shade would become me, Lucy. And now you
can see the results of your advice. What do you think?"
And with a toss of her head she turned around, showing off the outfit.

Jeffrey rolled his eyes, but Lucinda gave it serious consideration. "Any shade of blue is yours, of course, because of your eyes," she said. "But the deep, rich shades are particularly becoming to your hair and pale complexion. Yes, I admit it, I was right. Do you not think so, Jeffrey, my love?" There was a commanding look in Lucinda's eyes as she faced her husband. *Say something nice,* it said as clearly as words.

Priscilla might have found Jeffrey's struggle to find anything nice to say amusing if she had not been so unhappy.

"You look . . . less . . . frilly than usual," he managed at last.

Lucinda frowned, but Priscilla found herself smiling sincerely at him for the first time since she had known him. "Thank you, Cousin Jeffrey. I appreciate an honest compliment, even if it isn't . . . frilly."

Jeffrey grinned at her wordplay, but he looked a little ashamed as well. Priscilla thought he hadn't believed her capable of a joke, let alone one at least partly at her own expense. He would have been right, she thought, only a few weeks ago. Nicholas had given her the confidence to take Jeffrey in stride. Perhaps in time she would even learn to deal with her mother's hysterics without fear.

But where was Nicholas? The day after the most momentous night of her life and he was nowhere to be found. No message from him, no note. Nothing.

She sank back against the cushions and allowed herself a moment of self-pity and anger that he had not thought of her, of how she would feel to be left without a word. Then she pulled herself together. Until they managed to talk to her mother and father and make their escape to America, she could not risk having anyone else know of the depth of their feelings. Her mother was going to be difficult enough to persuade. If she thought the polite world knew of her daughter's attachment, she might never be reconciled to it.

Priscilla wondered if Jeffrey knew what had happened to send Nicholas on ahead. She was trying to find a way to ask without arousing suspicion when Lucinda saved her the trouble.

"Did Nicholas tell you why he left early?" she asked her husband.

"No, but the butler said a message came for him in the middle of the night and he left immediately. Scribbled a message for his grandfather and then commandeered one of their horses and set out immediately at about four this morning."

A message for his grandfather but not for her. As the carriage started out with a jerk, Priscilla was sunk in gloom. She did not look back to see Dalton trying to run down the drive on his tottery old legs, waving a piece of paper in his hand.

London at last! Nicholas was not a true horseman, though he rode through the streets of New York sometimes to avoid the worst of the traffic. By the time he arrived at his hotel off Grosvenor Square, he was exhausted and it was ten o'clock in the morning. Panic clawed at him.

Home! He had to get home!

Never had he felt so far away from what he loved and so helpless. What if his mother was not the only one to fall ill? What if Marcus and Melinda came down with scarlet fever as well? Was Mother getting the care she needed? Was the best doctor in attendance? How was the disease progressing? He refused to entertain the thought of the worst that could happen.

Shaking off his worry and fatigue, he went directly to his room, where he began to pack as he snapped out orders and directions to the hotel staff. Two hours later, having roused Jeffrey's lawyer and young secretary to help him, he was bathed, dressed, packed, and in possession of a ticket on a steamship for America leaving that night.

He was upset that his plans to take Priscilla with him would have to be put in abeyance. Still, he was sure she would understand that nothing mattered but getting back to America and his family. She could follow him, perhaps, or they could wait until he returned in the spring. Priscilla loved him. She would wait.

Ever since the messenger had arrived from London at three o'clock that morning, Nicholas had been in a state of confusion and apprehension that had boiled just below his calm, businesslike surface. He had been unable to think clearly about anything else.

Now he was on his way to the railroad station to catch a train for Southampton and the first leg of his long, painful journey. He was in a fever of impatience to get there, to get started. But before he left, he had to leave notes for Jeffrey and for Priscilla, explaining what had happened, why he had to go.

He knew a moment of doubt as to Priscilla's attitude. Could she perhaps think he should have waited at least to speak to her? He shook off the thought. She would understand. His mother lay deathly ill. His sister and brother could be infected as well. Priscilla had never had brothers or sisters, and her mother was not what Nicholas regarded as a proper parent, from what Priscilla had told him. Nevertheless, Priscilla would understand.

He directed the large black cab the hotel had called for him to Jeffrey's house. He left the letter with the butler, giving him careful instructions as to the delivery of the letter to Mr. or Mrs. Bancroft as soon as they returned to the city.

His next and final stop was the Harrowbys' house. He had never been inside and, upon being admitted, looked around with frank curiosity. The decorating style was ornate, with gold abounding everywhere. Yet he noticed the housekeeping was not up to the standards he would have expected, given Priscilla and Lucinda's attention to every detail of household and personal adornment.

There was dust on the surfaces of the gilt-trimmed mahogany tables. Servants gathered in clusters in the corners of the entrance hall, but there was no butler to be found. He was admitted by a maid with a distracted air, and was left to wait wherever he chose, rather than being shown to a withdrawing room.

After several minutes, his impatience overcame his manners. He stopped a manservant on his way somewhere and asked if he could see either the master or mistress of the establishment on an urgent matter.

"Tell them Nicholas Cannon begs for a word," he said, conscious of the passage of time. The train would not wait for him, and he had very little time to waste. Perhaps if he could not see anyone, he would write Priscilla after he was on board the ship.

No, that would not do. "I really must see one or the other, please," he added.

The man left without a word, and Nicholas was about to give up hope when a middle-aged woman drifted down the stairs toward him. She was dressed in the same pastel ruffles and bows he had deplored on Priscilla. The family resemblance was unmistakable, though Mrs. Harrowby's mouth was marred by a discontented droop and her blue eyes had none of Priscilla's warmth.

"You are Nicholas Connaught," she said. It sounded like an accusation.

"Nicholas Cannon," he corrected her automatically. "Yes, ma'am. I would like to leave a note for your—"

"The grandson of the marquis of Bellingham?" she swept on as if he had said nothing.

"Yes, ma'am. About the note for Miss Har—"

"And the nephew of the earl of Ashden?"

Time was hurrying past, and Priscilla's mother was concerned with his exact relationships to the Connaught family. He felt his temper begin to fray. "Yes, ma'am. I have been called home on urgent family business and I wanted to leave a note."

"For my daughter?" The tone was distinctly frosty. "That is most improper, young man."

Nicholas shrugged impatiently. "Yes, ma'am, but under the circumstances—"

"And just what are the circumstances?" Edwina Harrowby's eyes narrowed, and Nicholas thought she was a great deal less silly than her doll-like features and fluffy clothes led him to believe.

"Miss Harrowby has been very kind to me," he said. "I wish merely to bid her farewell."

"Very well." She dismissed him. "I will tell her."

He extended the note, wishing he had left it at the Bancrofts'. "And you will give her this?"

She smiled, but it did not reach her eyes. "Of course," she said, reaching out a hand.

Nicholas hesitated, unsure for some reason if he should give the letter to Priscilla's mother. "The letter," Edwina said. Reluctantly, Nicholas handed it over. With one swift movement, she placed it in her reticule and gave him another patently false smile. "Good-bye, Mr. Connaught," she said.

"Cannon." He corrected her automatically. "My father changed his name when he went to America."

"Really." She could not have been less interested. "I am sure you want to be on your way now."

Nicholas smothered his doubts. "Yes, of course. I have to catch a train to Southampton. Thank you, Mrs. Harrowby."

"Not at all, young man." She wanted him to leave.

He realized with shock he did not want to go. But he must leave, and right away. "Please be sure Priscilla gets the letter."

Her eyes narrowed, and he realized his mistake. "Miss Harrowby gets the letter," he corrected himself, feeling a fool.

"You are very insistent. It will perhaps be improper, but I will do it, since you insist. I probably should not tell you this, it not being public knowledge as yet, but Priscilla has received a most flattering offer from your uncle."

"What! You cannot mean it!" Nicholas was shaken out of his pose of deferential courtesy by the news. "He has been in the country with me."

"He came to see my husband this morning. It was very early for a morning call, true, but I thought it spoke of his care for Priscilla."

"Nonsense!" Nicholas refused to guard his tongue. "He only cares for her money. She will never marry him!"

If possible, Edwina's manner grew even frostier. "She will do what an obedient daughter should, Mr. Connaught—marry to gratify her mother. Now I think you should leave. I do not suppose we will meet again. I never travel."

"Oh, but I will return in the spring." He had written that in his note and he wanted Priscilla's mother to be aware his intentions were serious.

"Really." If her expression could have gotten any colder, it would have. It was clear one member of the Harrowby family would not welcome his return. "Then you had best leave now so you can return in time for the wedding."

He ignored her. It was absurd. Priscilla would never marry his uncle. "Just give her the letter. Please."

"Of course."

He did not believe her, but what could he do? Time was of the essence, and neither the train nor the ship would wait for him.

The door shut behind him almost before he had crossed the threshold.

A mere two minutes later, the Bancrofts' coach drew up in front of the Harrowbys'. Priscilla frowned at her mother, who still stood in the entrance hall.

"What are you doing here, Mama?" she said as she went forward to give Edwina a dutiful kiss. "Was that a cab I saw pulling away? Who came calling in a cab?"

"Mildred Lamington," her mother replied. "She was on her way from a tea somewhere and stopped in to—to—"

Priscilla frowned. What was the matter with her

mother? "Mrs. Lamington?" she said, surprised. "In a common hack? Amazing."

"Her carriage is—is broken," Mrs. Harrowby said. "What a lot of fuss about it! It is of no importance. You must tell me all about the house party. And then your papa has some wonderful news for you!"

Beaming at the idea of hearing all about the elegant house party her daughter had attended, and bursting with the news of the earl's visit, Edwina led the way up the staircase. Priscilla lingered for a moment, frowning as she looked around the marble-floored entrance hall. It looked somehow unkempt. She noticed the morning newspaper lay crumpled on the round walnut table in the center of the room. The newspaper was always taken by the butler to his private room and ironed before being presented to Priscilla's father at the breakfast table. It was a ritual, one that never varied. Yet today . . .

She tried to put her finger on what was amiss, but it was too vague, and her mind was still filled with Nicholas. Her love, her true, true love. She told herself that over and over, and she believed it. But she would be happier if he would come and they could tell their news to her parents and then begin to make plans.

"Priscilla?" her mother called from above, her voice still bubbling with excitement.

"Yes, Mama." Priscilla turned her back on the entrance hall and followed her mother up the stairs.

Fortunately for Priscilla's sanity, her mother stayed only a little while in her room, peppering her with questions but not listening to the answers, flinging dresses from the trunk to the chairs and bed in untidy heaps. When Priscilla began to pick them up and smooth them out, her mother frowned.

"Do not be bourgeois, Priscilla. Let Clara do it. Come and we will have tea in my room. Your father will want to speak with you later." She gave Priscilla a beaming smile.

If she had been less preoccupied with thoughts of Nicholas, Priscilla might have wondered at her mother's air of excitement. As it was, she excused herself, telling her mother she was tired from the journey. Though it had taken less than half a day, her mother found nothing strange in this and went off to have tea alone in her room.

Alone, Priscilla put away enough of her things so her room was livable. She lay down and stared up at the ceiling, trying to banish the sense of deep foreboding that oppressed her. Nicholas would come, of course he would. This evening—or if not, surely tomorrow.

Only a half hour later, the housekeeper knocked softly on her door. "The master wants you," she said. "He is in his study."

The only other summonses Priscilla had received from her father had resulted in painful interviews. She had overspent her allowance, broken a vase and tried to blame Lucinda. Those memories were very painful. She had been, she could now acknowledge, not a very nice little girl.

Priscilla took a deep breath and decided she could knock on the door to her father's study. She had never done so before, but this time felt different. She was not that needy, greedy little girl any more. Perhaps it was the frailty and fatigue she had sensed in him, or possibly her own sense of empowerment.

The praise she had received from the Connaughts for helping their Christmas celebration had helped her believe she had some value as a person. Whatever it was, she could face the coming interview with equanimity.

Blowing out her breath, she raised her hand and knocked.

"What?" It was a muffled sound. "Who is it?"

"It is Priscilla, Papa. May I come in?" She was amazed. Her voice did not shake.

"A moment, please." There was a scuffling sound from within and then her father said, "Come in, Priscilla."

She looked inside and was startled at the disorder. Her father was usually meticulously neat, both as to his person and his possessions. But now there were papers everywhere, not neatly stacked, but strewn on every surface, as if he had thrown them. Her father, too, looked disheveled, his thinning hair standing on end and his cravat askew. His gray complexion and bleak eyes as he stared at her distressed and upset her.

"Papa?" she said, uncertain what to do now that she had gained entrance to the inner sanctum. "I wondered—I thought—" She looked closely at his face and saw despair in his eyes. "Papa! What is wrong? Let me help!"

She walked up to him and did something she never had before. She put her arms around him and kissed his cheek.

Then he did something that shocked her, it was so unlike him. He laid his head on her shoulder and gave one long, shuddering breath that sounded almost like a sob. Priscilla instinctively tightened her hold on him.

"Tell me, Papa."

He took another long breath, straightened, and looked her in the eyes. His hands reached for hers. "We are ruined, daughter. Everything is lost."

She stood paralyzed for a moment, uncomprehending. Lost? Everything? How could that possibly be? They were rich. Then the ghost of an overheard conversation came back to her. "The Welsh railroad, Papa?"

He stepped back, looking as stunned as she felt. "How did you know?"

"I overheard Jeffrey talking about it at Bellingham Place."

"Yes. I took a flyer. I was so tired of seeing other men make fortunes by buying into railway schemes at the outset. This time, I had a chance to do that, to buy in early." He shook his head, looking a little shamefaced. "I wanted to show it was not your mother's money but my judgment that made us prosper."

Priscilla's eyes filled. Her father wanted what everyone wanted, to be important. She had wanted to be as valued as Lucinda, and her father wanted to be regarded as a financial success.

"And now it is all gone?" Priscilla could think of nothing to say. "What does that mean, Papa?"

He looked impatient. In the world of men that he inhabited, everyone would understand immediately what that meant. "Ruined. Lose the house, of course. No more parties or dresses. Only the bare necessities left—a few servants to care for your mother."

Priscilla was silent, still overcome by the enormity of this disaster. No parties or dresses? Then life as she knew it was certainly over. She tried to think of what she knew of girls whose papas had been ruined, but she knew nothing.

Such girls simply disappeared. She remembered vague rumors that they had retreated to the country or moved to some unfashionable part of town or a seaside resort where life was supposed to be cheaper. With a chill, she remembered giggling with other girls about one of them who had gone to live in Margate and married a country curate. "All she could expect with no dowry and no expectations," someone had said, and that had been the end of it.

What would happen to her, Priscilla Harrowby, with her golden curls and china blue eyes, now that she did not have a rich papa? Then she relaxed. Nicholas. She had Nicholas, and surely, after what they had shared, he would not care she no longer had a dowry.

Would he?

Her father, misinterpreting her silence, hastened to reassure her. "We will not starve. There is your mother's dowry and a small inheritance she received from an aunt. I have kept those safe. But her father's money is gone. We will have to move to another house. And I am afraid any hope of a dowry for you from my estate is lost. I regret that most of all, Priscilla. Which brings me to another matter. The earl of Ashden came to see me today, with a proposal of marriage. I did not tell him of my disaster. I thought it possible that Jeffrey Bancroft might see his way clear to—"

Priscilla surprised herself and her father by laughing. "Jeffrey give me a dowry so I could marry Lord Ashden? Not likely. He would hire me as their scullery maid before he would give me a groat."

"The earl was very insistent. He said he had fixed his interest with you at Bellingham Place over Christmas. He was sure you would accept. Unfortunately, your mother—"

There was a flurry of taps on the door. Before her father could answer, her mother flew into the room.

"Did you tell her? Did you explain what a coup this

will be? No other girl this season has captured an earl. Not that there are that many earls waiting to be captured!" Edwina's high, fluting voice grated along Priscilla's nerve endings.

"The earl was mistaken in the size of my dowry, Mama. He will likely withdraw the offer once he finds that out." Priscilla spoke dryly. She would not marry the earl in any case, but—

"There is no need to tell him of the size of your dowry." Edwina interrupted her thoughts. "He has made a formal offer. He cannot cry off without scandal. All we need do is send a notice to the *Times*. Then he will be caught!"

"But Mama—"

"Besides, where did you get the idea your dowry was small?"

Priscilla did not speak. She looked at her father, but Barnabas had lowered his head. Now, once again he raised it and said, "I am sorry, Edwina. I had hoped never to have to tell you this, but one of my investments has gone awry and we will have to retrench for a while."

Edwina nodded. Priscilla thought she had not comprehended what he said, that her mind was still on weddings and earls, until she said, "Then Priscilla will certainly need to marry, and soon. At the very least she will be off our hands. If she stays, she will have to act as my maid. I cannot be expected to live without one, you know."

"Perhaps you could go upstairs and rest now, Edwina."

She nodded brightly and left, pausing to pat Priscilla's cheek. "My little girl a countess. And later a marchioness."

Priscilla did not say anything until her mother was out the door. "I cannot marry the earl of Ashden, Papa."

"Why not? Did you not like him?" Her father gave her a piercing look from under his brows.

"He is an odious man and I detest him."

To her surprise, her father smiled. "I confess, I did not care for him very much either, Cilla. And your marriage must be your choice. I know how much anguish can be caused by a failure to take that into account. I will not force you to marry him."

"Just as well, Papa," she said with a sardonic smile of her own. "Not only do I detest him, but he invested in the same Welsh railroad you did."

"Then he needs someone's dowry. I think he might cry off even if you accepted him now."

"Possibly, though I would imagine his father would pay his debts if he had to."

"Yes," said Barnabas, patting her hand, "he will always have enough to live a pleasant, if not extravagant, life. You should consider that well, daughter."

"I cannot marry the earl, Papa." Just the memory of that slobbering kiss was enough to make her shudder.

Her father must have noticed her reaction. "We will say no more about it then, my dear."

She did not tell him that he need not worry she would not marry. Something—Nicholas's absence perhaps, or simple prudence since she did not have an engagement ring—kept her silent. But she tried to give him some of her confidence.

"Oh, Papa, we will come around. You will be able to do something wonderful with the money we have left. Do you not think so?"

He gave her a wan smile. "No, daughter, I do not.

I have no confidence in my ability to pick investments any more. I am going to see Henry Blankenship tomorrow, to see if he has some employment in his office I might be able to undertake. With a small salary and our remaining investments, we should be able to live if we are careful."

"Employment? You are going to be a clerk, Papa?"

He frowned and stood a little straighter, releasing her hands and turning away from her. "There is nothing shameful in honest work, Priscilla. Your cousin Lucinda knows that, and so does Henry Blankenship. He started on the streets with nothing. I am willing to work for my bread."

Shame for herself and pride for her father overcame her and she hung her head. For the first time that evening, tears came to her eyes. "I am sorry, Papa. You are right, and I am a selfish, spoiled wretch to think otherwise."

He turned back to face her, a surprised look on his face. She grimaced. "You did not think I had enough character and love for you to see how noble it is not to hide away but to face the future bravely. I will try very hard to be a help and not a hindrance."

Mr. Harrowby then did something that meant more to Priscilla than all the new dresses and parties in the world. He smiled at her and, putting his arms around her, gave her a hug and kissed her forehead. "With your help, I am sure I can pull us through," he said and smiled.

"Very well, Papa. I will see you at dinner. Shall I ask that your tea be sent in to you here?"

"Thank you, daughter. I would appreciate that." He patted her arm a little awkwardly. "Do not worry, Priscilla. Tomorrow things will look brighter."

"Yes, Papa, tomorrow will be better."

Priscilla left the order for tea and made her way to her bedroom. Tomorrow would be better.

Tomorrow Nicholas would come.

Twelve

But Nicholas did not come the next day.

Sure that he would, Priscilla had dressed in one of her new day dresses, a soft wool in a deep rose red color that brought out the delicate bloom of her complexion and the bright gold of her hair. She was satisfied that she looked her best, and waited in the drawing room for almost an hour.

The household staff, already reduced by the defection of several of the maids who had sensed disaster and left, not to be replaced, was demoralized by the unspoken sense that something was very wrong.

Mr. Harrowby had not as yet told them anything, but he had spoken to Mrs. Harrowby this morning. Afterward, she been heard sobbing for an hour and had remained in seclusion with the shades drawn. She had sent her daughter away with a shriek after Priscilla had tried to make her see that life could continue in a reasonably comfortable way, but their social life would have to be curtailed.

"Get out!" Edwina had cried. "You do not understand! I might as well be dead as to be too poor to entertain! And you refuse to help me! Refusing an earl when we are about to have to beg for our bread! Go away! Send me my maid."

So Priscilla had gone downstairs. Her father was

just finishing his breakfast when she came in. "Good morning, Papa. I am sorry your talk with Mama did not go well."

"I have assured her we will not have to move for another month at least. The rent is paid through that time. We will keep the cook and housekeeper and three of the maids."

"We can afford to do that?"

"For the moment. The rent is paid through the end of the month, as are the servants' wages for the quarter. We have rented this house for a number of years. I had hoped to buy it at one time, but the property owners in this neighborhood do not sell. Still, I do not think they will evict us when I tell them we will vacate peaceably."

Priscilla wanted to do something—anything—to feel she was helping her father. This new closeness between them was worth a little discomfort. After all, it would only be until Nicholas came and took her away. She felt a twinge of guilt at the thought of leaving her father alone with only her mother, who could find nothing to talk about but her ungrateful daughter, who was not a countess and would never be a marchioness. Perhaps they could all go to New York. A new life for all of them. She would ask Nicholas.

Now she looked around the drawing room and saw sad signs of neglect. She walked through the downstairs and saw dust and disorder everywhere. This would not do. She went through to the servants' wing and summoned the housekeeper and cook.

"I know you have more work to do now that we have lost some of the younger maids, but I am sure you can arrange to keep the rooms dusted and the fires made up." She tried for a calm smile and a confident demeanor.

"Yes, Miss Priscilla," the housekeeper said.

Priscilla felt better. Perhaps if she appeared as if nothing were amiss, she would begin to believe it herself. Meantime, she would try to fool the servants.

"Thank you, Mrs. Crawford."

The housekeeper's eyebrows went up and she almost smiled as she curtseyed.

"Mrs. Grant, we will be simplifying the meals from now on. My father's digestion is not what I would hope for," she improvised. "I think simpler fare and fewer courses would benefit him greatly. I would appreciate any suggestions you may have for how we can do this without his noticing we are changing his diet."

Mrs. Grant smiled as well. "Yes, miss. I am sure a simple roast chicken with boiled vegetables would answer."

"That sounds fine. Thank you both."

They left the parlor and Priscilla let out a relieved breath. She had remembered their names from Lucinda's mentioning them the last time she had visited. She had tried to sound like Lucinda. Apparently, she had succeeded in her imposture. A simpler diet would save them money, she was sure. Was there anything else she could do?

She paced for awhile in frustrated agitation. Where was Nicholas? If he did not come by this afternoon, she would go to Lucinda's and find some excuse to ask after him. Her spirits, which had been lifted by her father's unexpected affection, now sank beneath the weight of the future.

After a few minutes of pacing, she reached inside her sleeve, where she had tucked a handkerchief, and began to dust the tables. She was alone, no one would know, and she hated the sight of the grimy table tops. She had no sooner begun her task when the one remaining maid came to the door and announced she had a visitor.

"Nic—"

Radiant, she turned to face the door, only to see the slight figure of her cousin Lucinda framed in the doorway instead of Nicholas's lean height.

She schooled her face to a welcoming smile. "Lucinda, how nice of you to visit."

Lucinda came in, and Priscilla could see by the look of concern on her cousin's face that she knew about the situation. "Jeffrey knew and told you about the Welsh railway," Priscilla said. It was not a question. "I imagine he was only too delighted to picture me without a shilling to my name."

Lucinda flushed, and Priscilla knew she was right. She sighed. "It was nice of you to visit. I am going to need your help, Lucinda. If you do not wish to come to my aid, do it for my father. I know you have always been close to him."

Lucinda hurried over to Priscilla and took her hands. "My dear, of course I will help you any way I can. Please. We have put our past behind us, have we not?"

Priscilla smiled and laid her cheek for a moment against Lucinda's. "I cannot tell you what your friendship means to me at this time, Lucy. I am so grateful."

"Nonsense. Tell me what I can do. How is your mother taking the news?"

"Not well. Do come and sit down by the fire. I can ring for tea, if you would like."

Lucinda shook her head. "Your mother has taken it

badly? She is in bed, I take it. That was always her refuge."

"Yes. She is resting with her various patent medicines by her side." Priscilla sighed. "She prefers her maid to me, I am afraid. I tried to cheer her up, but she does not wish to see anything but blackness ahead."

Lucinda smiled. "I am afraid you are going to have to be the mainstay of the house now, Priscilla."

"Yes." But she wouldn't, would she, if Nicholas would only come? A sudden, cowardly desire to throw herself into his arms and wait for him to carry her away swept over Priscilla. Where was he?

"Lucinda, you may as well know that the earl of Ashden has offered for me, and I have asked Papa to refuse him. Mama will never forgive me. That is half the reason for her sulking in her room." She longed to ask Lucinda about Nicholas, but something kept her from it. They would cause enough of a scandal when they left for America immediately after their wedding. It would seem frightfully hole-in-the-corner to many, especially after her father's losses were known. She didn't want to involve Lucinda in her socially unacceptable behavior.

In another twenty seconds she was profoundly grateful she had not told her cousin.

"Was it not the oddest thing that Nicholas Cannon left for America so suddenly?" Lucinda interrupted her.

With an instinct born of a thousand nights under the scrutiny of a hundred jealous eyes, Priscilla bent over a table and fumbled with a bouquet of roses in a crystal vase. After a moment, she had schooled her expression to impassivity, and she faced her cousin with what she hoped was a calm look.

"Did he leave so soon? I did not know," she said. For a moment, she was sure she read pity on Lucinda's face.

"Yes, he left a note for Jeffrey, saying there was illness in his family and he must return at once." Lucinda avoided her eyes. "I am surprised he did not tell you. I thought you and he had reached some kind of understanding during our stay at Bellingham Place."

"No, no." Priscilla managed a light laugh. "It was merely a holiday flirtation. Something to pass the time. We were not serious."

"Oh." Lucinda sounded doubtful. "Well, you must let me know what I can do. And do ask uncle to come to talk to Jeffrey. He will have ideas about how to recoup uncle's losses. These things happen, Jeffrey says. Fortunes are won and lost and then won again with a shrewd investment."

"Yes, I am sure that is true," Priscilla said, her voice sounding high and thin to her own ears. She did not believe the soothing words. She did not even care if they were true. She wished for nothing so much as for her cousin to leave so she could stop having to pretend and go to her room. Like her mother, at this moment, Priscilla wanted darkness and privacy.

"I must go, Cilla, but I did want to tell you of our support." Lucinda rose and embraced Priscilla before taking her leave.

Alone at last, Priscilla hurried to her room and shut the door after herself. She leaned against it and let the waves of grief wash over her.

A family illness! A likely story. The very story she

had suggested to him as the best kind of excuse for a sudden absence.

But even if it was a lie, he should have told it to her directly. Not even a note! Priscilla hugged herself, afraid if she let go she would fly into a million pieces.

She had thought she would cry, but tears would not come. She felt waves of alternating hot and cold. Fear and rage and humiliation warred for primacy in her heart. How could he? What a fool she had been. How he must have laughed as he left London—and her—behind him. How many girls had fallen victim to his practiced charm, she wondered.

Seduced and abandoned—how banal. Ten thousand girls a year must succumb in the same way she had, believing the false words, dreaming of a life with the beloved one. The pain was physical in its impact, yet not one bit less fierce because others suffered the same way. She did not know what to do, whom to turn to.

No one. No one must know. She couldn't bear it if anyone else knew how stupid she had been. How blind and foolish. No, she would bear it alone. Then the thought hit her with a force like a physical blow.

What if disappointment was not the only thing she had to bear? What if she was pregnant? The very idea made her gasp for breath as a wave of fear washed over her. Oh, God, what would she do? She had heard whispers. There were things one could do. She would ask Lucinda. A nurse would know.

This final blow sent her to the floor. She sank down in a swirl of rose-colored skirts as the enormity of what she might have to endure came home to her. The disgrace. The exile—permanent in her case, she was sure, because she knew with absolute certainty she could not ask Lucinda for a remedy for the situation.

She would bear the child. She would have to. She simply could not contemplate any other answer. She did not know how or where, but somehow she would get through whatever she had to.

If she had to. If it were true. *Please, no, God,* she prayed, as ten thousand other girls had prayed. *Do not let it be true. Please.*

She truly tasted despair in that moment. Life had dealt her two devastating blows in quick succession, and she was reeling as if she had fallen and hit her head. She was dizzy and sick with worry and anger. What could she do? Without some activity, she thought she might go mad.

As if in answer to her unspoken plea, there was a knock on the door. She gained her feet and raised shaking hands to her hair. A glance in the mirror revealed that the earth-shattering emotions of the past half hour had left no trace on her face. Except for a rather blank expression, she did not think anyone would know she had been through hell—and had not left yet.

It was the housekeeper, Mrs. Crawford, with some question about the duties of the reduced staff. She dealt with that, tried several times to see her mother, but was turned away by Clara. Finally, in a frenzy of nervous energy, she slipped away for a twilight walk.

She returned in time to dress for dinner with her father, and noted with approval that he ate more than he had in the past several days.

"Congratulate me, my dear," he said as he looked up from his plate of chicken and brussels sprouts. "I have obtained employment."

"Then you were able to see Mr. Blankenship?" she asked as she took a bite of Mrs. Grant's succulent roasted chicken. The vegetables, she noted, still needed work. Perhaps less cooking time? Perhaps they could afford peas. She made a mental note and raised her eyes to her father again.

"No," he was saying, "the family is still away for the holiday season. Visiting Blankenship's sister in Bath, I understand. So I went to another acquaintance and he hired me as a sort of manager." To Priscilla's surprise, her father sounded a bit proud of his new, lowly position.

"Who did you see, Papa?"

"Jeffrey Bancroft," he answered.

"Jeffrey has made you his clerk?" She was furious. It was one thing for him to make fun of her. But to put her father in a position where he could be laughed at was another matter entirely.

"No, no, not a clerk, my dear. I am to manage his office and see to his various enterprises. It is a responsible position and he is paying quite handsomely for it."

Priscilla found herself seething with rage. Jeffrey Bancroft, once again patronizing her family, making fun of them, trying to show how superior he was. But one look at the bright expression on her father's face showed her how unkind it would be to point out Jeffrey's underlying motives to him.

"Good for you, Papa! Glad to be working again, I can see that."

"Yes. And with the bit we still have, I should be able to provide for your mother in reasonable comfort. She cannot bear very much unpleasant reality, you know."

She was touched by his concern for her mother. Edwina had never been a thoughtful or dedicated wife, but her husband was going to look after her regardless.

"That is wonderful, Papa," she said and tried to mean it.

"I am only sorry about you, daughter. I have nothing to offer you but a quiet life at home. I am sure your friends will still wish to include you in some of their activities. You were always such a popular girl." He smiled at her and her heart lifted. "Are you sure you do not wish for the earl? I have refused him, but—"

"No, no, Papa, a home with you is far preferable."

She did not wish to disillusion him, but she knew better than to expect invitations from her friends. No one in the social circles she traveled in would include her now. The women her mother called friends and their daughters, who were most of Priscilla's friends, would cut dead anyone who could no longer keep up at least the appearance of wealth. It would be worse now that her father had taken a paid position with another man's business.

Work was acceptable in Priscilla's circle, unlike that of the Connaughts, if a man owned his own business. But to work as a clerk, except for a young man on his way up the ladder of success, was completely beyond the pale. Mr. Harrowby had never concerned himself very much with the niceties of social behavior, but Mrs. Harrowby lived and died by it, and she had taught Priscilla all the nuances.

Now that there was no more money, there would be no more invitations. But there was no need to tell her father that. He had enough burdens for one man.

"Yes, Papa," she said with a sweet smile. "I am sure our friends will stand by us now. However, I do not think Mama will be well enough to go out, and I will probably be very busy myself. So we may have to disappoint them."

"You are not to undertake any of the housekeeping yourself, Priscilla. It is not seemly, and we have not yet sunk that low."

"Do not worry, Papa. I will not do anything you would not approve of."

"You have always been a good girl, Priscilla."

That was music to her ears and was the one bright spot in a day of disasters. At least her papa had drawn closer to her and had changed his opinion of her, though he had now decided he had always thought highly of her.

"Thank you, Papa. Would you like me to read to you after supper? I know I cannot converse with you as Lucinda did, but I can read to you and spare your eyes after a day of work. I believe Mr. Dickens has a new serial beginning in *Household Notes*."

Mr. Harrowby smiled at her. "That would be most delightful. You will see, Priscilla. We will do very well with a few changes in our habits."

Priscilla smiled again. This time it took an even greater effort. "Yes, Papa."

She could see the years stretching before her, as arid and featureless as one of those deserts she had seen pictured in her father's books of travel. Nicholas was gone, not even caring that she might be carrying his child.

Nicholas landed in New York a mere eighteen days after embarking from Southampton. The new steam-and-sail ships were turning the Atlantic into a mere lake! Worry about his mother and a growing anger at Priscilla—the countess!—kept him pacing the deck at all hours. For hours he would relive their romance and then remember her mother's insistence that she was to marry Granville. He avoided the young—and not so young—ladies on board, who cast many flirtatious glances in his direction. In fact, he did not even see them.

When he slept, he dreamed of Priscilla and how wonderful it would be if she were with him. They leaned over the rail, talking of their future and his family, her golden hair tangled and blowing in the sea breezes.

And the kisses. He dreamed of their kisses during the long winter nights. She was wrapped in her midnight blue cloak and they stood at the rail, his arm about her. No one else would brave the cold. They could kiss in the darkness.

And afterward, when they went to their cabin, they could once again share that incredible fusion, that heat and passion and laughter. He woke every night with tears on his cheeks and began to shake with need.

Once he was ashore, he could write her, and she would write him. Then he would know. Did she still love him? Had she gotten his letter, or had her mother simply thrown it in the fire? Could she believe he would leave without a word?

And what if she were pregnant? Oh, God, what would she do? Would she sleep with Granville, marry him, and pretend the baby was his? Many women did—but could Priscilla?

"Oh, Priscilla, I miss you so." He was sure she could sense his yearning all the way across the water. "Don't leave me for a title!" He could not help but remember that Jeffrey had said Priscilla would never disobey her mother in any important matter.

Once the cab dropped him at home, he bounded up

the steps and pounded on the door. When it flew open, he rushed past the man who opened it with scarcely a glance.

"Marcus! Melinda!" he called at the top of his voice. "I'm home!"

No one answered and he began to mount the stairs, taking them two at a time, heading straight for his mother's room. "Mother! It's me, Nicholas. I'm home!"

One of the closed doors on the corridor opened, and his sister stepped out. She hurried to him and put her arms around his waist and her head on his chest. "Oh, Nicky, I am so glad you have come. It has been so awful!"

He held her away from him, shocked at the change. His vivacious, bubbly sister had blue eyes that sparkled and curly chestnut hair that danced around her face. But this girl was pale and drawn. There were deep blue smudges under her eyes, and her dress hung on her too slender figure.

"Mellie, tell me, what has happened?" A sudden fear clutched at his heart. "Is Mother—"

"She is better. The doctor was just here. You must have met him in the hall."

"Yes, he opened the door for me. I thought he was the new butler!"

They looked at each other, and their ready sense of humor got the best of them. Melinda chuckled and at once looked more like her old self. "He is the best doctor in New York. He is fond of Mother, or he would not come back after such an insult."

Nicholas hugged her. "Where is Marcus? Has he fallen ill, too?"

"No, he is at your office, trying to keep everything together. He will be so relieved to have you back."

"And Mother? You said she is better." At Melinda's nod, his heart, so heavy with dread for so long, began to lighten.

"She was napping, but with all the noise you've been making . . ." Melinda smiled up at him. "Welcome home, Nicky. I am so glad you are here at last." She took his hand and with him walked to the big room at the end of the hallway. Motioning for him to be silent, she opened the gleaming mahogany door and whispered softly, "Mother? Are you sleeping?"

"What is it, dear?" His mother's soft voice was the sweetest sound Nicholas had heard in many days.

"I have a surprise for you," Melinda said and stood aside.

"Nicholas!" His mother, who was propped on a number of fluffy, lace-edged pillows, beamed at him. "Oh, I am glad to see you! Come and tell me all about the Connaughts. I have always longed to know, and your father never liked to speak of them."

Nicholas thought of his Uncle Granville and could easily understand why his father preferred not to think about his family. "I will tell you about them, but only after I discover how you are feeling." He went over and sat down on the plump little boudoir chair pulled up to the bed and took her hand. His gaze searched her face and found her thinner and paler, but still looking much younger than her forty-odd years. She smiled at him, and he looked into her eyes. His father used to say they were blue as a highland loch and it was a pity only Melinda had inherited them.

"I leave you both for a mere two months and when I return what do I find?" he asked with mock severity.

"The two of you looking as if you hadn't eaten or slept since I left. I am going to have to speak to the house-keeper about nourishing meals for you both."

His mother gave a soft chuckle and patted his hand. "I am on the mend. The doctor said I have been a model patient, improving every day and obeying every rule. He has limited me to a little thin gruel and—"

"That is ridiculous. I will talk to the man myself. I am sure you misunderstood him. He must have meant a good beefsteak and a glass of claret!"

His mother shook her head, smiling fondly at him. "Now you sound like your father. Go and see Marcus now, dearie. I'm sure you are perishing to get to the office and he is perishing to have you there. We will talk more later."

Nicholas bent and kissed her cheek. Thank God, his mother was mending! Now if he could straighten out his business affairs, he could gather his family and hurry back to Priscilla.

It should be only a matter of a few weeks, he told himself. A month at the most, and he would be on his way back to her.

After a few weeks, Priscilla found the pain in her heart had steadied and slowed to a dull ache. Nicholas was gone. There would be no baby, and for that she was both grateful and, perversely, disappointed. It would have been something of his, a little person with his sparkling brown eyes and aquiline nose. She knew she could not have kept the child and that her life would be destroyed by such a scandal. Nevertheless, some small, stubborn part of her heart yearned for the child that never was.

The rest of her life was dull beyond measure. She tended to the household duties required to make their home function. Her father was looking for a smaller house in a less fashionable part of town, and Priscilla dreaded the day they had to move. She knew her mother, who never left her room, would be bewildered and hysterical at the change. She was still furious with Priscilla for refusing the earl. Moving from the house they had rented for years would set the seal on their downfall.

Her father made a gallant effort to appear pleased to be working for Jeffrey. He came home in a calm and pleasant mood, ready to talk over dinner about interesting things that had happened in the office or news of the day. Priscilla had begun reading newspapers so she could converse intelligently with him. Unlike Lucinda, she never grew interested in the endless political machinations of Palmerston and Lord John Russell.

The dispute over Britain's position with respect to the growing quarrel between the American states interested her more. Would Nicholas go to war? She ruthlessly suppressed the idea. What did she care what became of Nicholas Cannon? If he went to war and was blown to bits, she would be happy. She would cheer. She hated him.

She avoided any thought of Nicholas, because no matter what she told herself, when she thought of him, she cried. She even avoided Lucinda because she might hear of him from her, and then she would cry in front of Jeffrey—the ultimate humiliation. Nicholas and Jeffrey were friends and he probably wrote to them. But Priscilla received few letters, just one or two from Elinor, writing from the seminary where her aunt had sent her—to get her out of the way, Elinor wrote.

But no letter from Nicholas. Of course not, she told herself. She did not expect it. He had shown his true colors and she expected nothing but silence. And she would not cry about it. She would not.

The mail seemed to interest everyone in the house. The only times she saw her mother leave her room was to wait for the postman. Edwina insisted on having all the mail brought to her room for inspection before it was distributed—mostly to her father. When the mail was delayed, for whatever reason, Edwina would dress and come downstairs. Priscilla thought it was good for her mother to leave her room. She held up the mail deliberately several times, but when her mother saw Priscilla holding the letters, she screeched with rage and snatched them out of her hands.

Her mother was becoming more and more odd, and Priscilla did not like to cross her, so she stopped delaying the mail delivery and let Edwina receive all letters.

Priscilla was growing more restless with only housekeeping duties to occupy her time. She hated to see the worried lines around her father's mouth deepen when he looked at the bills. If only there were some way she could help him. If only there were some way a lady could earn money without losing any more social standing than they already had.

She puzzled over the problem, but no answer came to her. She read about women who aided the poor, either as nurses, like Lucinda and her friends, Catherine and Rose, or as social workers, going among them in the worst slums of London.

Mr. Dickens seemed to admire such women. At least

he wrote admiringly of them in his journal. But Priscilla knew she was not the stuff of which saints were made. There had to be an answer that did not involve danger and dirt.

In the midst of this worry, she received an invitation. Mrs. Henry Blankenship, who had been so kind to her before the disastrous house party at Bellingham Place, came to call one morning. Priscilla was surprised to find she felt neither apologetic or ashamed to greet her guest wearing a simple morning dress several seasons out of style. Mrs. Blankenship probably already knew of their financial status. Priscilla's father had spoken to Mr. Blankenship about it. She found she did not care. Mary Ann Blankenship judged people by their actions and their attitudes, not their bank accounts.

"Miss Harrowby," she said, with her warm smile, "I am so glad to find you home. When you did not reply to my notes . . ."

"What?" Priscilla was startled. "I did not receive any notes from you, Mrs. Blankenship. I would certainly have replied. I cannot understand what could have happened."

But, of course, she did understand. Her mother had misplaced them. That was what came of allowing someone whose mind was not completely clear to have charge of something so important as mail.

"It does not matter. What matters is that we are having a reception on Friday evening and we would very much like you—and your family, if they can—to attend." Once again, she enveloped Priscilla in a warm smile.

Mary Ann Blankenship did not understand the social niceties. While she might have Priscilla to tea privately, as it were, she really could not have Priscilla and her father, who was working as a clerk, to a reception. Priscilla opened her mouth to try to explain the realities of life to Mary Ann when she decided she was entitled to one evening of fun and flirting and delicious food. And so was her father. Let the Blankenships' social standing take care of itself. They had never seemed very concerned about it. Why should Priscilla?

"We would love to come," she said with a beaming smile. "I do not think my mother will be well enough to attend, but my father and I will be there. And rest assured, if you send any more notes, I will answer."

Thirteen

Immediately upon Mary Ann Blankenship's departure, Priscilla went to her mother's room. Edwina had not allowed her to visit except for short, formal calls once a day. Ever since she learned of the family's fall from financial grace and Priscilla's refusal to come to the rescue, Edwina had grown more bitter and withdrawn.

Priscilla had great sympathy for her. Nothing in her life had prepared Edwina for the slightest adversity, and nothing had taught her how to perform the simplest task. She had passed on to her daughter the idea that being pretty and well-dowered was all that was required of young women.

Now Priscilla knew better. She also knew her mother was living in a kind of shadowy, dream-like world. Her conversation consisted of irrelevant snatches of invented news.

"Have you and the earl of Ashden set a date for your wedding yet, my dear?" was her greeting to Priscilla, as she entered her room. She was still in bed, dressed in a ruffled bed jacket and a lace cap.

"No, Mama," Priscilla replied calmly. "I am not going to marry the earl."

"Oh, well, perhaps in a few days you will change your mind. I think a spring wedding would be nice, though I am not sure we can be ready by then." Edwina looked critically at her daughter. "That dress is sadly out of style, you know. I cannot think why you have not given it to one of the maids already."

"It does well enough for a quiet morning at home, Mama." Priscilla had learned better than to confront her mother with any unnecessary truth about any of her delusions. To do so resulted in tears that escalated to hysteria very rapidly. Best to let her live as much as possible in a world she could cope with.

Her mother shrugged. "Well, you may go now, Priscilla."

Some problems, however, had to be dealt with. "Mama, are you sure you have sorted through all the mail correctly?" Priscilla asked. "I have learned that a letter seems to have gone astray—"

"No!" Her mother's shrill voice shook with hysteria. She shrank back against the pillows. "No! It is not true! I have done nothing but what any good mother would do!"

Priscilla tried to soothe her. "I am sure it was only an oversight, Mama. No one is accusing you of anything. Truly. But it has come to my attention that a letter addressed to me from Mrs. Blankenship did not arrive and—"

Her mother seemed to rally at that information. Her face regained some of its color. She sat up straight and said, with a semblance of her former dictatorial manner, "Nonsense. One cannot rely on the mails, you know. It no doubt went astray. It was nothing important, I am sure. Let us say no more about it."

Well, Priscilla thought, she had her answer. If there had been a letter from Nicholas, her mother had clearly taken it. Shrugging, she decided it was not worthwhile to risk sending her mother into another fit of the vapors by questioning her further.

"It would be very bad if any bills were to be mislaid," she said, as she stood, ready to leave the room. "I believe I should receive the mail from now on to be sure Papa has all of them." She slipped out the door and shut it, cutting off her mother's shrill protest.

No, it did not truly matter if a letter had been intercepted. Nicholas could have written again. He could have sent a message by Jeffrey or Lucinda. But he had not. And that meant only one thing. He did not care.

She drew a determined breath and reached for a more cheerful thought and found it in considering what to wear to the Blankenships' reception.

The Blankenships' reception was very like the one she had attended when Nicholas was in London. She ruthlessly suppressed any thought of that golden time. Her spirits rose as she dressed.

Her mother's maid, Clara, slipped away from Edwina long enough to help Priscilla arrange her hair and fasten the tapes at the back of her dress. How fortunate she had purchased all those new dresses with Lucinda. They were so becoming and so well-made she was sure she would not mind wearing them for years.

She stopped in to see her mother before she and her father left, thinking that to see her daughter dressed for an evening's entertainment would cheer Edwina. She was mistaken.

"Where did you get that ugly dress?" was her mother's first remark. "It must be one Lucinda picked out for you. I should have known she would try to make you look old and less pretty than she is. What a fool your father was to insist on it."

"I have received a number of compliments on the dress," Priscilla remarked mildly. She would not think of Nicholas, she would not! She clenched her fists in the folds of her cobalt blue skirts and smiled.

"Pooh! Compliments from women, I have no doubt," Edwina scoffed. "They always say nice things when you look particularly ill, hoping you will wear the same ugly outfit again."

"I really must hurry, Mama," Priscilla said.

"Where are you going? Is Mildred Lamington giving another musicale?" Her mother's voice perked up.

"No, Mama. We have not received an invitation from Mrs. Lamington in some weeks now." A small dose of reality might perhaps help her mother face the truth as time went on.

Edwina ignored the comment. "Where are you going?"

"The Blankenships are giving a reception and we—"

Rage made Edwina forget to guard her tongue. "No! No! I took that invitation. You never saw it!"

"Mama!" Priscilla shook her head at her. "You took my mail. That was very bad of you. You must not do that again."

Edwina pouted. "I only took some of it. It was for your own good. The Blankenships are not people you should know, Cilla, dear. They are common. They reek of the shop."

"Mama! They have been very kind to me. They are good people. Papa wishes me to know them."

"Your father does not understand. Men do not, Cilla, as a rule see the value of—"

"I do not have time to discuss this, Mama. But believe me, tomorrow we are going to talk. And I expect to receive every letter as well as every bill from every tradesman that you have been hiding these weeks."

"Oh, very well." Edwina shrugged and then turned her head into the pillows.

Priscilla did not tell her father what her mother had done. He had enough to worry about, enough trials in his life. Looking for a smaller house had been very difficult for him. It was the visible symbol of the loss of their money and status.

"Do you mind if we arrive a bit early?" he said. "I would like to talk privately with Mr. Blankenship if it is possible."

Priscilla felt a bit awkward arriving early for a party. The hostess usually had a great many things to do at the last minute and did not need someone to entertain unexpectedly. Perhaps she could make herself useful, she thought.

As it happened, she made herself extremely useful. When they arrived at the Blankenship mansion, Henry Blankenship greeted them with all the warmth he had shown in the past. Proclaiming that he wanted to talk to Mr. Harrowby, he led him off to his study. Mary Ann, however, wore a worried frown and seemed not to be her usual serene self.

"Oh, Miss Harrowby," she said, "I wonder if you could help me. Emily has come down with a severe cold. She is most uncomfortable, and I have promised to bring her a bowl of chicken soup and sit with her while she eats it. Could you see to the last-minute arrangements for me?"

Priscilla had no idea what Mary Ann thought constituted last-minute arrangements, but she agreed willingly. She could not help but think that Mary Ann, a stepmother for less than a year, was more devoted to Henry's children than Priscilla's own mother was to her. Edwina would never forego a party to look after Priscilla when she was sick. Still more unlikely to see her neglect a party she was giving to feed soup to a sick child. Priscilla shook her head and marched with a determined tread into the dining room.

Chaos greeted her eye—servants standing about with trays and platters in their hands, flowers stuck every which way into vases. Ah, here was something she could deal with, a problem she could solve. Self-pity vanished as she smiled with assumed self-assurance and greeted the two servants she correctly identified as the butler and housekeeper.

"Good evening. I am Miss Harrowby. Mrs. Blankenship has asked me to help you. She has to be upstairs with Miss Emily for a few moments."

Far from resenting her as an intruder, the servants were only too happy to be told what to do and shown how to do it. And Priscilla found herself perfectly able to do whatever was required to set the party to rights. By the time Mary Ann hurried back downstairs, just in time to greet her first guests, everything was in perfect readiness.

"I cannot thank you enough," she murmured to Priscilla, giving her hand a squeeze. "You have made everything beautiful. Putting those roses in the silver pitcher was a wonderful idea."

Priscilla smiled back, a little bleakly. "This is the only thing I really know how to do. If only I were a nurse, like you and Lucinda, I could earn something and help my father. It is so painful to sit and pretend to be a lady of leisure like before when Papa is working so hard."

"You would consider working?" Mary Ann's eyebrows rose.

"Of course! I have never thought work was demeaning, Mrs. Blankenship. It is just that I am so useless." And for the first time in weeks, a giggle rose to her lips.

Mary Ann looked very thoughtful, but before she could say anything, Jeffrey Bancroft's sardonic voice cut through their conversation. "Ah, Priscilla's giggle. Some things never change. London's filthy fog, Lord Palmerston's self-importance and—"

"My giggle." Priscilla found she was not afraid of Jeffrey, but she was annoyed at being interrupted. "Yes, Jeffrey, I take your point."

His eyebrows rose. "My excuses. I merely wanted to ask if you had heard from Nicholas recently. He writes me of his mother's illness and I wondered if he had told you any more of his plans to return to England in the spring."

"No. I have not heard from Mr. Cannon." She inclined her head in a regal bow. "Now if you will excuse me." Let Mary Ann be polite to Jeffrey if she cared to. Priscilla had had enough.

"Cilla, what has been going on?" Lucinda stopped her with a hand on her arm. "I have sent several notes around, but you have not replied to one of them. Jeffrey said you were ashamed of your father, but I do not think that is it. Is it because of Nicholas?"

Lucinda always was too clever by half. "No," Priscilla assured her, "of course not. Mama has been seeing to the mail. It gives her something to do, but it also means that some letters have accidentally gone astray."

Lucinda gave her a skeptical look. "Astray? Accidentally?"

"Yes. Mama is not well, you know. This loss of Papa's has been a great blow." Whatever she thought privately, Priscilla would defend her mother to other people.

"Staying in bed, isn't she?" Lucinda said. "She always did avoid any trouble."

Lucinda had lived with the Harrowbys and taken charge of the household for a number of years, until she left to go to the Crimea with Miss Nightingale. She knew Edwina's tricks and foibles as well as Priscilla and had far less sympathy for them.

"It makes it easier to have her in her room since she cannot seem to deal with the reality of the situation."

The two smiled at each other in perfect understanding and agreement. Then Lucinda shattered the moment. "What does Nicholas write to you?"

"Oh, nothing much." Priscilla tried for airy nonchalance. "We do not correspond. It would be very improper, you know."

Lucinda was not persuaded. "Oh, pooh! I am surprised. Jeffrey has not heard from him for a while because he is so busy trying to get his affairs in order so he can take several months this spring and bring his family here to meet the Connaughts." Lucinda looked closely at Priscilla, who felt as if she were under a magnifying lens. "What happened between you and Nicholas?"

"Nothing," Priscilla assured her. "Nothing at all. It was a mere flirtation to pass the time. Otherwise that house party would have been very uncomfortable. The earl was trying to court me in a very ungentlemanly way and all the cousins were flirting with Nicholas, but they were not joking. So we spent time together because we knew we were not serious."

So many lies in one little speech. She hoped she did not look as dishonest as she felt. Apparently, she did.

"I am sorry. I will not tease you about it." But Lucinda did not let go of her arm. "Nor will I ask you about the rumor that you are engaged to the earl. I know that cannot be true. You find him as odious as I do. I know you, Cilla. Not even your care for your mother would induce you to marry such a man. Come, let us find some of that delicious food Mary Ann is so famous for." She led Priscilla through the crowd of guests and to the dining room. "Oh, look, Mary Ann has put out platters for us to help ourselves. What a clever idea! And those roses in the silver pitcher—very pretty and unusual."

"Yes, it is nice, isn't it?" Priscilla said in a noncommittal voice. She was not going to reveal the fact that the ideas had been hers.

"I am so glad you are having a good time." Mary Ann bustled around the table and smiled at them. Then she turned serious and said, "I have been looking for you. I would like you both to come to tea tomorrow, just the three of us. I have an idea I need your help with."

"Some new scheme to help the widows of Crimean soldiers?" Lucinda asked. "You have already done more than anyone else to help them."

Mary Ann shook her head. "Four o'clock? I will tell you all about it then."

The rest of the party was a treat for Priscilla. She

had not realized how much she missed parties—the people, the food, the brilliant clothing. All of it stimulated her and made her feel more alive. It was too bad she would have so few opportunities to enjoy the social scene now.

On the way home, her father seemed more content than he had in some time. "Did you and Mr. Blankenship have an interesting conversation, Papa?" she asked.

He smiled. And for the first time since their crash, he looked as if he meant the smile. "Yes, we did indeed, my dear. He gave me several good ideas, just as Jeffrey has done. I have hopes, Priscilla, that things may improve for us."

She squeezed his hand. "I hope so, Papa. For your sake, I do hope things go better."

He gave her a long, searching look. "You are turning out to be a very good daughter, my dear. I appreciate everything you have done recently. I know I have not said so, but I do notice and I do thank you for it."

Priscilla blushed with gratitude and pleasure. These were the words she had long wanted to hear from her father. She had always thought she would hear them only if she managed to marry a rich and titled man. Yet now he had granted her permission to decline an offer from a titled gentleman and had given them to her for something as mundane as looking after him. Something Lucinda had done so successfully. Priscilla finally felt appreciated and loved by her father, the thing she had always longed for.

"You are very, very welcome, Papa. I am so glad I am able to add to your comfort." She put her hand on his arm and rode like that to their house.

Although she had been forced to talk about Nicholas, her father's praise and Lucinda and Mary Ann's warmth and friendship had made it a very good evening indeed.

The next day, Priscilla presented herself at her mother's door soon after she had eaten breakfast with her father. Edwina was up, sipping tea and looking warily at her daughter.

"I looked for any letters I might have . . . overlooked," she said with dignity. "These are all I could find." She held out five envelopes, three addressed in Lucinda's flowing writing and two in a clear, dark hand. She looked at them first. They were from Mary Ann Blankenship.

Her heart sank. For a moment she had hoped they were from Nicholas. But they were not, of course. Nicholas had not written to her. She would have to face the fact that he had gotten what he wanted from her and had cast her aside like a soiled glove. But just in case she was wrong, she would keep an eye out for the mail from now on.

"You are sure these are all you took?" Priscilla was not going to give her mother the benefit of a polite fiction. She had taken what was not hers, and Priscilla had not forgiven her yet.

"I am certain." Edwina looked her daughter in the eye as she spoke, yet Priscilla saw something shift and dart away in the depths of those guileless, china blue eyes, so like her own. She did not trust her mother, but there was nothing she could do short of ordering the room searched, a step she was not willing to take without authorization from her father.

"Very well, Mama. I hope I do not discover that

you have lied to me." Priscilla turned and left without another word.

She was more shaken than she would admit to find her mother had lied to her and manipulated her trust. She knew Edwina was capable of duplicity—life in society was full of subterfuge and manipulation. Only a few months ago she would perhaps have been capable of the same kinds of actions. Yet now she was appalled.

She was not sure what had changed her. Getting to know her straightforward cousin Lucinda better, she told herself. But that was not the whole answer and she knew it.

"Nicholas." She whispered the name to herself as she entered her room and prepared to read the letters her mother had turned over to her. "It was Nicholas."

Regardless of his caddish behavior at the end of their time together, during that time he had given her the confidence she needed. "I should be grateful to you," she said aloud. "But I am not. I hate you." And despite her resolutions to the contrary, a few scalding tears trickled down her cheeks before she could stop them.

Why could she not forget about him? Everyone's heart was broken sometime. They got over it and got on with their lives. Why could she not manage to do the same?

Well, she would! She would go to tea with Lucinda and Mary Ann and she would laugh and talk and behave as if nothing was the matter—as if she had not been hurt and humiliated. She had thought she would get over her hurt more easily if she acted as if nothing had happened, and if no one knew that she had been cast aside.

Now she found her pain existed deep within her, independently of whether anyone knew or not. Gossip might make it harder to bear, but the source of her misery was within. Her heart truly was broken, and the only remedy she knew of was to act as if it were not so.

Tea at the Blankenships' was as cozy and pleasant as evening parties were. Mary Ann welcomed Priscilla and led her into a small parlor that looked out over Mecklenberg Square and was furnished with old fashioned mahogany pieces and several upholstered sofas covered in flowered fabric. The walls were painted a sunny yellow and a fire crackled on the brick hearth. It was not a fashionable room, but it was warm and welcoming and Priscilla loved it.

When she said so to Mary Ann, her hostess smiled. "I am so glad you like it. Henry thought I might prefer all new things when we married. Even a new house. He told me he was prepared to give me anything I wanted. But this was home to his children and to Henry for a good many years. I don't think any place new would be as happy for them."

"And so it wouldn't be as happy for you," Priscilla guessed.

Mary Ann nodded. "I did have some curtains and chair covers redone, but for the most part I like it the way it was."

"It looks like you."

Mary Ann laughed. "Old and comfortable. Yes, I think so too."

"No, no." Priscilla shook her head, smiling. "I was thinking mellow and gracious, Mrs. Blankenship."

"Thank you, but I wish you would call me Mary Ann. Almost everyone does."

"I would love to. And I am Priscilla." They smiled at each other, and Priscilla was certain she had made a friend. It was a warm feeling, one she had not felt since she had last seen Elinor Connaught at Bellingham Place. Friendship had not come her way very much, and she found it was a great pleasure.

Lucinda arrived shortly thereafter and the three settled down to tea. The food, as always at the Blankenships', was delicious, including savory little scones as well as cakes. The tea was hot Indian tea and strong instead of the usual pale China variety. Lucinda and Mary Ann talked a little about the hospital, and the more she heard the more Priscilla was sure nursing was not work she could do as a profession.

She must have looked a little sad, for Lucinda asked, with a note of censure, if she was bored. "Not at all. I am sitting here thinking how admirable you both are and that I do not think I could even attempt what you both do so well."

Lucinda looked startled. Clearly, she had not expected Priscilla to look with favor on women working, particularly at such dirty, physically demanding work. "Do you really think so, Cilla?"

"Yes. I have learned to value work. I only wish there was something useful I could do. I would so like to help Papa. He is working very hard, though I must say he seems to enjoy it." She smiled a little at Lucinda.

"Jeffrey says he wants to make your father a partner. He has taken on so much of the work and keeps the office running so well that Jeffrey has time for other things." Lucinda blushed and looked down at her teacup.

"Other things such as his wife?" Mary Ann asked with a smile.

Lucinda blushed even more and then looked up and met Mary Ann's eyes. "Something like that. We are still more or less on our honeymoon. And Jeffrey's business is growing so he has been looking for a partner. Uncle Barnabas is the perfect person, according to Jeffrey."

Priscilla was delighted. Her father had seemed happy, though worried, during these past weeks. A partnership might add to the happiness and end the worry! Of course, it would mean Priscilla would have to see more of Jeffrey and endure his sarcastic remarks at her expense.

"That would be wonderful," she said. "But I would still like to be able to find something I can do, something I am good at and can be paid for. If I have learned anything over these past weeks, it is that you never know what is going to happen. It must be wonderful to know you can always support yourself. Unfortunately, my talents are all useless in the business world."

Mary Ann looked at her with new respect. "Yes, it is wonderful to know you can survive no matter what, tnough you must never forget all the work that goes into earning your living."

"I am prepared for work," Priscilla said. "But there is nothing I can do. I do not know enough to be a governess, even if it would not horrify my father." She shook her head and could feel her shoulders droop. "It is a hopeless quest. Best not to dwell on it."

Mary Ann leaned forward, her face a picture of concern. "I may have thought of just the thing," she said. "Though it could cause you to lose some status with your debutante friends."

Priscilla laughed, a short, bitter sound. "They are no longer my friends. When my father lost his fortune, everyone of them dropped us. I could not complain too much, for I had done the same thing to others."

"Does it matter so much to you?" Mary Ann asked. "Do you miss your friends?" There was a wealth of sympathy in her eyes.

"Not a bit," Priscilla replied and lifted her chin. "I still have a roof over my head and food to eat. I cannot complain about my life. I certainly do not miss those shallow creatures. I am only happy I think I am no longer one of them."

"No, indeed you are not." Lucinda sounded surprised at the thought.

Priscilla had to smile. "You must stop listening to Jeffrey. I am not nearly as silly and stupid as he thinks. I am not sure I ever was, but he frightened me so much I became exactly as foolish as he thought I was."

Lucinda looked chagrined. "I know Jeffrey is not always kind."

"Jeffrey is never kind," Priscilla said with a chuckle. "He is a lion, and he protects his own. He has always thought I was unkind to you, and I have to admit he was not wrong about that in the past. But you may tell him you have found me much improved. And my father has decided I am a good daughter. That plus the fact that I am not going to marry his friend Nicholas Cannon and ruin his life should make Jeffrey more kindly disposed toward me."

Priscilla listened to herself, appalled. Not a word she had said was untrue, but she did not wish to hurt Lucinda's feelings. Lucy had been more than kind to her recently, and Priscilla had heard Lucinda stand up for her at Bellingham Place. She did not want her cousin, who clearly adored her irascible husband, to feel bad.

She had started to say something of all this to Lucinda, when she was startled to hear her begin to laugh. "You are completely correct about Jeffrey. He is terribly fierce about me, and that makes him a little difficult to deal with. I know how much you have changed, Cilla, and I salute you for it."

"I did not know you before," Mary Ann said. "But I certainly salute you now. You have been faced with a difficult situation and you have not reacted as many others would have. You have picked up your burden and carried on. I can understand why you want to earn some money to make things easier for your family. And I want to put forth an idea for your consideration. Lucinda told me," she said to Priscilla, "about all the work you did behind the scenes at that house party. And I saw what you did for me last night. I don't know what I would have done without you."

Priscilla waved her hand in a gesture meant to convey that her work had been nothing out of the ordinary. But Mary Ann would have none of that.

"You have a gift for arranging things, making a party a success. And I think you could use that talent. There are a great many people who would love to entertain if they knew how. You know how. You can help them, arrange the tables, the decorations, the menu. And you won't want credit, so everyone will think they have done it all themselves."

Priscilla stared at her friend for a long moment. "I have never heard of anyone doing something like that. Do you really think it can be done?"

"Absolutely. And the best thing is no one will know you are working because you will do it quietly, with no advertising or gossip. You will like that because your mother and her friends will not know, and your clients will like it because they can pretend they have done it all themselves."

Lucinda sat up in her chair and clapped her hands. "That is a brilliant idea! Jeffrey and I are going to have to give a dinner party and I have been postponing it and dreading it! Now, I can turn it all over to you. Would fifty pounds be enough of a fee?"

"Fifty pounds! For one evening!" Priscilla was dumbfounded. "It is much too much."

"I do not think so." Mary Ann poured another cup of tea for each of them. "Henry always says people value what they have to pay a great deal for. And we want you to be valued."

"Absolutely. All right, seventy pounds it shall be. For a large party, we will make it a hundred. That should have people flocking to you." Lucinda grinned. "In secret, of course. No one will know if their neighbor's party was a raging success because of the neighbor or that clever Miss Harrowby!"

"How will I get clients?" Priscilla wondered. She had already accepted the fact that she was going to do this. "Who will pay me to do what their relatives will do for them?"

"Do not give that a thought. First of all, their relatives cannot do what you can do. You must learn to take your talent seriously, Cilla. As for clients, after my dinner party, Mary Ann will have a small dinner, will you not, Mary Ann? Or one of my friends will— Catherine's father, the baronet, or Rose's in-laws. The countess is known for her entertainments, and I believe she likes you, Cilla. We'll find someone." Lucinda gestured expansively. "After that, you will not have

enough time to handle all the parties people will want
you to organize for them."

Mary Ann laughed. "Listen to her, Priscilla. This
woman organized Florence Nightingale. She will have
no difficulty bringing London society to your door."

"Well," said Priscilla, drawing a deep breath and
leaping into the future on faith, "I shall do my best!"

"That is all that is necessary," said Lucinda, raising
her teacup in a toast.

Fourteen

Four months later

Nicholas leaned over the rail and watched the waves dance away from beneath the hull of the ship. He could feel strength seeping back into his body after two weeks on the water. The doctor had tried to tell him that after the long bout of scarlet fever and the relapses he had suffered, he should wait until late summer to leave for England. But Nicholas could wait no longer.

The doctor had tried to insist they take a sailing ship rather than one of the new steam or steam-and-sail vessels, but Nicholas had balked at that, too. He had been right to insist on taking the faster ship. Two weeks on the water, and he was ready to dive overboard and swim toward the white cliffs of Dover, now only a day away.

Priscilla.

What had happened to Priscilla? He had heard nothing from her directly. But he had heard, via a letter from his cousin Elinor, that the family was rife with the rumor that his uncle and Priscilla were engaged, though neither seemed to have any money left, which made them both ineligible. The marquis had refused to pay any more of his son's debts and the family thought the earl was desperately in need of ready funds, as was Mr. Harrowby, though no one Elinor had overheard really knew the true story. Some were saying the earl must still have money or he would not be courting Priscilla. Elinor was passing these rumors on for what they were worth, but she knew *for a fact* (that phrase had been underlined twice) that her dear friend Priscilla, would never marry the earl.

Unconsciously, he beat his fist on the rail. What had happened? One letter from Jeffrey and scarcely a mention of Priscilla in it. They had been so careful to keep their relationship a secret that his best friend did not think to mention her. Of course, it could be that Jeffrey knew Priscilla was engaged and did not wish to be the bearer of bad news.

Nicholas had written once from the ship, but in New York illness had claimed him before he could write again. When he had recovered enough to sit up, the news of her possible engagement to his uncle had hit him like a roundhouse punch.

Helen. Could Priscilla be just like Helen? Did he have some sort of blind spot that caused him not to see traits in women others saw only too clearly? His mother had not been fooled by Helen, and Jeffrey certainly disapproved of what he saw as Priscilla's hunger for money and status.

His answer had been to bury himself in the details of his business. Marcus had not been able to handle every problem that came up in Nicholas's absence by himself. The thorniest problems had to await Nicholas's return and had kept him busy far into the night. He was glad to be able to push the thought of Priscilla to the back of his mind.

But it had not worked for long. He had to sleep sometime, and with sleep had come dreams of Priscilla. She haunted him, and the memory of the love they had shared—or what was love to him, if not to her—had taunted him every time he closed his eyes.

Was she like Helen? He did not think so. There was a sweetness to Priscilla that others had seen as well as he. Elinor liked her, and so did Lucinda, even though Priscilla admitted she had been less than kind to her cousin when they were younger. Jeffrey was less forgiving, but that was understandable. He loved Lucinda.

Finally, he decided he had to know. He finished up the most pressing business and had broken free, given his mother and sister two days to pack, and told Marcus he was going to England and the business could go hang for few months if their trained clerks could not handle it. Despite the doctor's demand he use the trip as a rest, he booked passage on the fastest ship he could find.

He had told himself there was no use in writing Priscilla when he would be leaving so soon. He would wait to confront her. But there was more to his silence than that. Out here in the solitary darkness he admitted to himself he was afraid. When he received no word from her, he began to fear her mother had influenced her against him. Jeffrey's letter had confirmed Elinor's story that Barnabas Harrowby had lost a great deal of money in a railroad scheme that had failed. Lucinda added a postscript in which she said Priscilla had been seen at a number of society parties recently, looking very pretty.

That added up to only one thing in Jeffrey's mind—she was looking for a rich husband, just as her mother wished. The earl would be out of the running if he had truly lost a fortune, and Priscilla would not do for Granville now that her father had lost his money.

Nicholas had never told Priscilla just how wealthy he was. She would assume there were bigger fish in the London social pond than he would ever be. What a fool he had been not to wait until he had seen her before leaving London. If he'd had any idea that his mother was on the mend, or that he would lose touch with Priscilla entirely when he left, he would have camped on her doorstep until he had seen her and they had told her father about their engagement.

Damn! Stupid infectious diseases, sparing Marcus and Melinda and hitting him. Hitting him so hard that even now he found himself shaking with fatigue and sweating after the slightest exertion. His mother had recovered from the fever without relapse, but he had time and again found himself trying to dress for a visit to his office only to fall back in bed, the fever once again wracking his body.

He gazed at the wake the ship was making, glistening white in the moonlight, and wished Priscilla were there with him to admire the view. Instead, he was condemned to inactivity while Priscilla attended parties in London, parties filled with men far more eligible in her mother's eyes than he was.

And what did she think of him, with no word from him after the beautiful lovemaking they had shared? Had she lost faith completely? He couldn't blame her if she had. Nicholas was not a letter writer, but he had tried.

Had he given up too soon? He had a sinking feeling he had. He knew he wasn't good enough for her, but he would try to convince her that his love for her made up for having to give up her gay and frivolous life in London. There was social life in New York. Helen had certainly found enough to do and enough things to spend money on.

"Nicholas." His mother's soft voice still carried the hint of a Scottish burr. "It is growing cold and your sister and brother are waiting for you to make a fourth for whist." She came up to stand beside him and wrapped her tartan plaid cloak more closely around her. "Otherwise, they will be forced to play with that Mrs. Thomas, who has no card sense. Melinda will say something really rude if Mrs. T. trumps her ace one more time."

He tried to smile but could not. "In a minute, Mother."

"Nicholas, what happened in England?"

He shrugged, unwilling to discuss Priscilla, unable to lie to his mother. "Just what I told you. I met the Connaughts, most of whom I can see why Father crossed the ocean to avoid. The old marquis is a sharp old bird, but Father's brother, Granville, is a snake and a stupid one at that. Still jealous of Father after all these years."

"Your reaction is exactly what I expected. But that isn't what I meant." Jean put her hand over his clenched fist, still resting on the rail. "Who is she, Nicholas?"

He sighed. "I never could fool you, could I?"

Her lips quirked in a faint smile. "No, never. And it would save a great deal of time if you would stop trying. Tell me about her."

"All right. Her name is Priscilla Harrowby." He took a deep breath. "She is twenty and very pretty. From a wealthy family, though her father seems to have fallen on hard times since I left. Used to the social scene. Follows her mother's lead in most things—everything but me, I think. Mama did not approve of me. Much preferred Uncle Granville. I had to leave suddenly, after I declared myself but before we could talk to her family. I haven't heard from her since, though a young Connaught cousin I met at Bellingham Place wrote me that there are rumors that she and Granville are engaged. And Lucinda Bancroft wrote that Priscilla was being seen at many social events, apparently having a wonderful time." He shrugged. "That's it in a nutshell."

"Ah." Jean looked out to sea for a long moment. "So you love her, but you are afraid she is just like Helen."

He winced a little. His mother had little use for tact. When she had something to say, she said it. Usually, he found it an endearing and even a soothing trait. He always knew where he stood with his mother. But this time the truth, as the saying went, hurt.

"I want to meet her."

"She may well try to avoid me, but I am sure we will see each other. I can ask Jeffrey and Lucinda to arrange it. Priscilla is Lucinda's cousin."

"I will know. I never liked Helen. She had the soul of a trollop and the heart of a moneylender." No, his mother did not mince words. "If this girl is the same," she said, reaching out to pat his arm, "I will know."

He squeezed her hand. "At least I will always have you."

The same day the Cannons sailed from New York, Priscilla leaned back in her chair and eased her cramped fingers. She was making out menus for two dinners to be held on consecutive nights and preparing discreet bills, labeled only "For Services Rendered" to be given to two clients whose reception and musical evening respectively she had "helped to arrange," as she put it.

So far, Lucinda and Mary Ann had been right. Her business was going well, and so discreet was her work that it seemed to the uninitiated that Priscilla Harrowby was once again being invited to all the most interesting entertainments at all the best homes.

She had to smile. In truth, she was enjoying herself more now than when she had gone to parties and had nothing to do but giggle and fan herself and wait to come to the notice of some eligible young man. Now she had duties to see to, but in as unobtrusive a fashion as possible, lest anyone think the hostess of a party did not do everything herself.

She found she loved earning money. It was crass, she knew, even for a man to admit he liked working for money, and completely unheard of for a woman. But she did not care. To herself she could admit she not only loved having her own money, she liked what she did to earn it. Planning parties, seeing a gathering she had organized work and make people happy, was a joy to her. The fact that very few people knew she worked and fewer still knew whether she had planned a particular event or was attending as a guest fed her sense of humor.

She would like more work, for they could use the money. Her father's partnership with Jeffrey was slowly building up their bank account, but the steady drain of bills kept up. Soon they would have to pare their expenses more drastically. If they could not find two thousand pounds by the end of the month, they would be evicted.

They had not as yet found another house. She knew it was because her father hated the idea of moving. To him that would be an admission of permanent defeat. To her mother it would mean deepening depression and confusion. If only she could find a way to earn that much, her father would not have to ask Jeffrey for a loan and risk refusal.

Priscilla clenched her fists. If Jeffrey were unkind enough to refuse, she would have a few choice words to say to him. But what she really wanted was to avoid the problem altogether by finding a way to make the money herself. She gave her mind over to the problem as she made out her monthly bills. Sending them out gave her a thrill, and receiving money back by post was even more exhilarating.

In fact, if it were not for the steady, unending ache in her heart, she would be quite happy. She had faced the fact she would never marry, and it did not bother her. Only one man had ever made her think of a lifetime with him and he, it turned out, was not who she had thought he was. If he had been, he would have contacted her, if only because she might be pregnant. For all he knew, she was expecting his baby at this very moment, frightened and alone, turned out of her house by her disgraced parents.

She could not marry another man even if she wanted to. There was the matter of her virginity—or lack of it. Her husband, whoever he was, would know and she would be disgraced. If she considered marriage to anyone, she would have to tell him about Nicholas first, and the very idea of what that conversation would be like made her cringe. So, no marriage of convenience, which was the only kind possible—except to Nicholas.

She never asked Lucinda about him, but her cousin

had nonetheless volunteered the information he was ill with scarlet fever. *A likely story,* Priscilla thought. Just as likely as the tale of his mother's illness that was supposedly the reason for his sudden departure. And if he was truly ill? *Good!* she thought viciously. *He deserves it!* Then she immediately repented of such an uncharitable thought. *Not terribly ill,* she amended her order to the Almighty. *Just sick enough to feel dreadful for a while. And perhaps You could arrange for him to develop a disgusting rash and look ugly!*

If only she meant it, she thought. But somehow her love had survived Nicholas's neglect, even his callousness. It was pathetic, stupid—anything you wanted to call it—but it was there, and in her heart she refused to deny it. She sighed and hoped he would never return to England. If they were to meet again, she was afraid she might not be able to pretend indifference.

"You have a caller, Miss Priscilla." The housekeeper, who now doubled as a butler—a sign of their fall in the world—announced, breaking into her reverie.

She fished her shoes out from under the chair and rose, shaking out her skirts and pasting a smile on her face.

"The earl of Ashden," said Mrs. Crawford, handing his card to Priscilla.

Her jaw literally dropped, and it was all she could do to close her mouth before the tall, languid figure of Granville Connaught appeared in her doorway.

"Good morning, Miss Harrowby," he said, his pale brown eyes surveying her with an insolence he would never have shown when she was rich.

Priscilla drew herself up and looked at him with an

equally appraising gaze. "My lord," she said and waited for him to state his business.

"You are looking lovely, my dear. No, do not stiffen up that way and draw your enchanting mouth down in that unattractive frown. I have not come to importune you to marry me. You must know that is quite out of the question now."

"It was always out of the question, my lord." She was proud of her cool, ironic tone, though inside she longed to slap him.

"Ah, yes, my nephew. Not been around recently, I take it."

"I believe he is in New York. A bit far to drop in for tea."

He chuckled, but his eyes never lost their cool watchfulness. "Actually, I have come to you on business, Miss Harrowby."

"I believe you have me confused with my father. Or perhaps my cousin-in-law." She gave him a small smile, but did not ask him to be seated. It was extremely rude to leave a guest standing like this, but Priscilla did not care. The earl was not only uninvited, he was unwelcome. She did not care if he knew it.

"I have not, however, scotched the rumors linking our names that someone—your mother, perhaps?—has been circulating."

"My mother does not leave her room. She is not the source of any rumors about you, my lord." Scorn dripped from her tongue, and she longed to slap his sneering, imperious face.

"It really does not matter. I have not revealed their inaccuracy because they served my purpose. I have been able to woo—and win—another young lady without arousing suspicion. One actually possessed of a fortune, not a parvenu whose money can be lost overnight."

"Congratulations, my lord. Finding a suitable victim must have been difficult."

He flushed and his eyes turned even colder. "Do not reveal your disappointment so clearly, my dear. I can still offer you a relationship, just not the one you were perhaps hoping for."

Priscilla took a deep breath and fought down her rage. "I presume you did not come here just to insult me, my lord. If you have anything important to say, please do so. I am very busy."

"Ah, yes, I understand you have gone into the catering business," he said with a raised eyebrow. "Quite the enterprising little bourgeois. My hat is off to you. So few women go into business, and those who do tend to businesses of another kind."

She raised her hand in a gesture that told him quite clearly to stop. Occasionally, the husbands or sons of would-be clients became overly familiar, and Priscilla had learned how to discourage them. "Please. I do not know what you have heard, but I am afraid I cannot—"

He took a step nearer to her. "I truly need your help. No one but you can do it. My future papa- and mama-in-law are the very highest sticklers. They do not, I fear, quite approve of me as the lord and master of their little dormouse."

Something in the way he said 'lord and master' made Priscilla shiver. She felt very sorry for the 'little dormouse,' whoever she was.

"I do not see what I can do."

"I am planning a house party at Bellingham Place in their honor, to demonstrate what I have to offer them, as it were. If you were to come, it would make it clear to them—and the world—that we have never been more than friends."

"I am afraid I cannot—" Nothing would induce her to return to the Connaught family home.

"Not if you were to plan the party? Not for a thousand pounds?" He gave her a wolfish smile.

"Not for a—" Priscilla caught sight of the stack of bills waiting for her on her desk top. "Not for a thousand," she amended her statement smoothly. "But for two thousand, I would consider it."

The earl looked at her for a long moment. Something in her expression must have told him she meant it, for he shrugged. "I can see you drive a hard bargain. Blood will tell, I suppose, and yours is clearly that of shopkeepers and foundry owners."

"Your nephew is a foundry owner, I believe," she said before she could stop herself.

"A fact I never cease to deplore. Fortunately for the family, my marriage will bar him forever from the succession." His smile was triumphant. "I will expect your best efforts for the extortionate sum you are charging me."

"There are some rules you will need to understand," Priscilla said in her most businesslike tone. She picked up some papers at random and pretended to study them so she did not have to look at the earl. "I always appear to be a guest at the affairs I supervise. I assume that will not pose a problem for you?"

"Not at all. That is precisely what I wish. My soon-to-be betrothed's parents will wish to see for themselves that I have not jilted another, poorer woman to woo their darling. It would not suit their ideas of propriety, you see. Of course you must appear to be a guest. It will make the situation much more piquant to know how hard you will be working."

Priscilla managed to keep her expression bland and her tone businesslike. "Very good, my lord. You will let me know the dates and what sort of entertainment you have envisioned and how many guests there will be. Oh, and I will need an initial payment of half of what we have agreed to within the next few days."

He shook his head as if in admiration. "What a businesswoman you are. You have found your true calling in life at last. No wonder you never married, my dear! How delicious that you still look like a normal young woman."

"Good day, my lord." She waited until the door had closed after him to stick out her tongue.

Fifteen

It was odd being back at Bellingham Place. It had not changed at all in the nearly half a year since Priscilla had last seen it, yet she had changed so much.

She looked around the drawing room and leaned back into her hands to ease her aching back. The huge old place looked better than it had in years, according to Mrs. Sandles, the housekeeper, and it certainly was an improvement over its appearance the first time Priscilla had visited. It had taken a great deal of time and elbow grease to achieve it, but now the place had the look of a home that was loved and cared for.

The guests were arriving in less than an hour, and she was at last satisfied. Time to hurry upstairs and transform herself into a house guest. She had purchased several dresses suitable for a spring house party. It had eaten into her funds, but it was necessary. She could not appear as a welcome guest who was just helping with a few last minute details if she did not look the part.

"Here, miss," said Gillie, who had asked to be assigned to wait on Priscilla. "I have the flowered muslin all ready for you."

"Thank you, Gillie. I don't know what I would do without you." Priscilla slipped into the dress and surveyed herself in the pier glass. She would do. The dress was ivory strewn with pink and blue flowers. China blue ribbons the exact color of her eyes set off the spring freshness of the garment.

She had been assigned the same room she had the last time she had visited. It added to her sense of dislocation. The room, the house, the people—all were the same, but her world had been transformed. Nicholas, of course, had left with no plans to return so far as anyone knew. The marquis appeared to be unconcerned with his grandson's defection, according to Mrs. Sandles. The marquis might not care, but Priscilla did.

"Sit down a minute, miss, and I'll do your hair."

Gratefully, Priscilla sank onto the padded boudoir chair that was placed in front of the dressing table. She was tired, but she knew when the guests arrived she would be full of energy, eager to see to it that everyone enjoyed themselves.

She had avoided the earl up to now, and the marquis had never summoned her to visit him. She did not know exactly what the earl had told the old man about her visit, but she had enjoyed a peaceful and pleasant week. The servants seemed happy to have her in charge, and for once she felt as if it were her party, for no nervous hostess got in her way with impossible demands and sudden changes.

Several of the Connaught female cousins were coming, so there would be at least a nominal hostess to welcome the bride-to-be and her family. The guests who did not know better would assume that whichever one arrived first and took over the role had planned the entire event.

Hearing voices in the hallway below, Priscilla got to her feet, draped her new blue cashmere shawl over her elbows, and prepared to descend. She only hoped Granville had explained her presence so the cousins would not require long explanations.

Smiling, she came into the entrance hall, where Dalton and Mrs. Sandles were already seeing to the comfort of the first arrivals.

"Elinor!" she said, hurrying over, both hands outstretched to greet her young friend. "How wonderful to see you again!"

Elinor looked a little subdued, the worried frown between her brows more evident than ever. "It is good to see you, too, Priscilla." Priscilla was surprised to hear constraint in her voice. "You have met my Aunt Margaret, I believe."

"Yes, indeed." The woman who always looked as if she smelled something bad when she looked at Elinor. "And your two cousins. Annabelle and Susan, so nice to see you again."

Mrs. Sandles took the ladies off to inspect their rooms. Elinor lingered behind and put her hand on Priscilla's arm to keep her from following the others.

"Could I speak to you for a moment?" she asked.

"Of course. There is a fire burning in the library just upstairs. Why don't we go in there?"

Priscilla led the way up. She had taken special care with the library, making sure the furniture was polished to a dark, perfect gleam and there was always a cheerful fire burning on the grate. She paused inside the door and turned to look at her friend. "What is it, Elinor? You look worried to death. I won't eat you, you know."

"I wouldn't blame you if you felt like it." Elinor twisted her hands in the folds of her dark green traveling dress. "I wrote to Nicholas. And—and I told him about the rumor you and Granville were engaged." Elinor's eyes glistened with tears and her expression was anguished. "I didn't mean to hurt you, or gossip. I wanted Nicholas to know, because I thought he would be hurt. And so I—" Her voice broke and the tears overflowed. "Oh, Priscilla, I am so sorry."

Priscilla put her arms around Elinor's shaking shoulders. "It is all right, truly it is. Do not think you caused any trouble, my dear. It was just a holiday flirtation, not serious in the least. Nicholas would not care a rap if I were to become engaged to the Prince of Wales much less his uncle. Please don't cry, Elinor. You'll spoil your looks, and we wouldn't want that."

Elinor sniffed. "You are just being nice to me. But do not think because I am young, I am stupid. I know what I saw and Nicholas cared for you. And you cared for him, too, Priscilla. Do not tell me you didn't!"

Priscilla managed a tiny chuckle. "Very well, then, I won't tell you anything you don't want to hear. But now we had better get you upstairs where you can wash your face and change your dress for tea."

"You aren't angry? I may have cost you the man you love."

Priscilla tried for a warm smile. "That is a little dramatic, Elinor. You did not change anyone's mind. Truly." She reached out and squeezed the younger girl's hand.

Elinor smiled. "Thank you. You have relieved me of a great weight."

The rest of the afternoon was busy. Priscilla greeted guests and family members, not as hostess but as an unobtrusive presence, making things easier for everyone.

About four o'clock, the earl's intended bride and her

parents arrived. Miss Hester Allison-Hyatt was small and plump, with mouse brown hair and large hazel eyes that seemed a little frightened of the world. She was dressed very expensively but not very becomingly in a gray traveling dress with a matching coat and bonnet. Her front teeth protruded in a little overbite and the general effect was of a very sweet, very young dormouse. She was immediately surrounded by Connaughts eager to greet her and make her feel at home.

Priscilla turned to the girl's mother and father. They were a dour pair. The father, Sir Peter, in particular was large and red-faced and overbearing. Priscilla thought his manner went a long way to explaining his daughter's anxious look.

He was very suspicious of Priscilla, having no doubt heard of Granville's reputation. "And you are?" he said in a tone that bordered on rude.

"I am Priscilla Harrowby, a friend of the family," she responded. "Mrs. Sandles will show you to your rooms. I know where Miss Allison-Hyatt is to sleep. If you would like to rest a bit before tea, I will show her when the family has finished greeting her."

Lady Allison-Hyatt seemed more than willing to go to her room, but Sir Peter seemed inclined to linger and question Priscilla. "A family friend, eh?"

Just then Susan Connaught came up and took Priscilla by the arm. "We need your help again, Priscilla. The dining room must look wonderful for the dinner before the dance. I remember what a help you were when you were here for Christmas. So if you do not mind," she said to Sir Peter and his wife, "I will steal Miss Harrowby for a while."

Sir Peter seemed reassured by this speech that Priscilla was indeed a friend of the family and not a friend of the earl's and went off quite peacefully.

A few minutes later, Priscilla noticed Hester was looking a bit harassed. She managed to get her away from the group of young Connaught ladies and, with a friendly smile, offered to show her the room assigned her. Hester seemed almost pathetically eager to leave. She seemed to have struck up a friendship with Elinor, who was only a few years younger than she, but the other young ladies appeared to intimidate her.

"Thank you very much," she said to Priscilla, in a voice so soft it was almost inaudible. "It has been a long day, and I am tired. Do you think it would be very rude if I had tea in my room instead of coming down? I can feel a headache beginning."

Although Priscilla felt quite sure everyone would indeed find it odd, she could see Hester was truly worn out. "Of course not. No one will mind in the least. I can tell the housekeeper when I go down, if you would like."

"Oh, thank you. That is most kind of you. I want to be in my best looks tonight," she said naively. Her lips trembled a little and she clutched her hands together. "I want Granville—that is, the earl—to be proud of me."

"I am sure you have nothing to fear on that score," Priscilla said with an encouraging smile. "What time would you like your maid to come?"

Hester swallowed convulsively. "Do you think you—that is, I would like to invite you—" She took a deep breath. "Would you take tea with me here please, Miss Harrowby? I would appreciate it so much. I don't want—that is, I am nervous and I do not wish to be—alone."

There was an agonized look in Hester's eyes which Priscilla could not help but respond to. She had been in similar situations, situations where many girls would turn to their mothers. Like Priscilla, Hester obviously felt she could not confide in hers. Priscilla, who had not had a friend to turn to, did not want Hester to suffer similar loneliness.

"I would be delighted. I will go and find us some really delicious cakes and return shortly." Smiling, Priscilla slipped away to the kitchen. There she checked on the progress of the evening's dinner as well as the tea that was being readied. She filled a tray and then, shrugging off several offers of help by the over-worked staff, took it back to Hester's room.

There was a small sitting area near a bow window in the room, and Priscilla set the tray down there. Hester was delighted. Her face lit up when Priscilla returned, and she sat and helped herself to tea and cakes. In between bites, she told Priscilla all the thrilling details of Granville's courtship. It seemed to Priscilla that Hester was pathetically in love with the earl. She had never been courted except by several sons of nearby squires, and she believed they had been more in love with her dowry than her person.

Why she did not see Granville in the same light was perhaps due to the glow her first visit to London had cast over a sophisticated older man who paid her the first polished attention in her life.

"I know it is very wrong of me," Hester confided in a near whisper, "but I think I would do anything for Granville. He is a most unconventional and daring man. I do not understand what he sees in me. But I am very glad he sees something he likes." A shy smile lit her face, and Priscilla felt such pity for her she thought her heart would break. *Granville should be shot,* she thought furiously. To take advantage of a young, untried girl was worse even than attempting to seduce housemaids. This girl would be tied to the earl for life. No matter what she discovered about him, there would be no way out for her.

"How long have you and the earl known each other?" Priscilla asked.

"Three weeks," Hester admitted, blushing. "Mama and Papa think it is far too soon to be thinking of an engagement, but I think Granville is right. When you have met your heart's true companion, you know right away and there is no point in waiting."

"Do you really think so?" Priscilla allowed a little doubt to show. "I have always thought a long courtship, with plenty of flowers and dances and compliments, would be delightful. It seems a shame to miss it. The opportunity only comes once, you know."

Doubt crossed Hester's face, but only for a moment. "I thought so too, but then Granville said I could have all that after we are married. And that would be even more delightful, I think."

Her smile lit up her face, and Priscilla felt helpless to counteract Granville's careful work. Hester believed every word out of his mouth, Priscilla thought, enraged. She wracked her brain to think of something she could say to instill even a touch of doubt. Just then there was a knock on the door. Hester sprang up and went to answer it.

"Oh, Granville."

Priscilla heard the breathless love in her new friend's voice and despaired.

"You should not have come to my room. How very improper." Hester did not sound the least bit shocked.

"Fortunately, we have a chaperon. Miss Harrowby came to take tea with me."

Priscilla rose, ready to wait until midnight if necessary to prevent Granville from being alone with this helpless infant. But she was outmaneuvered immediately.

"Ah, yes, Miss Harrowby. She was one of my flirts before I met you, beloved, so you must promise not to believe a word she says about me!" Granville was smiling with what looked like blind devotion down at Hester as Priscilla came to the door.

"But she has said nothing about you," Hester protested. "Truly."

"How wise of you, Priscilla," Granville said under his breath. Raising his voice, he added, "Remember, you have promised to meet me a few minutes before dinner in the library, my love."

"Yes. Of course." From the look on Hester's face, Priscilla was sure she would meet the earl on the roof if he asked her.

Granville left, but before Priscilla could think of anything else to say, Hester announced her mama had made her promise to take a nap before dinner. There was nothing to do but leave, and Priscilla did, with a smile she was far from feeling.

The Cannon family arrived in London earlier that same day. Unable to wait to see Priscilla after all this time, Nicholas settled them in their rooms at Claridge's and took himself off to call on the Harrowbys. He told himself it wouldn't matter that he had behaved like a fool. Priscilla knew he loved her. He could persuade her to listen to him, and that would be all he would need, he was sure. He wouldn't talk to her, he would simply take her in his arms and—

"Miss Harrowby is not at home, sir," said the gimlet-eyed housekeeper who answered the door. A little surprised to find them still at their old address, if what Elinor had written him was true, Nicholas smiled at the woman and asked where Priscilla had gone.

Mrs. Crawford, like most servants, knew a good deal more about her masters' business than they thought. She believed this young man had hurt Miss Priscilla and would benefit from a dose of jealousy. Why should he think Miss Priscilla had been moping about waiting for him?

"She has gone to the country, to a house party," she said, telling him far more than was proper.

"A house party?" He remembered Lucinda's postscript to Jeffrey's letter, telling him how much Priscilla appeared to enjoy the many parties she was attending.

Nicholas thanked the housekeeper and strode off down the street, this time headed for his grandfather's. If Priscilla was away, he would go about the other business he had to take care of. He would arrange to bring his family to meet the marquis.

When he arrived in Grosvenor Square, Bellingham House was locked. He went around to the servants' entrance without a second thought. There his luck, he thought, changed, for one of the young bootboys was in the kitchen and came to the door.

"G'day, guv'nur," he said with a cheeky grin. "Wot brings you round to my side of the 'ouse?"

"Where has the family gone?" Nicholas said, getting right to the point.

"Country," the boot boy replied. "I'm on me way there with some plants for the big party."

"What party?"

"The earl's gettin' himself married," said the boot boy.

"Well, thank God," Nicholas said before he thought. He tipped the boy and left, wondering what to do now.

Then the thought hit him like a brick falling on his head. Was there some connection between Priscilla's absence and Granville's engagement? Of course not, he told himself. Priscilla would never marry Granville. Elinor had said so, and she would know.

But would she? If the Harrowbys had lost all their money, would not Priscilla's mother badger her into marrying a peer, even if one who was not as rich as he had been? After all, Granville would inherit the Connaught fortune when his father died.

For the first time, Nicholas wished his grandfather would leave him the family fortune. We would see how much sneering his Uncle Granville would do when he had to go to Nicholas for spending money! Nicholas shook his head, as if to clear it of these nonsensical thoughts. He would approach this in a sensible, calm way. He would go to see Jeffrey and Lucinda and learn the truth about Priscilla.

Jeffrey was not home, but Lucinda received him with every evidence of pleasure. She grasped his hands, gave his cheek a kiss, and then led him into her sunny sitting room and offered him sherry or Madeira.

"So," she said with a wide grin, "you could not stay away. It is about time you returned."

Apprehension slid along his nerve endings, tightening his muscles. "What do you mean, it's about time? Where is Priscilla? What has she been doing?"

"I wrote you," Lucinda said, her face a mask of innocence. "She has been enjoying herself."

"And where is she now?"

"Don't glare at me, Nicholas. It does not frighten me in the least. Jeffrey used to do the very same thing until he realized it was a waste of effort." She tossed her glossy black curls and gave him glare for glare from her deep blue eyes.

"Where is she?" he repeated, through gritted teeth.

"Why, I believe she is at Bellingham Place right now, for your uncle's engagement party. She's been there for the past several days. It is one of her most important—"

"Damn her! She is not going to marry him!" He had slammed the door and hailed a hackney almost before he could think what he was doing.

How fast could he get to Bellingham Place?

Sixteen

Priscilla had done everything possible to ensure dinner that night would be a triumph. From the flowers in the silver epergne she had unearthed in one of the sideboards to the gleaming glassware and china, everything looked beautiful. The food she had helped Mrs. Bennett plan was going to be delicious and, she hoped, still hot when the footmen handed it round. She left the selection of wine to Dalton, but was sure he would provide the finest.

As she dressed in the cobalt blue silk she had worn during the Christmas house party, her mind, busy with details of the party to come, suddenly turned and, like a compass needle, veered to her heart's true north.

Nicholas. She had worn this dress with Nicholas and he had admired it. Nicholas had admired her, had loved her. She had been so sure. How could she have been so mistaken?

Well, she had not been mistaken. He had lied to her and she had believed him. *Fool, fool,* she told herself. *You had better forget him.* Difficult to do anywhere—but here, at Bellingham Place, where they had been together, sworn their love . . .

Priscilla told herself there was nothing to do but get on with her job. She had agreed to arrange this party, and she was going to see to it that it was a raging success. Best to get on with it.

Gillie knocked and entered, ready to do her hair, and Priscilla sighed. One small pleasure amid all the duties and worries.

After Gillie had arranged her hair in a shining mass of curls, Priscilla left her room to descend to the drawing room. Thinking that perhaps Lady Allison-Hyatt had not thought to accompany her daughter, Priscilla stopped by Hester's room. She knocked softly, but received no response. Her mother must have come to escort her down.

Priscilla found most of the party in the drawing room, where the gentlemen were being offered their choice of Madeira or sherry and the ladies were given lemonade. Priscilla looked around and found Granville had not yet arrived. Since the Allison-Hyatts were already there, this seemed excessively rude.

Hester was still absent as well, and Priscilla began to feel a shiver of apprehension. No one in the family was ready to deal with the full-fledged crisis she could feel brewing. The marquis had planned to come down to dinner this evening, she knew, but he was not there yet.

Dalton entered the room, bearing a square of folded white notepaper on a tray, and Priscilla's apprehension grew when he approached Sir Peter and held it out.

Sir Peter quickly scanned the note's contents. His face turned an alarming shade of purple, and he crumpled the paper in his hand with a convulsive movement that told Priscilla he wished it were Granville's neck.

"The blackguard!" he exclaimed. "He dares to kidnap my daughter and tell me it is because he loves her. Bah! He loves her bank account and nothing else!"

"Peter, dear." His wife's pleading had no effect on him. He shook off the hand she placed on his arm and whirled to see who was available as a lightning rod for his wrath.

"Miss Harrowby!" He rounded on Priscilla. "What is the meaning of this? You are a friend of the family. There were rumors you intended to marry the earl. You took tea with my daughter this afternoon. What have you and that—that damnable man done with my Hester?"

Everyone else in the room began to whisper and twitter like birds while Priscilla simply stared at him for a moment. The accusation was so far-fetched she was at a loss for words. Then she managed to speak slowly and calmly, though anger made her heart beat faster. How dare this man accuse her? Everyone else in the room was related to Granville. Why was he not accusing them? Or perhaps that was the answer—he would not wish to blame any member of such a large and powerful family.

"I am so sorry, Sir Peter," she said, "but I truly have no idea where they have gone."

"He says they are eloping to Scotland to be married over the anvil. Did you know of this?" He took a step toward her. Priscilla was not brave, but she stood her ground. This pompous man picking on someone weaker and less powerful was not going to make her show her true cowardly colors.

"No, I know nothing of this."

There was the tapping of a cane on the hardwood floor of the hallway, and the marquis was framed in the doorway, leaning heavily on his stick. "I am sure she is telling the truth, Sir Peter. You have made your doubts about this marriage very clear. I am sure Granville talked your daughter into an elopement as a result. Probably told her he couldn't wait, that sort of stuff. Granville can be damned persuasive when he wants." The old man started toward his deep chair near the fire. Dalton was beside him in an instant, discreetly lending his arm.

Once he was seated, the marquis turned his bright brown eyes to Sir Peter again. "What do you wish to do about this, sir?" he asked. The first sensible thing anyone had said, Priscilla thought.

"I—I." Sir Peter blinked quickly, his eyes darting back and forth as he grappled with what he needed to do. "Go after them, bring them back. This makes it clearer than ever he is not worthy of my little girl."

The marquis's bushy white eyebrows shot up. "Really, sir? Then I wonder you are here."

Sir Peter flushed painfully. "What do you suggest, my lord?"

"Let 'em elope and make the best of it. Tell it as a romantic tale of star-crossed lovers." His scornful expression told what he thought of such a story, but Sir Peter looked doubtful.

"I do not know what is best to do. I cannot express how much I would regret such an alliance."

"Oh, we are agreed on that," the marquis shot back. "Your mousy little daughter can never adequately manage Bellingham. We all know that. Best get Miss Harrowby here to take on the task."

Priscilla blushed. She had no wish to be involved in this ugly, private quarrel and quietly began to leave the room to see what could be done about dinner, when the door burst open again. One of the younger footmen dashed into the room.

"My lord," he gasped. "There's been an accident. Man from the coaching inn rode to tell us."

"An accident." The marquis's voice was steady, but his hand clutched the cane until his knuckles were white. "My son?"

"Yes, my lord. The earl was hurt bad. They're bringing them back now. Should be here directly."

The man looked around as if waiting for orders, but no one said anything. Even Dalton seemed stunned, unable to speak.

"What should I do, my lord?" the man asked.

"I do not know," the marquis said. Suddenly an old man, he seemed to shrink in his chair as the enormity of what had happened closed in upon him.

"Go tell Mrs. Sandles what you know," Priscilla said after a minute, when no one else spoke. She had no wish to put herself forward at this time, but none of the Connaughts seemed able to act.

The young man looked around a little helplessly, unsure of what the marquis wanted done. "Do what she tells you, boy," the old man said, his hand covering his eyes.

Priscilla followed the footman out and proceeded to confer with the housekeeper. They prepared as quickly as they could for the arrival of the injured. They had time to gather blankets, brandy, and hot water. It was fully fifteen minutes later when the rattle of wheels on the carriage way announced an arrival.

"Go and see what help they need carrying them in," said Priscilla, when the young man stood as if frozen. She should not be here, and here she was ordering everyone around as if she knew what she was doing. Why did she have to put herself forward, as if she were the mistress of the house? Why was everyone else standing about waiting to be told what to do?

Two men entered, carrying Granville. He lay in their arms as limp as a discarded doll. Priscilla felt her stomach begin to revolt as soon as she saw the blood seeping through his coat.

She hated the sight of blood. It always made her want to faint. Her mother had told her this was a perfectly proper response, that all young ladies should react that way. It showed their delicacy, how unfit they were to experience the rough side of life.

Yet here she stood, she thought rebelliously, while everyone else stood like statues, their eyes turned to her as if she knew what to do. She snatched up a blanket and lay it on the floor. "Put him down and go fetch the doctor," she said, amazed at the cool sound of her own voice. "Where is Miss Allison-Hyatt?"

"Jem and Fred's bringing her in. Had to get a door from one of the sheds. 'Pears she has a broken leg. Leastwise it's turned at a angle."

Priscilla knelt down beside the earl's broken figure. Uncertain what to do, she dabbed at his blood-stained face. Two men appeared in the doorway, bearing a board with the slight figure of Hester.

Sir Peter hurried forward, all but wringing his hands. It occurred to Priscilla that he was totally useless, for all his self-importance and bluster, in a moment like this. His wife fluttered in the background, saying nothing, doing nothing.

Well, if her parents would not, it would seem she would have to. "Take Miss Allison-Hyatt up. Mrs. Sandles will direct you." Priscilla nodded to the housekeeper, who had brought clean cloths to be used to wipe away the blood. Thank God for someone useful.

The plump, black-clad figure beckoned the young man carrying Hester forward, and they began to ascend the stairs.

"Do not remove her from the board," Mrs. Sandles said. "Just lay it on the bed."

Priscilla turned back to the earl and began to try to loosen his cravat when an awful suspicion formed in her mind. She looked up to see the marquis moving slowly forward, leaning heavily on his cane, his face a gray mask of sternly repressed emotion.

"Is he dead?" he said, his voice a rasp.

Priscilla, whose emotions had frozen under the onslaught of the past half hour, opened her mouth to reply that she had no idea—she had never seen a dead body—when the great front door opened for the third time.

A figure in a swirling greatcoat stood silhouetted in the evening light. A glance and she knew who it was. She froze, on her knees next to the earl, as her heart skipped and her head pounded a rapid beat. He had come back.

Priscilla dragged her attention from the silhouette in the doorway, her emotions warring within her, wanting to hold him, wanting to strike him. Wanting him to feel the pain she had felt all these long months. Gritting her teeth, she turned her attention back to Granville, bathing the blood from his ashen face.

"What is going on?" Nicholas asked. "Cilla? Grandfather?"

Priscilla ignored his sharp, accusatory tone. She had more than enough to cope with. An unreasonably angry Nicholas would simply have to wait.

The marquis was staring at her. She could see he had not fully realized Nicholas was here. The old man focused on her and her hands, now dotted with the blood from Granville's wounds.

"Is he . . ." His voice cracked.

"Yes," she whispered to the marquis, pity all but swamping her, thickening her throat till she could hardly speak. "I am afraid he is dead. I am so sorry, sir."

The marquis moved forward. Dalton appeared at his side, lending a little help. Dalton, too, looked stunned. His throat was working, but he said nothing.

"Take him into the small parlor," the marquis said, his head lowered.

The men, who had waited on the fringes of the family group that had gathered in the hall, obeyed without a word. For a long moment, the hall remained silent. Everyone was still, absorbing the shock of Granville's sudden death. Priscilla still knelt on the marble floor, afraid to rise for fear her knees would not hold her.

"Was there a coachman driving?" the marquis asked one of the men who had carried the earl in.

"No, sir. Seems like the earl, he was driving."

The marquis shook his head. "He never could drive. Cow-handed. Used the whip." His voice was calm, but his hand shook as he swiped it in front of his face. "Poor boy. He never was the slightest use. Poor boy." He turned and began to walk slowly, almost haltingly, toward the stairs.

"Perhaps a tray in my room, Miss Harrowby," he said as he passed her.

"I will see to it, my lord." The old man looked gray and frozen, and Priscilla's heart ached with pity. She had no idea what to do about any of this. She wanted to continue to ignore Nicholas, who had all but shattered her composure by his attitude.

"Grandfather." Nicholas's soft word echoed in the silent room.

The old man paused and turned, grief and sorrow etched on his features. He gave a fleeting grimace that might have been a smile. "Dalt . . ." The marquis struggled to clear his throat. "Dalton, you will see to my grandson." The marquis looked back at Nicholas from the foot of the staircase. "You will forgive me for not welcoming you, my boy?"

"Of course, sir." Nicholas's voice held the warmth of true affection and a wealth of pity for the old man's loss. "If there is anything you want of me, please ask."

Dalton moved over to the door, where Nicholas still stood. "If you would care to come in, my lord."

Nicholas turned around, looking for the lord behind him. Then it struck him all at once. Granville was dead, and that meant more than a heartache for an old man who had already had too many. It meant he, Nicholas Cannon, was an earl. My God.

Moving automatically, he stepped farther into the room and shrugged off his coat. He turned to Dalton and gave a small smile. "I wish you would go up to my grandfather, Dalton. He looked very tired."

Dalton smiled, his eyes still serious, filled with concern for the marquis. "Thank you, my lord. I will go right away." He hurried off.

Nicholas turned to the rest of the family, all huddled now close to the drawing room doors. "What happened?" He looked at their more than usually festive garb and said, "Were you having a party?"

Elinor's Aunt Margaret stepped forward. "Yes. We were going to celebrate Granville's engagement, but—"

Something in his face must have given him away.

Margaret stepped back, silenced. Nicholas turned to look at Priscilla. She had risen to her feet and stood now, talking to one of the footmen in low tones.

"Assuming your duties already, Cilla?" he said, trying to avoid a sneer. "I am sorry to disappoint you, but your services as countess will not be required." He could almost feel the rage boil and hiss inside him like lava from a volcano. Never had he felt so angry or so betrayed. He loved her, damn it. How could she?

She glared at him, and he realized her eyes were glazed with shock. "I am only trying to help the family. I am going up to Miss Allison-Hyatt now. Would you please send the doctor up when he arrives?" She spoke to the footmen. "And be sure the marquis's tray is carried up promptly so it does not grow cold." With that, she turned on her heel and hurried over to the stairs.

"Who the devil is Miss Austin-Bryant?" he asked the room in general.

There was silence for a minute, as if the simplest question threw all the Connaughts into a panic. Then Elinor's voice, clear and precise, broke the silence and doused Nicholas's anger. "Miss Hester Allison-Hyatt was Cousin Granville's fiancée," she said. "They were eloping and the carriage overturned. She is upstairs, unconscious but not dead."

Elinor's Aunt Margaret, apparently thinking it unseemly that a mere schoolgirl should answer the new earl's questions, and in such a calm manner, spoke up at last. "I know we are all deeply grieved at Granville's death." Everyone nodded solemnly. Margaret continued, "However, you must be hungry after your journey, and dinner is prepared and waiting. If you would like, we could eat now. My lord," she added, her mouth pursed as if the words hurt her.

As they probably did, he thought. An evening with his Connaught relations deferring to him, calling him sir and bowing and scraping to him because he had succeeded to a courtesy title, was not an attractive thought. He had always found the idea of cheering a new king the moment the old one died ghoulish and coldhearted.

He nodded. "Why do you not go in? I believe I will go to my room and later visit my grandfather. I will see you all in the morning."

Once in his room, he realized he had done himself out of a fine dinner just so he could escape his relations. Well, there was no help for it. He would wash and go along to the marquis's room. At least he could see to the frail old man's comfort, if he could not gain his own. Going to bed hungry would serve him right. How could he have behaved so boorishly to Priscilla, who was obviously the mainstay of the household? Though how that had come about if Granville was engaged to another young lady had him puzzled.

A few minutes later, he tapped on his grandfather's door and entered softly. Dalton was standing by the bed, while the marquis sat propped up on the usual pile of pillows. He was picking at a tray of what smelled to Nicholas like heaven.

"Come in, my boy." The voice was dry and almost cracked. "I find I cannot work up an appetite for the delicious food Miss Harrowby planned."

"Perhaps a glass of claret, my lord?" Dalton suggested.

"I would be pleased to join you, grandfather," Nicholas said. He was disturbed by the pale, gray cast to the marquis's features. A glass of wine would do him good.

Dalton smiled and hurried over to a cabinet in a corner of the room where he had placed a decanter and glasses. He filled two and handed them to Nicholas and the marquis.

Nicholas gazed soberly at his grandfather over the rim of his glass. "I seem to have arrived at a very bad time."

"No, no, you can help with the arrangements. Granville will be buried here next to his mother, with space left for me." He twirled his glass between his fingers, staring pensively down at the rich red wine. "I will not keep them waiting long, I fancy."

Before Nicholas could reply, his grandfather raised his eyes. "I think you had better marry that Miss Harrowby. I know she's just a middle-class girl, but she certainly knows how to run a household like this. Has the servants eating out of her hand."

Nicholas leaned forward, consumed with curiosity. "What is she doing running your house, sir?"

"I think Granville hired her to plan the engagement party," the marquis said. "You are staring at my plate. Do have some of the roast squab."

Nicholas watched as the old man sighed, looking out the window at the dark night. His voice was flat and cheerless, yet Nicholas could see his color was beginning to return.

He pushed the plate toward Nicholas. "I am sure it is good. We had it a night or two ago. Miss Harrowby said we had to try out the menu to see if it would serve."

Nicholas remained fixed on Priscilla. He did not

care a rap for poultry. "He *hired* her? How can that be?"

The marquis shrugged. "I have not the least idea, my boy. You must ask her. And while you are at it, ask about the Allison-Hyatt girl. The doctor should be here by now."

"I will tell you in the morning, sir. You should get some sleep now, I think."

He rose and took his grandfather's hand. The marquis gripped his with a surprisingly strong clasp. "You will stay with me, Nicholas, won't you?"

"Yes, sir, of course I will. And I will bring my family. They are at Claridge's. I will send for them tomorrow, if you do not object." There was still a little doubt in Nicholas's heart as to whether his grandfather really would accept his mother and siblings into his home.

"I will write them myself, my boy, asking that they come as soon as possible." The marquis released his hand and leaned back against the pillows, closing his eyes. "Good night, Nicholas."

"Good night, sir." On impulse, he bent and kissed the marquis's forehead.

"Good night, my lord," Dalton said from the doorway.

"I wish you would not call me that," Nicholas said impatiently.

"You had best get used to it, my lord," Dalton replied with a stern look.

"Oh, God." It was true. He could not bear it. His mind in turmoil, Nicholas left the room.

Where was Priscilla?

Seventeen

Priscilla found Hester Allison-Hyatt lying, pale and still unconscious, on the board that had been placed on her bed. Either the men who had carried her up or Mrs. Sandles had placed her hands crossed on her breast, as if she had died.

"Put a lily in her hands why don't you, for heaven's sake!" Priscilla went to the washstand and poured water in the basin. The least she could do was clean the poor girl's face and uncross her hands before her parents came in and thought she'd died a horrible death.

When she took the cloth over to wipe Hester's face, Priscilla saw what looked like tear stains on her cheeks under the dirt. She prayed Granville had not ruined his last moments on earth by being unkind to this sensitive young girl who loved him. As she bent over, Hester's eyes fluttered open.

"Priscilla?" she breathed, her voice a thread of sound.

"Yes, Hester, it is Priscilla."

"I hurt so much. What happened? Am I at Bellingham Place?" Hester asked as tears began to leak out of her eyes.

Gently, Priscilla wiped them away. "Yes, dear. There has been an accident. We are waiting for the doctor to

come and look at you. Let me take your slippers off
and pull this quilt over you."

She suited the action to the words all the while sending up a silent prayer: *Please, do not let her ask about
Granville yet. Let her wait to ask the doctor or her
mother these impossible questions. Please! I am really
no good at this, Lord.*

Priscilla worked as carefully as she could, but Hester
gave a tiny gasp of pain when she removed the right
shoe.

"Does that hurt very badly, Hester?"

Hester shook her head. "Not if I keep it very still.
Granville is dead, isn't he, Priscilla?" There was a
wealth of sadness in the small voice.

"Yes, dear, he is. I am so sorry." Pity wrung Priscilla's heart at the sight of the small, woebegone figure.
She sat on the side of the bed and took Hester's hand
in hers.

Hester's lip trembled, and her hand closed on Priscilla's convulsively. "He did not love me, you know.
He was very angry at the horses and just before the
carriage turned over he told me he did not know why
he was going to all this trouble to marry a—a dormouse like me." Tears shimmered in Hester's eyes, and
Priscilla damned the late earl of Ashden to perdition.

She had to comfort this girl, and she said the first
words that came into her head. "Granville had a very
bad temper, Hester. He often said things he did not
mean in the heat of anger. Ask any member of the
family." Priscilla could only hope she sounded con-
vincing. There was no reason why Hester should go
through life believing Granville's last hurtful words.

"Really?" Hester looked hopeful and Priscilla
smiled down at her.

"Really. Ask anyone."

There was a knock on the door. When Priscilla called out to enter, a large, somewhat untidy man in a rumpled black coat came into the room and introduced himself as Dr. Matheson. He quickly examined Hester and determined that her leg was broken. He had splints and bandages in his carriage and he asked that Priscilla remain to help keep the patient quiet.

How could she keep Hester quiet, Priscilla wondered, when she herself was going to scream and go into strong hysterics at any moment? She could not do this. She hated pain. They would have to find someone else. Someone strong and invincible, like Lucinda. She simply could not do things like this.

But, like everything else this nightmarish evening, she found she could do it. It seemed she could do whatever she had to. It helped that Hester was very brave, giving only one sharp cry when the doctor moved her leg to set the bone straight. Priscilla was proud she had neither screamed nor fainted. She must remember to tell Lucinda.

The doctor seemed more concerned about the head injury than with her limb for, as he told Priscilla in a low voice when he was about to leave, one could never tell about the brain. He said he could not give Hester morphine because of that, and told her Hester would not experience great pain so long as she was kept quiet. Once a long bone was set, he told her, the pain would subside rather rapidly. By morning, she should feel much better. He recommended someone sit up with the patient this night. If there were no complications, then she might get up and sit in a chair for several hours.

Just as the doctor left, the Allison-Hyatts appeared.

Priscilla was surprised they had not been with their daughter all through her ordeal, but she welcomed them in. When she tried to slip away, however, all three asked her to stay. A little surprised, she agreed.

It took only a few minutes for her to realize Sir Peter dominated the family. His loud, braying voice rode over the softer, sweeter sounds of his wife and daughter. Even when they could be heard, he paid no attention to him.

He did not ask about what the doctor had done for his daughter's injuries. He did not inquire about how she felt. He did not comfort her after the tragic outcome of her elopement.

Instead, he ranted about what a bad girl she was, how ill-judged her behavior, how difficult it would be to find her a husband now. While Lady Allison-Hyatt looked unhappy and chirped ineffectually from time to time, she did nothing to stem the tide. Thoroughly under her husband's thumb, Priscilla decided.

After five minutes of this, Hester was looking drawn and miserable. Priscilla pasted a smile on her face and turned with false concern to the Allison-Hyatts.

"The doctor has ordered rest for Hester. He limited all her visits to five minutes. You can come back tomorrow."

"Humph." Sir Peter was not happy at the suggestion, but he was not at ease in the sickroom either. He left with considerable ill grace.

"Did the doctor really say that?" Hester asked.

"No, it was my idea," Priscilla confessed with a rueful grimace. "I only thought you needed to rest and your father was giving you the headache."

Hester smiled gratefully. "If only I could live here. It was not so much Granville as the idea of—"

"Getting away from your family. I know. I think many girls marry for just that reason. Do not worry. Your leg will keep you here for a while. And after your leg heals, we will think of something else."

Priscilla heard her own confident words and could have bitten her tongue. She had no way to guarantee Hester could stay. The Connaughts in all probability would wish her gone as soon as possible. She would be a reminder of a terrible day.

"I will stay with you tonight," Priscilla said. "But I had better go down now and find you some dinner. I hope the family ate the dinner I planned, but I hope they left a little, too. I think just broth and tea for you. That's what my cousin Lucinda always gives invalids. I will have it sent up. Gillie can come in and sit with you while I am gone."

No sooner had she shut the door behind her than Nicholas appeared before her like a figure in a dream. "Priscilla, I must talk to you. You have to listen to me."

That peremptory tone sounded to her ears exactly like the one Sir Peter used to his wife and child. Priscilla could feel her hackles rise. She had put up with a great deal this day, and she was not going to have the man who left her without a word issuing orders. It was the last straw!

"I have things to see to," she said, her voice shaking a little. "And I do not *have* to listen to you. I am not, thank heavens, married to you and I do not *have* to do *anything* just because you say so!"

Her crumpled blue silk skirts swirled, her crinoline and petticoats flashing around her ankles, and Priscilla was gone at a run, leaving Nicholas staring after her. Good! Let him stare. Men! Granville eloping with that foolish girl upstairs, Sir Peter bellowing, and now Nicholas ordering her to listen to him! Not a word about how tired she must be, how worried, how well she had handled everything. *Beast!*

Downstairs everything was going much better than she expected. She had thought the Connaughts would be upset, that at least some tears would be shed for Granville, who, after all had been a part of their family and their lives. But it was not so. Under the capable leadership of Mrs. Sandles, the elegant meal had been served and cleared away. Drinks and sandwiches were available on the sideboard and tea was being served in the drawing room.

Life, in short, was going on for the Connaughts very much as if the earl of Ashden, their cousin, was not lying dead in a nearby room. Priscilla found it very odd. She would cry for anyone in her family—even Jeffrey.

Elinor's Aunt Margaret was taking charge in the drawing room. And about time, too, in Priscilla's estimation. No woman had taken charge of this barracks since the marchioness died many years before.

No wonder it was so cheerless and, until she came, clean but not sparkling and far from comfortable. Now it sparkled. She had caused some of the furniture to be rearranged into more congenial groups.

She paused on her inspection tour to congratulate herself on a job well done. When she left tomorrow, she would leave a much improved home for Nicholas—*that beast!*—to come to.

She slipped into the kitchen. There she found the staff gathered around the long table, subdued and quiet. They were eating what was left of the dinner. They all stood respectfully as she came in. There were tears in some eyes as she told them how well they had behaved under such very trying circumstances, how much help they had been.

"I am sure the new earl will be down himself to thank you tomorrow," she said, making a mental note to order—yes, *order!*—Nicholas to do so. She issued orders for tea and broth to be taken up to Hester.

Back upstairs, she paused in the dining room and, realizing she was hungry, took a sandwich and bit into it thankfully. She sank into a chair near the sideboard and ate with relief. Only a few more hours, and then she could go home! Surely Lady Allison-Hyatt would want to stay to take care of her daughter. Priscilla was feeling more and more like an interloper, and she was sure the Connaughts would be glad to see the last of her before the funeral. Good. Back to London. She tried to be glad, but instead found herself sunk in gloom.

She did not want to stay. Granville's death and the marquis's tough but heartbroken reaction had moved her deeply. She might have stayed to help him, but she could not stay now that Nicholas had come back.

She wasn't still in love with Nicholas Cannon—no, she must not forget. He was the earl of Ashden now. Well, all the more reason. She was not in love with the earl of Ashden. Was she? What a humiliating thought. If he did not wish to marry her when he was plain Nicholas Cannon, American businessman, how much less he would wish to marry her now that he had a title and was the heir to a greater one.

She looked around for something to drink. There was a decanter and, next to it, a seltzer bottle. She looked around her, a mischievous thought coming full-blown into her head.

Why not? She had always wanted to try a brandy and soda. Why not now? No one would see her. The gentlemen were all in the billiard room and the ladies were taking late evening tea in the drawing room.

She found a big crystal tumbler and splashed brandy into it. Then she pushed the top of the seltzer container and watched it fizz into her glass.

She sat down and took a sip. *Rather good,* she thought. It warmed her. Feeling warm and relaxed for the first time since that awful scene in the hallway, she took another bite of her sandwich, then another sip of the brandy and soda. Delicious! She quite liked it. Why did ladies not drink it, she wondered. It was much more warming than lemonade. She stretched her toes out in front of her and wiggled them as she sipped.

"What the hell do you think you are doing?" It was Nicholas's voice, harsh and strained.

"Eating supper," she replied, unperturbed by his visible anger. Her hostess's concerns got the better of her fear and anger with him. "Have you eaten? The sandwiches are really quite good."

Without a word, Nicholas helped himself to a sandwich and a brandy and soda. He sat down opposite her. "What the hell are you drinking?"

"That is not very hospitable," she said, still feeling quite warm and happy. "No way for an earl to treat his guests."

"And why the hell are you a guest here?"

"That is not very kind. You are becoming a boor." She was enjoying herself. Correcting Nicholas was fun. She took another sip. "This is brandy and soda. I rather like it."

"I can see that." Nicholas smiled, that crooked half

smile he had when he saw a secret joke. "How much have you had?"

"Just this glass, though I am considering another."

She smiled at him, feeling quite in charity with him for the first time since he had left. The brandy made life look rather fuzzy around the edges, but definitely pleasant.

"Why did you leave without me?" she asked, sincerely wanting to satisfy her curiosity, emotions swathed in the fumes of brandy. No wonder people drank. You did not forget what pained you, but it ceased to cause you pain.

Nicholas paled and then turned red. "I left you a letter explaining that my mother had scarlet fever."

"Left it with my mother?" She was not angry, just curious, seeking information. She drained her glass. "That was silly. You must have known I'd never see it."

"I wrote you again once I was home. Then I got scarlet fever." Nicholas got up and moved to the sideboard.

"Get me another while you are up," Priscilla asked.

"You have had enough, Miss Harrowby," he said. "Gentlemen do not let ladies become inebriated in their homes."

"Pish and tush," Priscilla said. "I do not think I am a lady anymore. I work, you know." She nodded sagely and gazed up at him. "So you do not need to worry. Give me another brandy and soda."

"No. Tell me about your work. I did not know of it." He sounded strained but interested.

"You could have, if you had cared to. No. I have to get back to Hester. I promised I would stay with her. I do not wish to talk to you. You left me without a word and you stayed away for months. We cannot be friends. I think I detest you." That seemed to say everything. She was pleased with herself. They would not have to talk any more.

She rose to her feet, and found she was not feeling quite so steady. Happy that she could walk, for her head was beginning to spin just a trifle, Priscilla made her way carefully to the stairs, leaving Nicholas with no opportunity to speak for the second time that night.

Hester was asleep, her dinner tray on the table beside the bed. Gillie was smoothing the bed clothes over her when Priscilla entered the room. "Miss!" Gillie was shocked. "Have you been drinking?"

"How did you know?" Priscilla was a little guilty. Well-brought-up young ladies did not drink brandy. Ever.

"My dad used to smell like you do!" Gillie shook her head. "With all you've had to contend with, Miss, I'm not surprised. I think my mum took a nip or two on occasion!"

Priscilla smiled. She was forgiven.

"I will sit with Miss Allison-Hyatt, Gillie. I do not think she will awaken, but the doctor wants someone here in case she does and does not remember where she is."

"Very well, miss. But you need sleep yourself. Why not put on this nice wrapper I brought from your room and pull the chair up to the bed? You can cuddle yourself in this nice blanket." Gillie moved the chair and handed Priscilla an afghan knit in soft blue wool.

Gratefully, Priscilla allowed Gillie to help her remove her dress and the complicated undergarments that went with it. When her stays were released and she stepped out of her high-heeled evening slippers, she gave a sigh of relief. She sank down on the chair and leaned back. There was physical relief, but the warm, fuzzy feeling the brandy had given her was beginning to seep away and she found herself tired and depressed. What a horrible day! What a ghastly way for anyone to die, even the earl of Ashden. And poor Hester!

And poor Priscilla, too, if it came to that. She had not hated her second visit to Bellingham Place, although it was far from the romantic idyll the first one had been. But now with Granville's death and Nicholas's return, she felt her anomalous position as both employee and guest and wanted to be gone.

Nicholas. He looked wonderful. Thinner than he had before, more careworn, his eyes tired. Perhaps he *had* been sick.

Not that illness was an excuse for leaving her without a word for months and months when she might have been pregnant. No, it did not matter to her in the slightest that he looked wonderful and virile and that she was sure he was as full of life and humor as ever, once he recovered from scarlet fever. He had deserted her. That was all that mattered.

For some reason, reaching that conclusion, though she was sure it was the right one, did not cheer her. She opened her eyes and stared into the darkness. Here she was, a semi-servant in this house, in love with the new master, who had seduced and abandoned her. Every female servant's nightmare, and for her it had come true.

She tossed her head, trying to dislodge the thoughts that plagued her. Once she returned to London, she would see things differently. She could continue her work. Her father would continue his partnership with

Jeffrey. She had friends. She had her work and her father. It would be enough.

Oh, Nicholas, why didn't you love me? Why? Was Jeffrey right, was she just a frivolous, brainless creature, no good to anyone? How much better Lucinda would have handled this evening's events. Calm, competent, always in charge—

Priscilla slept.

Nicholas did not know how long he sat over the decanter of brandy and a plate of sandwiches. He had lost his appetite, knowing what Priscilla thought of him.

In vino veritas. His father had told him what that saying meant and now he understood exactly. Priscilla had told him he was every kind of cad, and she was right. That was the horrifying thing—she was absolutely right. He never should have left without her. Never. Another day would have made no difference. His mother was on the road to recovery when he left and was all but well when he got home.

But what if she had been dying? What if one day later had meant he would not be there to say good-bye? That thought had filled his mind from the moment he got word his mother was ill. Still, he should have waited to take Priscilla with him as he had planned.

Because what was he going to do without Priscilla? Bad enough when he had only to go back to New York and try to make a life without her. But now he had this entire, unknown new life ahead of him, filled with people he did not know and did not wish to know and duties he did not understand. Without the woman he loved beside him, he didn't know how he could face it. All his freedom, gone. Everything he and his father had built, abandoned.

His mind twisted and turned for a while, trying to find a way out.

He could renounce the title, stay in America. But then he would be sentencing Marcus to take his place, and it would be no easier for him than for Nicholas. If Marcus renounced as well, the title would go to one of the cousins, none of whom had the wit or grit to do it.

If he renounced the title, would his grandfather follow through on his threat to leave him the money and estates, knowing Nicholas would feel duty bound to take care of the family property—and the family?

Oh, damn. The future loomed ahead of him, full of responsibility and boredom. He needed Priscilla with him. From the way his grandfather reacted to her, she knew how to handle the family and the house. If only he could make her listen, make her understand.

He had been so worried about his mother, and Marcus and Melinda, too. Perhaps no one but another immigrant could understand how important family was. And how small his family was! He had never met his grandparents or aunts or uncles or cousins. He had just his parents and his siblings. And they had been threatened by this disease. He could have lost them all in the space of a few days—a few days when he wasn't there.

Could Priscilla understand that? Priscilla, whose family was not affectionate, whose parents did not seem to care whether or not she was around them? And if she could understand, would she care? He had left her, had not been in touch with her—to her mind, had abandoned her.

He hadn't, of course. He had missed her every minute, had thought longingly of her every day. He had tried to write until he had received Jeffrey's letter with Lucinda's teasing little postscript. Then the poison of his relationship with Helen had started to work on his brain. Jeffrey thought Priscilla a silly, mercenary creature, as Helen had been. Somehow, once he was away from her, that doubt began to seem more and more acceptable.

He looked into his heart. Did he doubt her still? Now that he had a title and vast riches to offer her, did he believe those were the things that mattered to her?

No, now that he should doubt, he did not. If Priscilla married him, it would be for love. If she did not—but that did not bear thinking of.

Nicholas looked at the glass of brandy in his hand as if he had never seen it before. Then he tossed it off and got to his feet. He would sleep and then he would deal with his grandfather's sorrow, the practicalities of a funeral, the needs of this new burdensome family.

Somewhere in all that he would find time to woo the woman he loved.

Eighteen

The next morning Nicholas lay in wait for Priscilla in the breakfast room, but to no avail. He drank endless cups of weak coffee, reminding himself with every swallow to ask his mother to teach these heathens how to make it properly. There would have to be some changes made in the household if he were to survive early mornings in England.

He paused, his cup halfway to his lips. Had he then already decided to take up the challenge? Was he going to stay in this alien land of his fathers?

He had no answer to that question. Perhaps, he thought, he could arrange a compromise with his grandfather—agree to manage the money while refusing the title. He could manage money with no difficulty from New York. A trip to England, perhaps two trips, every year, and he could discharge his responsibilities.

Because without Priscilla, he could not take on the task of being the marquis of Bellingham. By himself it was impossible. And marrying anyone but Priscilla was equally impossible.

Where was she? It seemed to him he spent the better part of his life waiting for Priscilla. He wanted her where he could always talk to her, be with her. Feel her.

The memory of their night together swept over him. He had managed to hold it at bay since those nights on board ship when, on his way back to her, he had allowed his mind to recall every kiss and touch. The feel of her skin, the look in her eyes—vulnerable, open. And he had betrayed that trust.

Priscilla entered the room, talking to Elinor, who was right behind her.

"Good morning, Cousin Nicholas," said Elinor. "Or should I say, 'my lord'?"

"Don't you dare," Nicholas responded, with a welcoming smile for the only member of the Connaught family he liked. His grandfather he respected, even loved, but Elinor he felt was his friend.

"Good morning, Priscilla," he said, his smile turning tentative and pleading.

She ignored him. "After I leave this afternoon, you will look in on Hester, won't you, Elinor?" she said. "I think you two could be friends. She hasn't many, I don't think."

Leaving? She couldn't leave. He would be tied up here for weeks, probably, no matter what he decided about the title. He could not leave his grandfather to cope alone. But he needed Priscilla with him.

"I would like to talk with you, Priscilla. In private."

She raised her eyebrows. She was totally in command of herself this morning, but no less angry and hurt. She simply was not going to reveal it. "I do not believe I will have the time, my lord." Ice crystals formed around the words. "Before I leave."

"It is very important."

"To you, perhaps. I, on the other hand, cannot think of anything you could say to me that would interest me in the slightest."

There was a muffled gasp from Elinor. Then he heard her hurry away and close the door after her. Good girl, she knew when to leave.

He could apologize, explain—or try to. But that should come after. He should say the most important thing first, take the biggest chance of his life. Give her the opportunity to destroy him once and for all. He took a deep breath.

"I love you, Priscilla. I want you to marry me."

He could see he had disarmed her. She had expected arguments, excuses. Now her face did not look angry, it looked anguished. But in the end he lost his gamble.

"No." No explanations, no accusations, nothing he could try to argue away.

"Please, Priscilla. I need you. Now more than ever." Instinctively, his hands reached for her. "And I love you. Now more than ever."

She shook her head and bit down on her lower lip. Still, it trembled and she turned away, taking a deep breath, her shoulders hunched.

"Please, Priscilla, take a walk with me. Talk with me. Tell me how you feel, tell me what you have done since I left. Be as angry as you must, but come with me, tell me. Don't shut me out." He cast about for something more to say, but nothing occurred to him except, "I am sorry, love. I hurt you. I did not mean to, but I did, I know I did, and I am so sorry."

"Go away."

"I wish I could." He meant it. "But I must stay, at least for a while, and I want you to stay with me."

That seemed to make her mind up. "No."

She turned and faced him then, for he stood between her and the door. She drew herself up to her full height and said, with terrible dignity and finality, "Let me go."

He had no choice. He could only talk to her. He could not physically force her. He stood aside.

"If I have to follow you to London, I will, Cilla. You cannot run away from me forever, love. You will have to listen to me, and talk to me sometime."

She fled.

Dalton found him in the library half an hour later, turning the pages of a book he was not looking at. He accompanied Dalton to his grandfather's room.

The marquis looked older today. Nicholas did not have the heart to tell him he was not sure he could bear the burden life had handed him. He went over to the bed and took the old man's hand in both of his.

"Grandfather, I am so sorry about Granville. It must be a terrible loss."

"Yes. I have suffered great losses. Losing your father. Being too foolish to welcome his chosen bride. Great losses indeed, my boy." There was a wealth of sadness in his face. The brown eyes were dull today, as if nothing could interest him anymore.

"Well, you will have a chance to make up for disapproving of my mother," Nicholas said. "I have written her, and she and my brother and sister should be here by nightfall."

His grandfather only smiled at him. "I know how you have dreaded this day, but now that it is here, I must ask you to help me. No matter how you feel about the family or the English aristocracy in general, I cannot get about as I ought. You will have to speak with the vicar and with the family. The funeral will be private, but notices must be sent to the *Times*."

Nicholas nodded. He knew he had to face the responsibility, even if only for a little while, and help his grandfather. "Yes, I will do everything that is necessary. My mother can help. We had to do much the same things for my father last year. Perhaps Margaret will be able to help until my mother arrives."

"Margaret! She cares for nothing but marrying her daughters off as soon as possible. A head stuffed with feathers! No, she cannot help. Her niece, now, Elinor, she might be of some use."

Nicholas was surprised at how much his grandfather knew about all the members of his large family. "I will ask her. I am sure she will be available for the rest of the day until my mother arrives. We will do the best we can."

"Thank you, my boy. I find I am not as able as I once was to rule. And believe me, without someone in charge, the family will go to rack and ruin." He stared straight at Nicholas, and now his eyes were snapping with life again. His family could do that, make him come to life, ready to do whatever was necessary to keep the Connaughts functioning.

"They ought to learn to be self-sufficient, grandfather." Nicholas did not relish spending the rest of his life as a glorified nanny to a family of people who had never been required to shoulder any responsibility.

"A lovely idea, my boy. But very difficult to implement."

"You control the purse strings, do you not?"

"Yes. As is customary, the head of the family controls the family fortune." The marquis looked up at Nicholas. "What do you intend to do about it?"

Nicholas shrugged. He was not sure as yet, but he certainly was going to do something. He wanted to travel with Priscilla, visit all sorts of places, go to New York to spend time with Marcus and Melinda. He did not plan to be tethered here by the needs of the Connaughts.

"I am not sure yet. But rest assured I will do something. Parcel out some of the money and cut them off from the rest."

"I tried that. Everyone got in trouble, some with the law, some with other families. They all had to be rescued."

Nicholas gave the marquis a grim smile. "No, they did not. You chose to, to save the family name. But I do not care about the family name. I care that individuals learn to survive on their own."

His grandfather stared at him for a moment. Then a reluctant smile played about his lips, and he said, "Go away, my boy. You tire me with your theories. It is time for my nap. Dalton! Move my pillows, please."

Nicholas received the vicar in the drawing room and interviewed several of the younger cousins in the study later. They wanted to be sure their tuition would be paid. They did not want to risk any interruption of their lives at university because of Granville's death.

Nicholas was not the scholar Marcus was, but he had graduated from Columbia College in New York while working at his father's business. These young sprigs did not seem to spend a great deal of their time studying. He made a note to see about curtailing their allowances depending on their grades.

It still lacked an hour until noon when a rattle

sounded on the drive below the study windows. Nicholas, who had dismissed the last of his feckless younger cousins, looked down to see who had come now. The vicar and the undertaker had already come. Who could this be?

Then he saw and his face cleared as if by magic. He was downstairs in a series of bounds and outside before his mother had put a foot on the steps leading to the front door. The sun was warm on his face and he regretted the morning spent dealing with the family. He regretted Priscilla was not here to be introduced as his promised bride.

But he was happy to see his family, particularly his mother.

He swung her into his arms and twirled her around. "Oh, you cannot know how happy I am to see you," he said fervently. "These people will drive me mad before they're through."

Jean chuckled. "Well, we just won't let them, laddie. Come, Melinda, Marcus. We are here. Your father's family home."

Marcus looked around at the enormous house and whistled. "Whew. No wonder he wanted to leave."

Nicholas grinned at his irrepressible younger brother and, linking arms with him, turned to wait for Melinda to join them. She was craning her neck to look at the roof. Her bonnet fell down her back, only the blue silk ribbons holding it on. She linked her arm with Nicholas's so she and Marcus flanked him.

"Let them try to ride roughshod over you, Mr. Nicholas Cannon, Earl of Whatever. You have your family here now." She grinned up at him.

"Everybody in that castle is my family," he replied with a rueful smile. "More's the pity!"

"We'll lick them into shape!" said Melinda.

"I would like to freshen up a bit, and then I would like to meet your grandfather." Jean's quiet voice put an end to their foolishness.

"Of course, Mother. And there is someone I would like you to meet."

"The girl." Jean smiled at him. "I would be delighted."

Jean met "the girl" before she had a chance to greet the man who had disowned her husband. As the housekeeper was leading her down a long hallway toward what she hoped was a bedroom where she could wash the travel dust from her face, one of the doors lining the wall opened and one of the prettiest creatures Jean had ever seen came out.

"Mrs. Sandles," the golden girl said, "I think Miss Allison-Hyatt needs some tea or barley water. Something to drink. I wish my cousin were here. She would know what to do."

Peering down the hall, into the sunlight that poured through the bull's-eye mirror at the end, the girl discerned another figure behind Mrs. Sandles. "Oh, I beg your pardon, I did not know anyone else was here." She gave Jean a sweet, apologetic smile. "I am sorry, should I know you? I cannot see you very well. The light is dazzling."

Jean smiled back, sure she had just met Nicholas's love. She extended her hand. "I am Jean Cannon. I expect you know my son, Nicholas."

She was encouraged to see the blush on the girl's face as she extended a hand and said, "I am Priscilla Harrowby, looking after the late earl's fiancée. She broke her leg in the accident yesterday and is still feeling sadly out of frame."

Jean nodded. "Yes, I remember when Marcus broke his leg. It was a week before he felt able to get out of bed and use his crutches. Of course, he liked being waited upon, so that could explain the last two days!"

Priscilla, who had grown very stiff after the introduction, had to smile at that.

"I will perhaps see you at luncheon, Miss Harrowby."

Priscilla nodded.

"I will look forward to it," said Jean.

"What a nice young lady," she said to Mrs. Sandles as the housekeeper ushered her into a large room, done in mahogany with hangings and window curtains in a soft shade of blue brocade.

"Yes, indeed. She has been a godsend these past few days," said Mrs. Sandles, always ready to share a confidence or two. "A shame the party can't go on, such a lot of effort she put into it. Of course, it is too bad the earl is dead." She did not sound the least bit sorry, Jean noted.

"Really?" said Jean, puzzled but unwilling to ask any questions for fear of damming the flow.

"My, yes. A wonder she is with planning and entertainment." Mrs. Sandles put Jean's portmanteau on the chest. "Well, I had best leave you now, Mrs.—Cannon. It does seem odd to call a family member by that name. Never could get used to it with Mr. Nicholas. Of course, now I won't have to, will I?" And with that the housekeeper was gone.

Jean unpacked and waited for Melinda to come in and share her impressions of the house. Then they could find their way downstairs together. When a knock came at her door, she hurried over, a smile on her face.

The figure at the door was not her fresh-faced daughter, but an elderly man with a shock of white hair and a pair of twinkling blue eyes. "Mrs. Cannon?" he said.

"Yes, I am Jean Cannon," she replied, drawing herself up.

"The marquis would like to see you, ma'am, if you would be so kind."

"Now?" Surely it was time for luncheon. Jean had only had time to gulp a cup of coffee in London before boarding the marquis's traveling coach for the journey to Bellingham Place. She was looking forward to luncheon.

"If you please, ma'am. The marquis naps directly after luncheon. He is wishful for you to eat with him so you can talk. Otherwise it would be tea time before you could meet, and he is most anxious to meet you."

The marquis of Bellingham had managed to contain his eagerness to meet her for twenty-five years. Jean did not say anything so churlish, but her expression must have revealed her doubt as to the marquis's enthusiasm.

"He is very desirous of making amends, ma'am. While he can." With that unsubtle reminder of the marquis's age, Dalton won Jean's cooperation.

A few minutes later, she stood at the entrance to the marquis's chamber. *Oh, Bart, if only you were with me now!* The thought of her late husband gave her courage, and she resolved to be a credit to him and their son, no matter what provocation his father offered her.

"My dear Mrs. Cannon! Jean!" The marquis beamed at her from the tapestry wing chair set in the window alcove. "I am delighted to meet you. So glad you could come so quickly. Nicholas needs you, I think. We all do, come to that. Come and sit down and we will have luncheon served right away."

Jean moved slowly over to meet Bart's father. That was how she always thought of him. Not the marquis, but simply a father.

"Sir," she said, extending her hand. "I am glad to meet you at last, but sorry it had to be under such circumstances."

"Yes, indeed." The brown eyes that looked intently into hers were strikingly young and amazingly shrewd. "Sit down, my dear. Dalton is going to serve us luncheon right here." He smiled. "So we can get acquainted."

"I am very sorry for your loss, sir. And I am sure Bart would be as well."

"It has been a loss," the marquis said, nodding to Dalton, who placed soup plates before them both. "Though I have to confess to you that, while I will miss Granville—who was, after all, my firstborn son— I always suspected he would not outlive me."

Taken aback by the marquis's matter-of-fact way of announcing that view, Jean could only murmur, "That must have been difficult. To see your son and believe he would not live long. Was he ill, then?"

"No, unless you consider drunkenness and inveterate gambling sicknesses. Granville was simply lacking in whatever it was that enabled Bart to persevere and prevail." The marquis began to spoon his soup, no emotion showing on his face.

"You did not like your son very much." Jean decided to return plain speaking for plain speaking.

"I loved him," the marquis said, giving her a crooked little smile that reminded her of her husband and Nicholas. "But I did not approve of him or like him. He was not a very kind man." He looked up at her then, and she could see the depth of sorrow in his eyes.

"I am very sorry," she said. Impulsively, she reached out to lay a hand over his. "You have lost both your sons now. I hope Nicholas and Marcus will help you with your sorrow."

"Ah, yes, Nicholas," the marquis said.

He nodded to Dalton, who cleared away the soup and served them each a plate of cold roast beef and salad. Jean looked at him expectantly. This was what she had come to hear—the marquis's ideas about Nicholas. She had her own ideas, but she wanted to hear his first.

"He is the earl of Ashden now," he said. "Do you know what that means?"

She had a very good idea. "Why do you not tell me?" she said gently.

"The Connaughts are one of the great families," the marquis began. "And the earl of Ashden, whoever he may be, is the heir. If he is fortunate, he is brought up at Bellingham Place and he learns the history of his family." He sighed and took a small forkful of salad, then laid it down on his plate, too intent on what he was saying to eat. "Nicholas did not have that advantage. He was not brought up here, with servants who have served the family for generations, with tenants whose great-great-grandfathers were tenants of my great-great-grandfather. It is too bad. I understand America does not have that kind of tradition. I have seen Nicholas does not value tradition as I would wish him to do."

Jean smiled. It was this kind of refusal to see the value of Nicholas's ideas that would drive him away, as it had driven his father. "No, he does not. Nor did Bart, my lord. It is not a trait limited to Americans."

"Do you think he will be willing to learn? Or will he refuse the title and go back?" There was anxiety in the question.

"Are you willing to let Nicholas be Nicholas? Or will you demand everything be done as it always has been? You cannot train a man like Nicholas the way you would a horse, you know." She placidly cut her roast beef. Before she ate she gave him some food for thought. "It is the mistake you made with Bart. You would be well-advised not to treat his son so high-handedly."

He glared at her. "You are outspoken, madam."

"Yes, I am. I find it makes things much simpler. Now we know where we stand with no time wasted. You do not have the advantage here, you see. Nicholas can simply leave and go back to America. He will still be the earl of Ashden, still be your heir. But he is rich, so you do not have the power of the purse over him to keep him here doing your bidding." She chewed her beef, swallowed, then said thoughtfully, "Of course, you would not have that power over him in any case, any more than you did over Bart. Independent young men do not like being kept on a tight leash. You lose them that way."

The marquis was turning an alarming shade of purple. Jean noted with some amusement that he was trying hard to curb his tongue. "I thank you for the advice."

"Which you have no intention of heeding." She shook her head and rose. "I cannot make you see reason, I suppose, but I do hope you will consider my ideas. I may be only a woman, and a Scottish woman at that." She smiled faintly. "But I was Bart's wife for over twenty-five years, and I have been Nicholas's mother for nearly that long, and I think I understand them both better than anyone else."

The marquis grasped the hand she held out to him and held on. "Will you help me keep Nicholas here? Will you use your influence? Whatever you have built in America cannot compare to this." His gesture was meant to include the entire estate.

She shook her head. "I would not use that argument with Nicholas, if I were you. What he has in America he and his father built. It is important and very large indeed to Nicholas. You belittle it at your peril. Good day to you, my lord." She swept out with the dignity of a royal duchess.

The marquis lowered his head. Then he looked up to meet the sympathetic gaze of Dalton, his butler and factotum. "I have lost any chance with her, have I not?"

Dalton considered. "I do not think so. Mrs. Cannon is very fair. She knows it is her son's destiny, however she may feel about it." He paused for a moment, then gave the marquis one of his rare pieces of advice. "I think you should listen to her, my lord."

"Yes," the marquis sighed. "So do I, Dalton. I am just not sure I can."

Nineteen

Nicholas knew he was the topic of every conversation anywhere in the vicinity of Bellingham Place. It made him nervous and edgy. The fact that the only person he wanted to talk to refused to speak to him and was planning to leave this very afternoon added an undercurrent of anger to the mix.

He requested his overcoat from a footman who bowed and scraped and generally made much of the new earl. Several other servants managed to find their way to the hall to see the new earl, all of which annoyed the new earl greatly. As he went outside he heard the sound of voices coming from the far end of the terrace.

Marcus and Melinda. He would know the sound anywhere. His friends. His family.

As he came up to them, he could see they were improvising a game of hopscotch on the terrace paving stones. He grinned. "Well, children, I see all the splendor of a stately English home has no effect on you ragamuffins."

Marcus grinned back at him. "Tell your baby sister it is not at all the thing to play games in such a setting. She refuses to listen to me. A little conduct, Mellie, if you please."

Melinda tapped her toe and crossed her arms in front

of her chest. She was a pretty girl, Nicholas thought, with her chestnut hair and blue eyes. But what made her memorable was her vitality and charm. The vitality was very much in evidence, he thought with a grin. The charm less so. She looked worried.

"This is an enormous pile, Nicky. And everyone seems so stiff and formal. I know the earl has just died, but nobody seemed to like him very much."

His mother's candor had been born again in Melinda.

Marcus looked at him, gave his arm a punch and said, "You do not look at all happy to have become an English lord overnight, Nick. It sounds to me as if you have fallen into a tub of butter, but you don't seem to see it!"

"Oh, Mark, for goodness sake!" Melinda gave Nicholas's arm a gentle pat and then linked hers with his. "It is a great deal of responsibility. Isn't it, Nicky?"

"People bowing and scraping, huge house, money and land and pretty girls dying to marry you. Sounds pretty soft to me!" Marcus's brown eyes danced, but Nicholas was not in the mood for his brother's teasing.

"Well, since you are so thrilled with the prospect, how would you like to take over this mausoleum and everything that goes with it, not to mention everyone in it? After all, you are next in line."

"Good lord, no. You are the one they are all busy bowing to. I could never get used to it. 'Yes, my lord.' 'No, my lord.' " Marcus shook his head. "You and our esteemed grandfather are welcome to all that. My lord," he added with a low bow and a flourish.

At that moment, Dalton emerged from the house and hurried toward them. Nicholas hurried over to the old man. "What is it, Dalton?" he asked, hoping nothing had happened to his grandfather.

"His lordship wishes to see you. And if they can spare the time, he would like to meet his other two grandchildren as well."

"Splendid idea! Come along, children," Nicholas said with a big grin. "Time to pay your respects."

Getting to the marquis's room involved a bewildering series of corridors. As they rounded one on the first floor, Nicholas spied a golden haired figure on her way into what looked like a small parlor.

"If you will excuse me," he said to his three companions. "I will meet you later. I have some important business to take care of."

A moment later, he entered the small parlor. "Good afternoon, Cilla," he said softly.

She whirled around. She was not dressed for travel, he noted, but instead wore a soft afternoon dress of a deep gray wool, in keeping with the mourning that was supposed to be taking place.

"No one misses him, do they?" he said.

"I think Hester Allison-Hyatt does," Priscilla said. "She is very low in spirits. I have tried to cheer her up, but I cannot seem to do so. At any rate, I have agreed to stay on with her here for a while. The marquis has given his permission," she added defensively.

"You are welcome for as long as you wish. You would be welcome forever," he replied. "Priscilla, I think you need to listen to what I have to say."

"I do not think you can say anything that would change things," she said, beginning to twist her hands together. "It is better to just leave things as they are. There is nothing—"

"I thought you were going to marry Granville," he

burst out. "Jeffrey indicated it, and when I returned, you were here. I thought—"

"How could you!" She turned on him, fury in her eyes. "How could you possibly think I would marry anyone—least of all your uncle—after all you and I had been to each other? What were you thinking? That I was some mercenary creature who would just as soon marry one Connaught as another? Just so I married a title? Is that it?"

She whirled away from him and hurried over to the window. Staring out, avoiding his eyes, she said in a calmer voice, "I know Jeffrey thinks me capable of that, but I thought better of you. I thought you knew me." She turned to face him. "I thought you loved me."

"I did. I do. I know how wrong I was to think for even a second—" He broke off and went to stand beside her. He ached at the anger and disappointment he heard in her voice. "Listen for a moment. I know I was wrong. But I was jealous. I had been very sick and I was not thinking clearly. Then Jeffrey wrote and Elinor wrote and I—please forgive me."

"It could never work between us, Nicholas. I was so disappointed in you. And you did not trust me."

"I did, Cilla. It was myself I did not trust."

She shook her head. "Fine words, but you left me and believed the worst of me. You thought I would marry your uncle. I cannot seem to forget that."

"Priscilla, I—"

The door to the little parlor opened and Dalton stood framed in the doorway, shifting apologetically from one foot to the other.

"Excuse me, my lord, but the marquis requests your presence. Immediately."

"Tell the marquis," Nicholas began, his temper rising.

"Go along, Nicholas," Priscilla said, smiling faintly at Dalton. "It is a difficult time for his lordship. He needs you."

"Very well." She had said she was not going to leave immediately. He would have a chance to explain, plead, kiss, convince—to do something!

He left her looking pensively out the window.

Had she done the right thing? She was still angry, still hurt. But she knew one thing as well. She still loved him. She would always love him, no matter what misunderstanding they had. The trouble was, she could not count on his loving her the same way.

"Excuse me," a voice said from the doorway. "It's Miss Harrowby, now isn't it?"

Priscilla turned to see a small, middle-aged woman with rich chestnut hair and blue eyes smiling at her. The smile and the hint of the burr in her voice told Priscilla she was about to meet Nicholas's mother for the second time.

"Yes, ma'am, I am Priscilla Harrowby." She drew on all her social skills to present a calm demeanor. "How are you finding Bellingham Place?"

"I am still feeling a bit battered by all that has happened." Jean Cannon came into the room and, smiling, took Priscilla's hand. "Do you think if we pulled that bellpull that someone would come who could give me a cup of tea?"

Priscilla smiled back. "I believe so. Shall we try?"

Her hands were cold and shaking as she pulled the cord. She did not want Nicholas's mother to tell her she had better not be thinking of marrying her son. Poor, untitled Priscilla Harrowby, who worked for a living, might be acceptable as the bride of Nicholas Cannon, American citizen, not for the earl of Ashden. Fortunately, Priscilla knew it, even if Mrs. Cannon was too democratic to recognize it.

They sat in two small tapestry armchairs to await whoever would answer their summons. Of course, everyone in the house knew who had rung the bell, so Mrs. Sandles herself answered almost immediately. She nodded at their request and went off to fetch the tea and tell the staff that the two ladies seemed to be getting along a treat.

"My son wants to marry you," Jean Cannon said, while they waited.

"I know. He will get over it, Mrs. Cannon. There is no need for you to worry."

"Oh, my dear, I am not worried, except that you seem to keep saying no to him. That worries me, for it makes him very unhappy." She looked at Priscilla expectantly.

"You cannot approve."

"Whyever not?"

"But I am not titled and I have to be honest with you, my father is no longer wealthy." She paused. That should tell Mrs. Cannon all she needed to know.

"I know you are not titled, my dear, or I would be calling you Lady Priscilla. As for wealth, Nicholas has enough and to spare."

"He—he does?" This was not going as Priscilla had expected it to.

"Yes, quite a large fortune. And Marcus will probably make a good deal more for us all. He has the knack for it as well." She seemed quite comfortable with all this. Her wealthy, titled son to marry a poor commoner.

Mrs. Sandles brought the tea, and some little cakes as well. Priscilla, who had not been able to face luncheon, was glad for the cakes.

"You would not disapprove if I were to marry Nicholas?" Priscilla asked. "Not that I have decided to forgive him, for I have not."

"No, I would not disapprove. In fact, I shall be very distressed and disappointed if you do not. Nicholas has not been lucky in love before you, Priscilla. You do not mind if I call you Priscilla, do you?"

"No, ma'am, I would be honored."

"Well, Nicholas fell in love once before. I probably should not be telling you this. Nicholas would skin me alive if he knew."

Priscilla leaned forward. If Nicholas's mother stopped now she would drag the story out of her, by threat of torture if necessary. "He was in love?" she prompted.

"Well, say rather he thought he was. I knew better. Helen was a cold, scheming creature. My husband and I insisted on a long engagement. We asked that they spend some time apart. Helen did not like that idea. When Nicholas agreed, she broke the engagement and married someone else. Nicholas came over here to the Crystal Palace exhibition. He got over her pretty quickly once he learned her brother's creditors demanded immediate payment. She could not afford to wait the six months."

"You knew she was mercenary. But there are a number of people, including Nicholas's friend Jeffrey Bancroft, who would swear I am as mercenary as anyone in England."

302   *Martha Schroeder*

"Perhaps at one point you were. I don't know about that. But I do not think you are mercenary now." Mrs. Cannon smiled and poured herself another cup of tea. "I think you love Nicholas and that is why you won't marry him. You think he needs someone aristocratic, born in a place like this." She looked around and then gave Priscilla a conspiratorial smile. "If there *are* any other places like this. Bart, Nicholas's father, used to say that Bellingham Place was a dream and a nightmare combined. I am beginning to see what he meant."

"There are things between us that would always be stones in our path," Priscilla said, "aside from the idea of my being a countess. My mother always dreamed of it, but she never had the slightest idea of what it entailed. Her dream never went beyond the wedding. I do not think I can do this. I am not sure I want to. When we—when Nicholas was here before, I was looking forward to going to New York. Neither of us wants this." She looked down at her hands. "It is not a dream either for Nicholas or for me."

"I know, my dear. You understand what Nicholas is going through. He has to give up a very full life in New York to come here and learn an entirely new existence. Without you, I am not sure he can do it."

"What would his father have done?"

Mrs. Cannon paused and thought for a long moment, her expression rapt and far away. "He would have done it. Like Nicholas, he would not have wanted to, and he would have known I hated the idea, as you do, but we would have come. At bottom, he loved this place, but above all, he knew his duty. Family came first with him."

There was a pause, and when Mrs. Cannon spoke again, it was with quiet conviction. "Nicholas feels the same way," she said. "That is why he dashed across the ocean to New York without waiting to tell you. He was terrified I would die and he would not be there for his brother and sister. You see,"—and Priscilla noted there were tears in her eyes—"we have been so close for so long, and now that his father is not here any more, Nicholas feels he is the one in charge. He had promised Bart he would look after us all. So he had to come."

"I understand."

And at last she did. This glimpse of the tight-knit Cannon clan told her things Nicholas never could say aloud. It explained his need to return to America and the family he had left behind, as well as his trip to England to meet the Connaughts.

Family. He needed to try to interweave the strands of the New World with the old. Now it would have to be his life's work, leaving the adventure of empire building in America to his brother.

For the first time, Priscilla felt as if she understood the man she had loved from the first moment she saw him. She had always loved him. Now she understood him.

But could she trust him? He had left her before, and while she did not think he would do it again, he had done so in part because he thought she had betrayed him. She believed he regretted that, but she was not sure if such a misunderstanding arose in future he would trust her. He had said he would, and she believed he would try. But he had failed before. Could she move past that?

Nicholas's mother broke the silence. She got to her feet and said, "I hope you will give my son a chance,

Priscilla. He needs you. I am not sure he can do this without you."

Priscilla rose to face this outspoken woman who wanted her as a daughter-in-law. "I—I do love him. It will be Nicholas or no one, you know."

Jean Cannon smiled, a wide, relieved smile that crinkled her eyes. "That is all you need to know, surely. You wouldn't settle for a lifetime of emptiness because you can't have perfection, now would you? What sensible woman would do that? The human race would have died out long ago if we had all waited for the perfect man!"

Priscilla chuckled. "I will bear that in mind!"

She slipped away to look in on Hester. She found her playing backgammon with Elinor and looking quite a bit more cheerful. It seemed her parents were going to leave for home this afternoon, and Hester's mood had improved accordingly.

"They are leaving me here," she said happily, "until I am able to travel. I should be able to stretch that out for quite a while, if I am clever."

"I believe there is another young lady who might form part of your group. Nicholas's sister is here. When you can be carried downstairs, the three of you might find some amusements together."

Hester's face brightened still more. "Another friend! Besides you two. What richness! I have never had many friends. We live deep in the country, and my parents never took me to London before this year. Papa thought it a great waste. He said I would probably never receive an offer anyway, being plain and having no conversation."

Priscilla longed to box Sir Peter's ears. What kind of a father would say such things? Her father had not been affectionate and until recently had not thought very highly of her. But if he thought her stupid he had at least not said so to her face.

"Well, I must disagree with your father. I think you have both charm and conversation. And you should definitely return to London as soon as you can, if only to scotch any gossip that may have started."

She made up her mind to tell someone—perhaps Nicholas's mother—that room should be found for Hester at Bellingham House when the family returned to town. It seemed clear Hester's daydream of love and Granville had been only that—a daydream. Now that it seemed possible she was going to get what she really wanted—friends and even perhaps a family—she was happier than Granville had ever made her.

Priscilla slipped away again and decided to take a walk. She needed to think. She had almost made up her mind to take a chance and say yes to Nicholas. She loved him with all her heart. Her heart was bruised, and she needed soothing and judicious coddling to make it feel as happy as she had when they had first met. But she had a feeling Nicholas could do that, if properly directed.

She went to her room to get her cloak. She was about to leave via the French doors in the morning room when the marquis's aged butler found her. She thought he must have been looking for her, for he seemed a little out of breath.

"The marquis would like to see you, Miss Harrowby," he said.

"Now?" *Oh, please, not now. Just let me escape for a few minutes.*

"Yes, miss. It is almost time for tea and his lordship

always tries to come down for that. He sleeps a bit afterward. So now would be the best time."

Priscilla sighed. She supposed that now she would hear how unsuitable she was for the position of countess of Ashden, much less that of marchioness of Bellingham. She could not disagree, so perhaps this would be a short interview. Short, but unpleasant. Well, she had been dealing with her mother for years now. She should be used to that.

She squared her shoulders and prepared to follow Dalton into the jaws of hell, or however Mr. Tennyson had described the Charge of the Light Brigade.

The marquis was seated in his armchair when she entered. He looked older than he had the day before. Losing another son had aged him. "Miss Harrowby, thank you for coming."

She curtseyed slightly. "My lord." And stood, her hands folded at her waist, with what she hoped was an inquiring look on her face. She was prepared to wait in silence until he told her she was not the proper wife for the earl of Ashden, that he needed one who was bred to the role.

She was sure that in his grandfather's mind, Nicholas needed a wife who knew all the details of running a nobleman's castle—and his life. How to entertain the tenants at Boxing Day. How to raise proper noble children.

All the things a rich man's daughter did not necessarily know. The people in Priscilla's world might have as much money as the wealthiest aristocrats, but they did not have the same expectations, rules, or habits.

The marquis studied her in her gray dress and simple hairdo. Then, to her surprise, he smiled at her.

"So, Miss Harrowby, are you going to marry my

grandson?" His white, bushy eyebrows were raised almost to his hairline. He looked remarkably like Granville at that moment.

She never could explain afterward what made her say it. But she looked him straight in the eye and said, "Yes, my lord, I am."

"Good! Excellent! No one was sure, you know. Even Dalton did not know your mind, and Dalton, as you will learn, knows everything."

Priscilla clamped her mouth shut to keep her jaw from dropping. She swallowed hard and cleared her throat. "You do not object?"

He gave her a shrewd look. "You are not marrying him to disoblige me, I hope? Because you will not. You have demonstrated you can run the houses and the family with no difficulty. And Nicholas looks so besotted whenever he looks at you it is clear there is love on his side. So how could I object?"

"Because my birth is not aristocratic."

"A detriment, true, but much less of one than it used to be. Half the peerage have been elevated within two lifetimes at most."

"Because I have worked for money."

He smiled. "That is not a detriment for Nicholas. I happen to know his mother worked for a while when the family first went to America."

Priscilla could not leave it alone. She could put up with Jeffrey Bancroft's patronizing attitude, but she was not going to marry into it. "But for you, sir?"

He rose laboriously to his feet. Both Dalton and Priscilla hurried to help him, but he waved them off. Then, with great courtliness, he took her hand in his and kissed it.

"I welcome you to this family, my dear," he said.

"We could use some work, Priscilla. The house is not what it could be. I can see you have improved it in just a week. The family is not all it could be, either. Nicholas and Jean have both told me that. England is changing, and it is a blessing for the Connaughts that they will have you and Nicholas to help them change with it."

The first thing she had to do, she decided after she left the marquis, was find Nicholas and tell him he was going to marry her. Who knows? With their habit of misinterpreting everything the other said, he might have given up and proposed to another girl by this time!

She ran him to earth in the garden, standing and staring morosely at the overgrown climbing rose trellis.

"Someone should really prune those when they've finished blooming," she said as she came up to him.

He turned to her, his smile quizzical. "Two footmen and Mrs. Sandles have congratulated me on my wedding," he said. "That would not bother me. But just now Dalton wished me happy, so it must be true. I trust it is you I am marrying?"

"Yes," she said, and put her arms around his neck. Heaven to feel him again after all this time. "It is true. You are marrying me. The marquis and I have decided. Not to mention your mother. So if you have any objections, better speak now."

"Objections?" He took her face in his hands. "It is the only thought that has kept me sane. How soon, my angel? Do not say a year. Granville must not be allowed to be as difficult in death as he was in life!" His kiss was as heavenly as she remembered.

"Hmm. I should be able to organize a nice, quiet wedding by—"

"Next week?"

"Christmas." She raised her face for his kiss. "Remember, you are not marrying just anyone. Your bride will be a countess! Six months is not a moment too long to wait for such an occasion!"

"Ten minutes would be too long to wait. My bride will be you that is all that matters. Kiss me, love, and let us tell the two or three people who do not already know that we are betrothed."

Twenty

Christmas Eve

"Where is she? The vicar is here, Elinor is at the piano, I am here—where is Priscilla?"

Nicholas began to pace the floor of the small anteroom, usually used as a card room off the ballroom of Bellingham Place. The room was small, so it took him only three strides to reach the windows. Then he pivoted and retraced his steps.

"It is the bride's prerogative to take her time getting ready for her wedding. And in this case, I think it is probably the bride's mother who is holding things up. You know Edwina," Jean said, trying to soothe her impatient son. "Do stop pacing, Nicky. You are making me dizzy."

By contrast, she looked serenely beautiful in her dress of Christmas green brocade, which set off her chestnut hair and still unlined complexion. She wore a corsage of holly and red roses and looked ten years younger than her age, Nicholas thought.

He shrugged impatiently. "I have been ready since the first day I met her. Where is she?"

"You kept her waiting for a good part of that time," his mother replied.

"You don't think she's gone off to London, do you?"

"Nicholas, stop it. She will be here in a moment or two."

He peeked out to see if perhaps the bride had arrived at last. No sign of her. He looked around at Priscilla's handiwork. The ballroom at Bellingham Place was now decorated with evergreens and white satin ribbons. There were white roses from the estate's succession houses near the small altar and twenty or so gilt chairs set up in informal rows. The room was beautiful, as anything Priscilla had anything to do with was.

Nicholas sighed. Damn! She was doing it again. Tying him up in knots. For the past six months, he had felt as if he were tied up in those soft satin ribbons. He had spent much of his time conferring with his grandfather about the rest of the Connaughts while Priscilla had been in London, finishing the events she had agreed to plan.

Then had come the real torture. His visits to Priscilla had to be spent listening to Edwina prattle on about The Wedding. If the Prince of Wales ever settled on a bride, his wedding would not be any more meticulously planned than this one.

"We must let my mother do it, darling," Priscilla had said. "It is all she has ever dreamed of. Her daughter marrying an earl and the ceremony held at one of the great houses of England. She is in heaven. Once she accomplishes this, she will never bother us again."

Nicholas had been highly dubious. His encounters with Priscilla's mother had not led him to believe she had any sensible thoughts at all, nor that she would not expect to take up permanent residence at Bellingham Place. But he had every faith that Barnabas, his soon-to-be father-in-law, could prevent that. Barnabas had made a great deal of his fortune back, and with the money had come an ability to control Edwina he had never had before, according to Priscilla.

One thing had bothered Nicholas about the wedding. "You are not going to let her pick out your dress, are you?" he asked in some trepidation. "I don't like all those ruffles and flounces and what not."

"No. I have let her work with Mrs. Sandles to plan the wedding breakfast, and she has invited all her cronies to a reception after we return to London. But she realizes Granville's death has made a huge wedding impossible. And she has her own dress to worry about. I have told her she needn't worry about mine."

They had been snatching a few moments alone in the Harrowby drawing room. Alone at last, and still they had to talk about The Wedding. Nicholas at last understood why bridegrooms were so eager to get the damned ceremony over with—then they would no longer have to listen to the endless talk.

He wound one of her golden curls around his finger and nuzzled the side of her neck. "Have I told you today that you are beautiful and I love you?"

"Umm-hmm. But tell me again." She gave a soft little purr and turned her face for his kiss.

"Priscilla! How many guests did we finally decide—" Edwina Harrowby sailed into the room, talking at her usual gallop. "Oh, it is you, my lord. You must not kiss gentlemen in the drawing room, Priscilla. How many times must I tell you? Now, about this guest list."

Nicholas growled and Priscilla had smothered a laugh.

And that, he thought now, was the way the entire time had gone. His time had been spent wrestling with the problems of managing an enormous estate, consisting not just of the ten thousand acres of Bellingham Place, but at least nine other properties all over Britain, Scotland, and Wales, totaling at least one hundred thousand acres. In addition, there were investments in joint stock companies, partnerships, banks. Nicholas's head was stuffed with information. He was beginning to see his entrepreneurial skills would be put to good use managing all this wealth. He could be a force for progress and democracy.

He had not told his grandfather that as yet.

"Being the earl is no sinecure, I can see," Marcus had said to him when he had found Nicholas sitting over ledgers in the study of Bellingham Place in the middle of the night.

"It is like running a small country," Nicholas had replied, rubbing his aching head. "Fortunately, Priscilla has learned about bookkeeping and money from her father. There is nothing like earning your own for a while to make you appreciate the value of knowing where it is going. She will be such a help—if I can ever get her to the altar."

The other door into the card room, the one from the hall, opened to admit Dalton, who was pushing his grandfather in a wheeled chair. It was his one concession to advancing age, made necessary by a small stroke that had followed Granville's death. He looked far frailer than he had the year before when they had first met, Nicholas thought, but far happier, too. What a gallant old man, helping him learn the intricacies of his inheritance despite his sorrow at the death of the son he sorely missed, though he had been a constant disappointment to him in life.

"My boy, I wanted to see you before everyone else

crowded around you." The marquis held out his hands and Nicholas took them in both of his.

"Grandfather," Nicholas said, his throat tight with emotion. He loved this brave, fragile old man, the more so because he knew he would lose him soon.

"Best of luck, my boy. Though I have a feeling that in winning Priscilla you have had all the luck anyone can wish for."

"I agree, Grandfather." Nicholas smiled.

"Jean." His grandfather smiled fondly at his daughter-in-law. Over these past months they had become fast friends, making him regret more than ever the stubborn pride that had kept him from knowing her for so many years. "You have a very handsome family." He looked at Marcus and Nicholas. "Melinda is out charming the vicar, as she does every male she meets. You are going to have trouble with that one, my dear."

"I fear you are right, Father," she said. The marquis flushed with pleasure at hearing that name on her lips, and Nicholas found himself smiling with them. Family. It was all that mattered after all. His mother had always known that.

The marquis left then to find his place near the altar, where he and Dalton could see everything. Time ticked on. Marcus lounged on one of the small gilt chairs in the anteroom. He was dressed in formal evening wear and looked so like his father that Nicholas had caught his mother's eyes brim with tears when she looked at him.

Marcus watched Nicholas pace for a minute or two. "Remind me of this day if I ever am so lost to reality that I think of marrying," Marcus remarked with the wry little half smile that was the signature of all the men of the family.

"I will remind you of that remark on your wedding day," said his mother, smiling at him.

"Now, Mum, you're my best girl, always will be," said Marcus with a grin. "Don't need a wife when I have you."

"Go on with you! Nicholas, I think your bride has arrived at last."

Nicholas looked again out the half-opened door, and this time he caught a glimpse of Lucinda Bancroft, Priscilla's lone attendant, beautiful in ice blue satin. That was his signal, and he turned to his mother and kissed her cheek.

"I love you, Mother," he whispered. "You look beautiful."

"And I love you." She reached up and patted his cheek. "Your father would be so proud." She turned away to go to her seat on one of the gilt chairs in the front of the ballroom.

He and Marcus stepped out of the room to stand by the altar. Elinor began to play, Lucinda began to walk toward him, and then Priscilla appeared on her father's arm. It was only a few steps to the altar but it was time enough for Nicholas to be struck once again by his bride's beauty. Her dress was a simple ivory satin, and she carried white roses with sprays of holly. He loved her so much it almost hurt him to look at her. His brave, beautiful, funny love. Their eyes met, and they smiled at each other with their hearts in their eyes.

Their vows seemed to take only a moment, so deep was he lost in thinking of their meaning. Frighteningly solemn, yet they did not frighten him when they joined him to Priscilla forever.

They turned to face their guests afterward and he looked around the room. Jeffrey, the Blankenships, a goodly sprinkling of Connaughts, including Aunt Margaret. Elinor began playing a piece by Bach, the name of which Nicholas could not remember, as a signal that the ceremony was over.

"It was the loveliest wedding a countess ever had." Edwina sighed. "My daughter. Lady Ashden."

"Yes, Mama, it was lovely." Priscilla smiled. The wedding was the last thing she was prepared to do for her mother. From now on her life was her own. And Nicholas's. She smiled up at her groom.

"Is your mother more annoying than my Aunt Margaret, do you think?" Nicholas asked as they began to walk among their guests. He nodded to the table where food had been laid out. Aunt Margaret had planted herself in front of it and had already made considerable inroads on the contents.

"Well, at least we have your mother and my father to make up for them," Priscilla replied. She was prepared to smile at the foibles of the whole world this day. "And the marquis."

"Priscilla, Nicholas, congratulations." It was Jeffrey. She smiled. Yes, she was even prepared to put up with Jeffrey.

He nodded to Nicholas, who began to move off, ready to talk to Henry and Mary Ann Blankenship.

"I wanted to talk to you, Priscilla," Jeffrey began. He must have seen the resistance on her face, for he quickly added, "I told Nicholas I needed to beg your pardon."

"Whatever for?" Priscilla asked, though there were

any number of unkind remarks she remembered all too clearly. But as always with Jeffrey, she retreated to her pose of well-brought-up ninny, an exact replica of Edwina.

"For all the unkind things I have ever said to you or about you," he replied. "You have proved me wrong in every particular. Lucy told me so a thousand times, and Nicholas got quite angry about it from the very first time he met you. I do not know if you have changed or if I am simply seeing you more clearly, but you are a wonderful woman, Priscilla. You have helped your father, taken care of your mother, run a business. And you are kind as well. I am sorry I did not always recognize your qualities."

"I was very afraid of you," she said. "It made me foolish. So the fault was not all yours. I acted like a brainless flibbertigibbet out of fear."

"I am sorry for that most of all, I think." Jeffrey smiled at her ruefully. "Do you think we can be friends?"

"Well, since your wife is my best friend and my husband is yours, I think we had better try." And with generous smile, Priscilla held out her hand.

Nicholas had been watching the interchange from a stance near the buffet table. He stood surrounded by a bevy of young ladies—the Blankenships' two daughters, Elinor, Melinda, and Hester Allison-Hyatt, who was a permanent house guest of the Connaughts, sometimes staying with Elinor's Aunt Margaret, sometimes with Nicholas and his mother at Bellingham House.

Now he looked up and saw Priscilla had finished talking with Jeffrey. He came back and put his arm around her. "Now that you have accepted Jeffrey's

apology, do you suppose we can slip away, just ourselves?" Smiling down at her, he added, "So I can
begin to tell you again all you mean to me."

Priscilla smiled up at him. "I trust you mean to demonstrate your feelings as well, my lord. So that we can
make each other happy in our own special way. The
way we did last Christmas?" Nicholas nodded enthu-
siastically. "Not until luncheon and all the toasts and
speeches are over with," she said. "But then . . ."

Nicholas laughed. "Yes, then we will be alone at
last, just the two of us, in time to celebrate our very
own, very private, very merry little Christmas!"